The Geomancer's Apprentice

YIN LEONG

Kampung Kreepy Books

Copyright © 2021 Yin Wilczek
All rights reserved.
ISBN: 978-1-7371252-1-1
Library of Congress Control Number: 2021914898

No part of this book may be reproduced, or stored in a retrieval system, or transmitted in any form or by any means, electronic, mechanical, photocopying, recording, or otherwise, without express written permission of the publisher.

This is a work of fiction. Any resemblance to actual events or people is purely coincidental. For narrative purposes, I've taken liberties in the description of feng shui and certain Washington, D.C., landmarks. Where real agencies and public figures are mentioned, their interactions with the novel's characters are wholly imaginary, as are shape-shifting monsters.

Praise for
The Geomancer's Apprentice

"Junie Soong's journey from young coffeeshop-employee reject to unconventional hero in Yin Leong's *The Geomancer's Apprentice* is a rousing joyride! The pairing of Junie with on-the-brink-of-retirement geomancer Joe Tham as they rush to discover dragons and crush monsters is both humorous and inspired.

"While other books set in Washington, D.C., dwell on Capitol Hill and probe politics, this refreshing tale gives us a fascinating glimpse into the otherworldly orbit that might just exist in the shadow of the fabled Chinatown Gate. Quite simply, I couldn't put it down and read it in one sitting. I loved it."

—**Ellen Byerrum**, author of the Crime of Fashion Mysteries

Dedication

As any writer knows, it is a long and arduous journey from an idea to a novel. Thank you to my family and friends for their unwavering support. You know who you are. Love, always.

Prologue

She didn't know what possessed her to do it. She had always believed herself a traditionalist, content with the way things were. Yet, after she bought the house, she suddenly wanted something totally different, something open to the elements, something that would let in the light.

Dom would have tried to talk her out of it had he still been around. She could picture him shaking his head in exasperation. Her husband loved old things and old houses. He would have considered it sacrilege.

Now, a year later and after about a million dollars' worth of construction, the original residence was gone and another built in its place. And she was chagrined to find she didn't like it. The new house was ready but she was dragging her heels about moving in.

Millie unlocked the front door. When she entered, her eyes, as always, were drawn upward to the chandelier in the foyer. It had cost thousands of dollars and was one of the most expensive items she had installed. Its crystals were made from the finest Swarovski glass.

The late-evening light streamed in, transforming the crystals into delicate drops of fire. The crystals in turn reflected their golden phosphorescence onto the foyer's marble floor and window panes, causing the whole space to shimmer. She should have been delighted by the play of light. Instead, it oddly emphasized her feeling that there was something not quite right about her new home.

She shook her head to snap herself out of it. *What was wrong with her?*

She was the first to admit that the new construction probably was impelled by her midlife crisis. Midlife crisis with a side of loneliness, if she was being totally honest. She led a busy life, but Dom's death had left an emptiness that she couldn't seem to fill no matter how much she packed into her day, no matter how many people with which she surrounded herself.

Her husband had been her rock, her refuge for so long, ever since …

She stopped herself, refusing to dwell on the past. So what if the new house turned out to be a mistake? So what if it was too big for her? Some women went shopping as a form of therapy—she had the means to acquire and raze property. And everyone suffered once in a while from post-purchase regret. She should just enjoy the house—and the additional space that it offered—for what it was instead of nitpicking. No wonder the architect now was reluctant to take her calls. Dan, the general contractor, was still patient, but who knew how long his patience would last?

She glanced at her watch, a gold Rolex Lady-Datejust with diamonds that Dom had given her for her 50th birthday. *Could it be almost 7:30?* She meant to come earlier, but the meeting had lasted longer than she anticipated. People always wanted to chat after a board meeting. Then, just as she was about to drive to the house, Emma had called to discuss an invitation for Millie to speak at a medical conference.

She reminded herself to give Emma some time off even though she didn't know what she would do without her dedicated assistant. Emma deserved a nice, long vacation, preferably somewhere remote with no internet or cell reception.

Millie's mind involuntarily slipped back to the time she and Dom had gone to Santorini, the southernmost island in the Greek Cyclades. For two blissful weeks, they stayed in a whitewashed house perched on a cliff high above the Aegean Sea. They were suspended in their own bubble between the blue sky above and the bluer sea below. They didn't have phones, or television, or newspapers. They were cut off from the rest of the world, and it had been wonderful. It had been perfect.

Tears pricked her eyes and she forced herself back to the present. She was here, at her new house, the house she built without Dom, and he was gone forever. She should stop woolgathering and do what she came to do.

She headed purposefully for the cellar. It was really an omission on her part. She couldn't decide what to do about the enormous area under the house so the contractors had left it largely undisturbed, apart from removing most of the junk that the previous homeowners had abandoned there. The architect was right though—the cellar had to be dealt with if she intended ultimately to sell the residence. It was old and fusty, nothing but wasted space.

She recently had started collecting wine, the latest in a long line of hobbies. She thought the cellar might be the ideal repository for her growing collection. If so, she wanted the project completed before she moved in. Her plan today was to take another look at the cellar. She better have some concrete ideas before she contacted the architect.

She opened the door and turned on the light. She stood on the landing and looked doubtfully down the rickety wooden stairs. She could barely see the lower steps. She vaguely recalled Dan saying something about the deficient lighting. It struck her that she had never been alone in the cellar before. She should have been better prepared. Perhaps she should have asked him to meet her here. She definitely should have brought a flashlight. Good thing she wasn't afraid of the dark.

Millie trudged resolutely downward. About three-quarters of the way, there was a second landing where the staircase turned 90 degrees to the right. When she made the turn, she found herself staring into almost total darkness. The light she had switched on, already dim, was reduced to a faint glow this far down.

Sighing irritably, she stretched out her hands and held firmly onto the handrails on either side of her. It was a good thing the stairwell was narrow, although it probably wouldn't conform to today's building codes. She felt gingerly with her foot before descending onto the next tread. She was glad she was wearing sensible shoes. The echoes from the clack of her low heels made it sound as though someone was following close behind her. It was a little disconcerting. It must be something to do with the acoustics down here.

There were only five steps after the turning. When she—and the phantom stranger accompanying her—arrived at the cellar floor, she reached blindly for the pull chain to switch on the light she knew was somewhere above her.

Her hand swung in vain through the air. If she remembered correctly, the chain was almost directly above the base of the steps. Dan had showed it to her. But she couldn't find it now.

She was still swatting uselessly above her when she became aware of a *pressing* sensation. She paused with her arm still raised. The sensation was becoming not so much pressing as *choking*. She was finding it difficult to breathe. And did it seem darker than before? It was as if the darkness was crowding in so hard against her that it was constricting her throat and airways. She laughed nervously. *Where were all these bizarre notions coming from?*

When her laughter died away, she detected a faint rasping noise. It seemed to originate from deep within the cellar. Puzzled, she turned toward the sound and listened intently. *Could it be workmen?* Why were they still here at such a late hour and why hadn't they turned on any lights?

It took awhile before Millie identified the sound as scratching. Something was scratching persistently at the dirt floor in the older section of the cellar. It was strange that she could hear it here in the main cellar. It must be an auditory illusion, like the echoes of her footfalls on the stairs.

Whatever it was, it had to be much larger than a rat. She shivered and hugged herself. Her flesh felt cold; the skin on her upper arms was breaking out in goose pimples. *It's trying to break through,* she thought. *It's coming.* The words seemed to materialize out of thin air. It was as if someone had whispered them in her head.

She suddenly jerked and yelped in fright. Something was tugging at her hand. It was pulling her back to the staircase, toward the light at the top of the steps. It pulled so hard that her arm actually lifted in the air and she had to move to stop from falling over. She couldn't see anything in the dark, but her hand was clasped by what felt like … frigid fingers.

It's coming. It's coming. It's coming. This time she clearly heard the words outside her head. Her courage deserted her. She screamed and bolted clumsily up the stairs, running so fast she was fortunate not to trip and break her neck.

She didn't stop running until she was out the front door and well clear of the house.

Chapter 1

Junie stepped off the escalator. The morning rush hour was over, but she had to push through a family of tourists—complete with bulky kiddie strollers—to get out of the Gallery Place-Chinatown Metro Station.

Just outside the station, she was greeted by the sight of the Friendship Archway, the symbolic entrance to Washington, D.C.'s Chinatown. It was just past 10 in the morning, but the July sun already was beating down on the arch's golden pagoda roofs. Traffic streamed by on the roads under and around the monument. Exhaust fumes permeated the warm air. Jack hammers rat-a-tatted as a road crew dug up part of the intersection.

Following her mother's detailed instructions, Junie trotted briskly along H Street Northwest past the archway. A little further on, she turned up a side street lined with eateries and shops. As she walked, her reflection—Asian, nondescript, bespectacled—kept pace with her from the storefront windows. She could see her ponytail was disintegrating. It was limp, wilting like the potted plants she passed on the sidewalk.

Darn. It was too late to fix her hair. Judging from the sign on the door —in both English and Chinese—she had arrived at the Laughing Buddha Cafe. Her heart sank as she surveyed the building in which the cafe was located.

The architecture in Chinatown could best be described as eclectic. Its buildings were a mishmash of styles, shapes and sizes. Even so, the structure in front of her was singularly unattractive. It hunched, squat and shabby, like a troll amid fairy princesses. It was only three stories high, capped by a flat roof. The original brick front was covered by flaking white paint that looked grayish in the bright sunlight. The second and third floors each had three large windows that faced the street.

According to her mother, the Laughing Buddha occupied the first two levels of the building. Beside the cafe's glass door was a narrow wooden door. Junie cautiously opened it and found a dreary stairwell. She went in and climbed the stairs, which ended at a short corridor on the third floor. In the middle of the corridor was another door. A small sign on it announced: "Joseph HL Tham, Feng Shui Master/Geomancer."

Junie took a deep breath. She nudged her glasses higher up her nose and knocked timidly. A voice behind the door told her to enter. When she did, she saw a middle-aged Asian man sitting at a desk. His thick hair was cropped short and streaked with gray; his sloping eyes gleamed like polished black marbles.

"Yes?" A hopeful smile lifted the slightly droopy contours of his face.

"Mr. Tham? It's me, Junie Soong. I'm here about a job?"

The man's face fell. "Oh, right," he said without enthusiasm. "Your mother called this morning, TWICE"—he raised the index and middle fingers of his right hand to emphasize his point—"to remind me you were coming." He gestured to the chairs in front of his desk. "Please sit. Can I see your resume?"

"Yes sir."

Junie slumped down on the nearer chair. She reached into her backpack, extracted a sheet of paper and slid it in front of him. Rather than stare at him while he perused her depressing lack of achievement, she looked around the small office.

There was an entryway behind Tham's desk that led to a kitchen. Another desk was placed perpendicular to Tham's. The wall behind the second desk was occupied by a metal filing cabinet.

On the other side of the room were the three windows that Junie had seen from the outside. The window blinds were lowered most of the way, blocking out the sun. The depressing half-light and the grayness of everything in the office—furniture, cabinet, carpet, wall paint, old newspapers —culminated in an atmosphere of dinginess.

The one bright spot of color was a dry erase board edged in red that hung above the cabinet. Someone had written on it in thick black marker:

CHARGES (not inclusive of expenses):

Cleansing regimen: $1,888
Single cleansing: $888
Removal of curse: $300
Feng shui consultation: $250
Blessing: $150 per visit

TODAY'S SPECIAL: feng shui consultation + blessing: $350

"Today's Special" was underlined twice with a red marker. The film of dust on the board suggested the prices hadn't changed for some time.

Tham cleared his throat and Junie hastily shifted her eyes back to him. He tapped her resume. "Your mother mentioned something about you being fired from Starbucks?"

Junie's face reddened. "I wasn't fired," she said defensively. "I quit before that."

Unnerved by Tham's silence, she quickly added, "They threatened to fire me because I was rude to a customer. He was making disparaging remarks about my disabled co-worker."

The telephone on Tham's desk rang just then, saving him from having to respond. He picked up the handset.

"Hello, Joseph Tham speaking." He tried hard to infuse cheeriness, helpfulness and efficiency into his voice. "How may I help you?"

The speaker on the other end of the line was so loud that Junie could tell it was a woman. "Sure, I can be there shortly," he said, jotting something down on the notepad in front of him.

After more nodding and "uh huhs," he placed the handset back in its cradle and stood up. "I just got a new job," he informed Junie. "They need me there immediately. Want to tag along?"

She grabbed her backpack and scrambled to her feet. She was five-foot-four; Tham was only a couple of inches or so taller.

"Wait, does this mean I'm hired?" she asked.

"Let's see how you do on this assignment first," he said warily.

"Where are we going?"

"To a client's house in Kalorama. She's complaining about her cellar."

Junie waited while Tham went back to his apartment, which was accessed through the kitchen. When he returned to the office, he was wearing a sports jacket over his wrinkled button-down shirt and slacks. He carried a large leather bag, the kind doctors lugged around in movies depicting the Old West.

He filled Junie in on the cab ride to Kalorama, a wealthy residential area in D.C.'s northwest quadrant.

"Millicent Scarpini is a recent client of mine," he said. "I performed a blessing at her Watergate apartment not too long ago. She's interested in feng shui and all things Asian because her husband was a former U.S. diplomat and they spent a lot of time in India and China. The husband died about three years ago, I believe.

"Anyway, Millie's independently wealthy. Her family manufactured packaging for medical equipment, or something like that. She sits on a few boards and donates a lot of money to medical research. She bought the house we're going to about a year ago. It caused a big stink at the time. According to media reports, she tore down the historical brick manor that was there and replaced it with a glass and steel monstrosity. She kept the original cellar though."

"Have you been to the place?" Junie asked.

"No," Tham said. "I read about it in the *Washington Post*. I don't know if she's even moved in yet. Anyway, Millie thinks the cellar is filled with negative energy. She wants us to bless it or make it more feng shui-friendly."

"Oh." Junie mulled the phrase "feng shui-friendly." *What did that even mean?* Those words weren't part of her usual vocabulary. "Will you charge her the 'today's special' price?"

He looked blank for a second before he recalled the rates recorded on his dry erase board.

"We'll see," he said. "Who knows, we may be able to elevate this to a cleansing." He brightened at the prospect.

The cab dropped them in front of a gorgeous mansion. It was in the modern minimalist style, glass rectangles stacked on top of each other, like something you would see in southern California or Miami. It looked distinctly out of place among its stodgy Federal-style brick neighbors.

Tham clicked his tongue and shook his head as they walked up the front path, set amid a lush lawn that was obviously new. "This place has too many sharp angles," he grumbled as he rang the doorbell. "Poison arrows everywhere. Very bad feng shui."

The door was energetically thrown open by a large-boned woman clad in a stylish pantsuit and expensive jewelry. "Joe, I'm so glad you could make it." She looked genuinely worried, even frightened, as she ushered them in.

Standing behind Millie was a beefy African-American man dressed in a denim shirt and jeans. He had grizzled hair and kind eyes. His broad face wore a harassed expression. She introduced him as Dan Groskind, her general contractor. Tham and Dan shook hands and traded business cards, after which Tham introduced Junie as his apprentice-slash-associate.

Junie gazed around in awe while the others made small talk. They were in an impressive two-story foyer, spotlit by sunlight coming through wall-to-wall, floor-to-ceiling windows. A glistening chandelier hung high above them. In the middle of the foyer was a magnificent staircase with polished dark risers.

"Thank you for calling me," Tham was saying.

"Actually, I called Dan first," Millie said. "First thing this morning, as a matter of fact. He wasn't available at the time, so I called my architect, who also wasn't available. I couldn't think of who else to call, except maybe a pest control company, when I remembered the apartment blessing. Didn't you tell me at the time that you can fix … um … *unhealthy* atmospheres? Do you think this is something within your area of expertise?" She anxiously twisted a gold bangle around and around her wrist.

"Well, I'll be happy to take a look," Tham said smoothly.

She heaved a sigh of relief. "The cellar's this way. Anyway, Dan was able to come after all. I thought the two of you could look over the cellar together. I was just filling him in when you arrived."

She led them down marble corridors and through large and airy rooms that were as yet unfurnished. Finally, she stopped in front of a stout, wooden door.

Millie reached for the door's handle and hesitated. She backed away, a look of fear on her face. "Sorry, I can't go down there again," she said. "Joe, if you don't mind, I'll let Dan take care of you. He can answer all your questions—he's more familiar with the cellar than I am."

"That's fine," Tham said. "Before we go with Dan, can you explain again what the problem is? On the phone, you mentioned something about the cellar being dark and oppressive."

She rubbed her hands together, managing to look both frightened and embarrassed. "That sounds silly, doesn't it? It's a cellar. It's underground. Of course it's *dark*."

She exhaled loudly. "Well ... um ... I ... I went down last night by myself. I wanted to see if it was a good place to store my wine collection. Once I was downstairs, I ... er ... I got a very bad feeling." She paused, aware of how lame that sounded. "I thought I heard something," she added a little desperately. "Or rather, *some* things. And then something touched me."

"What kind of things?" Tham asked.

"I'm not sure. I thought I heard scratching or ... or whispering. And I don't know what touched me." She looked down at her bangle, refusing to meet Tham's gaze. "I'm afraid I chickened out so I didn't stay very long."

She smiled weakly. "I may be getting senile, but can you go down to the cellar with Dan and um ... check the atmosphere or something?" She turned to Dan. "Or you can fix it if it's a structural issue after all."

Dan nodded stoically.

"Sure." Tham's tone was reassuring. "Even if it turns out to be structural, we can still calm the environment with a simple blessing."

Chapter 2

Dan opened the cellar door and stepped onto a small landing. He reached up and pulled a chain dangling from the ceiling. An incandescent bulb lit up, revealing a set of stairs descending to another landing at which they turned.

"Watch your step," he warned. "There's no universal switch that turns on all the cellar lights at once. You have to pull on the chains for the individual bulbs."

He gestured downstairs. "There's another bulb at the base of the stairs. Unfortunately, the bulbs are only 25 watts—or about 200 lumens each—so they don't light up the stairs very well. It's especially bad where the stairs turn. My guess is the lighting was last updated in the 1970s. We can't install better lighting unless the cellar is completely rewired. That'll be one of my major concerns if Millie decides to do anything down here."

The cellar was very different from the sleek edifice that rested above it. Not only was it dark, it smelled dank and musty. Junie felt a little off-kilter as they followed Dan down the steps. She found the staircase especially claustrophobic.

At the lower landing, the contractor pulled a flashlight out of his pocket and turned it on so they could see the final treads. Junie's dizziness transformed into a tension headache. She blinked, trying to adjust her eyes to the dimness.

When they were at the bottom, Dan located the other bulb and turned it on. "I'm not sure if Millie told you, but the cellar is very old, dating back to the house that was built here in the early 1800s," he said. "Parts of it may be even older. There is some evidence that there was a dwelling here before that."

The bulb created a small circle of light around them. The rest of the cellar was veiled in gloom, but Junie got the sense of cavernous space. That could be due in part to the high ceiling—it was about 10 feet or so from the cellar's cracked cement floor to the floor joists of the house above. The brick walls closest to the light were badly gouged and chipped, with occasional gaps where the mortar had fallen out.

"This place was chock full of stuff when I first saw it, which isn't surprising considering the age of the original building, or buildings, I should say," Dan continued. "We've cleared a lot of it. My workers also shored up a few places. I didn't want trip hazards or the walls collapsing while my men were putting in new water and gas lines for the house." He angled his beam upward to show them the new pipes running between the joists.

"You should bring a flashlight if you come down here for any reason," he added unnecessarily. "There are bulbs throughout the cellar like the one above us. The bad news is they were put in rather haphazardly. You won't be able to find them to turn them on unless you already know where they are. The pull chains are virtually invisible in the dark."

Tham lowered his voice so Millie couldn't hear them from upstairs. "Do you think Millie might be imagining those noises? Have you ever known her to be fanciful? Has she done this in the past?"

"If I had to describe her as an employer, it'd be exacting. Fanciful? Not at all." Dan eyed Tham and Junie quizzically. "What do you two do again? Millie didn't fully explain."

"We're feng shui geomancers—we harmonize or improve the flow of energy within an environment," Tham said.

"I'm guessing we're not talking about electricity or natural gas?"

"No."

Dan's expression now was skeptical, but he kept his thoughts to himself. "Anyway, a few of my men were down here a couple of days ago and they didn't mention anything out of the ordinary. I'll turn on all the lights before we start our inspections. Wait for me to come back. I don't want you two wandering around in the dark."

"While we're waiting, I'll prepare for a blessing ritual," Tham said. "That may be all Millie needs to put her fears to rest."

Dan strode off with his flashlight. As lights started to come on in other parts of the cellar, Tham retrieved a large, flat box from his bag. He carefully placed the box on the floor, opened it and took out a wooden disk that was about an inch high and a little less than a foot in diameter.

Junie stared at the object in fascination. She could tell it was an antique. It was divided into quadrants by red vertical and horizontal lines etched into its black lacquered surface. Numerous thin yellow lines divided the disk further into sections and concentric circles. The sections were filled with tiny red and yellow symbols and characters that she could barely make out in the poor light. In the disk's center was a smaller disk covered with glass. A needle under the glass quivered from side to side.

"Is that some kind of compass?" she asked.

"It's a luopan, otherwise known as a feng shui compass," Tham said. "This was made specially for my great-great-great-grandfather, who was a very famous geomancer in China. It's been in the family for more than 200 years."

He looked down at his bag. "Say Junie, can you hold the luopan for a minute? I have more things to take out. Please, please don't drop it."

She grasped the compass gingerly with both hands. This was her first time holding anything so old. It was surprisingly heavy. The needle was now rotating rapidly. Tham didn't notice, having bent down to rummage in his bag. He took out a portable music player and placed it on the ground. He delved into his bag again and brought out several candles in glass containers.

"So Junie, do you know anything about feng shui, otherwise known as Chinese geomancy?" he asked as he deposited the candles beside the music player. She shook her head.

"Feng shui is a system of beliefs that's more than 3,000 years old." Tham's voice assumed a pedagogical timbre. "It's all about the movement of qi, the vital energy or essence—the life force, if you will—that flows within and from all things, whether animate or inanimate. Feng shui helps people to exist in harmony and balance with the natural forces that surround them."

She blinked, wondering if he expected her to take notes. But the lecture was over; he was now holding his hand out for the compass.

"So this is what we're going to do," he said. "Once Dan turns on all the lights, I'm going to use the luopan to measure the cellar's energy flow. The luopan is always the geomancer's first recourse."

She placed the instrument in his outstretched hand. His eyebrows shot up to his hairline when he saw the needle's wild rotations.

"Whoa," he said in astonishment. "I've never seen it do that before. Maybe it's finally broken." He squinted at the compass and tapped its glass bubble gently. "Hmmm. It's not moving anymore. I wonder what happened?"

He was still tapping the luopan when they heard Dan yell from the other end of the cellar. He and Junie looked up in shock. Dan screamed in terror. He screamed again.

Tham hastily thrust the antique compass into Junie's arms and sprinted toward the screams. Junie clutched the luopan to her chest and chased after him.

The cellar narrowed as they raced in the direction of Dan's terrified cries. Fortunately, the contractor left a trail of lights behind him. They dashed under a brick archway and down a tunnel-like passageway. The passage was paved with uneven cobblestones; the walls and ceiling were dirt and rocks. It opened up eventually into a chamber. There was a large pit near the middle of the room. Dan was in the pit, clinging desperately to the edge as the soil crumbled around him.

"Help!" he screamed. "Help me!"

Tham dropped to his knees and gripped Dan's arms. He must have been a lot stronger than he looked.

With Tham's help, Dan was able to half-scrabble, half-crawl out of the rapidly widening depression. When Tham judged they were a safe distance from the pit, he released Dan and the contractor collapsed to the floor.

"Thank God you heard me," Dan rasped. His chest heaved up and down in harsh pants. "I was turning on the light when the ground gave way beneath me. Where the hell did that hole come from? I didn't see it before. Nobody said anything about a hole."

"Is it a sinkhole?" Tham asked. "They're common in D.C., especially after rainy periods."

"Maybe."

"Can you stand?" Tham helped the contractor to his feet.

Dan winced in pain and leaned heavily on the geomancer. "Something's wrong with my ankle," he groaned.

"Let me look."

Junie took the opportunity to explore while Tham was examining the contractor's ankle. This peculiar area and the connecting tunnel must be the older section that Dan spoke about. The chamber floor was hard-packed earth. The ceiling was an uneven mishmash of joists and beams, only about seven feet or so high in parts.

The walls were hugged by ancient timbers, pitted and half-rotted away to reveal the yellowish clay endemic to the D.C. metropolitan area. The wood must have been shelving of some sort. Based on the fragments left behind, it looked like the chamber was used for storage once upon a time. Perhaps it served as a root or wine cellar for an abode that stood on the site centuries before Millie built her glass manor.

She wrinkled her nose. The room reeked of old, wet things. Underlying the acrid odor was something more metallic, somewhat resembling the smell of rusty iron. She looked up, curious to see whether there was an old trapdoor in the ceiling. Many old cellars were accessed that way. But if there once was a trapdoor, it was long gone.

The room's sole light source looked antiquated as well. The naked bulb hung from a cord, unlike the lights in the other parts of the cellar, which were set in porcelain fixtures attached to the joists. Instead of a pull chain, it had string that was black and frayed with age. The bulb swayed lazily over the pit. Dan must have been pulling on its string when he fell.

She wandered over to the pit and peered in, careful to keep clear of the shifting dirt. The oscillating light made it difficult to see how deep the depression was.

As she stared into the hole, her tension headache worsened, until it became a vise that squeezed the back of her skull. Her mounting discomfort was accompanied by a growing conviction that, creepiness aside, there was something very, very wrong about this place. A sudden movement caught her eye. She froze. Her grip on the luopan tightened.

Two red spots of light were glowing far, far down in the pit. The lights winked out for a second before they returned. Junie gulped. *The spots looked just like ...* The skin at the nape of her neck prickled when she realized what she was seeing. Eyes. The spots were EYES. Something was staring back at her.

She squeaked when she felt a touch on her arm. It was Tham. He gave her an odd look and said, "We should leave immediately. We don't know how stable the ground is—another sinkhole may open up."

She nodded and moved away from the pit.

They couldn't go very fast with Dan incapacitated. Junie, trailing after the other two, couldn't help stopping frequently to look behind her.

Once upstairs, they hustled Millie out in case the sinkhole had compromised the house's foundation. The homeowner insisted on driving Dan to the nearest emergency room to have his ankle checked out.

Joe called for a cab after Millie drove off with Dan. By the time the taxi arrived, Junie had convinced herself that what she saw in the pit was nothing more than a trick of the light. *Perhaps some kind of weird reflection from the swinging bulb?*

Back at the office, Tham told her she got the job. "If you still want it, that is. Bear in mind, though, that it's not always this exciting." He chortled. "It's not every day that we get to mount a sinkhole rescue."

"So, Mr. Tham, what is it exactly that I'll be doing?" she asked.

"As my associate, you'll organize our schedule, help me with the customers, conduct research, do some bookkeeping, keep the office clean, that sort of thing. As my apprentice, you'll get to learn the trade. And please," he added magnanimously, "call me Joe."

"Um, Joe, how much will I be paid? When I worked at Starbucks, I made more than minimum wage."

"You'll get a cut of the profits." Tham pointed to the dry erase board. "These are the rates. I'll pay you 10 percent of the profit we make from any work assignments."

"Including today?"

He hesitated. "Millie didn't get a chance to write me a check," he said at last. "But when she does, you'll get 10 percent of whatever is left over after we take out expenses, including cab fare. So, do you want to work for me?"

"Before I accept the offer, I have a confession to make." Junie hung her head. "I didn't quit from Starbucks. I made up the story about the disabled co-worker. They did fire me."

"What for?"

"I mixed up orders. And I might have forgotten to turn up for a few shifts. I also dropped things and broke several plates and mugs."

"Good thing then that we won't be providing coffee and snacks as part of our services," he said dryly. "At least not for the foreseeable future. See you tomorrow, if I see you, at tennish."

Chapter 3

Junie stopped at a bookstore on her way to the Gallery Place station. After a few minutes of browsing, she settled on a beginner's guide to feng shui. She walked to the station and boarded a Red Line train, transferring to the Blue Line at the Metro Center stop.

She received a text from her brother as she was walking home from the Franconia-Springfield station.

"How's it going fartface?" Patrick asked.

"Pretty good stinkbreath," she replied. "Got the job."

"Whoo hoo!" he texted. "Ma will be thrilled."

"BTW," Patrick added, "coming home in about a month's time. Have something to discuss with Pa and Ma."

"What?" Junie asked.

"Not sure yet. Still deciding. If I tell you and Ma knows you know, she'll pry it out of you in a nanosecond."

True. There were no secrets from Ma. "Whatever armpit sniffer," she typed.

"See you later butt scratcher."

Junie smiled and jammed the phone back in her jeans pocket. She and her brother had traded insults—usually related to the anatomy—since they were little. The name-calling was now their secret code.

She had arrived home. She glanced at the garage and scowled. The door was open, showing her mother's red Lexus inside. *Darn.* She tiptoed to the front door and inserted her key into the keyhole.

The door opened before she could turn the key. "Junie!" her mother gushed. "I expected you home a lot sooner! How did the interview go?"

"Um, good. I got the job. I start tomorrow."

"Congratulations!" Stella threw her arms around her daughter. "I'm so happy for you. Tell me all about it."

Junie spent the next 20 minutes being quizzed by her mother about the new job. Stella's eyes grew wide over her daughter's sinkhole adventure. She frowned when Junie told her what Joe had promised to pay.

"Only 10 percent?" She rubbed her chin absently with one finger, topped by a vermilion fingernail. "Hmm. We'll have to renegotiate that. If today's any indication, maybe you should get extra for danger. How about health insurance?"

"He didn't mention that."

"Oh well. I guess that means you're staying on our plan."

Junie finally made her escape. She went to her room and shut the door. "She means well, she means well, she means well," she muttered to herself as she turned the latch.

And her mother did mean well. That only made it worse.

Ma couldn't help being pushy. In fact, the pushiness, plus her initiative, optimism and enthusiasm, were what made her one of the top realtors in the area, if not the region. She could sell *anything*.

The problem wasn't so much Stella as the fact that Junie came from a family of achievers. In addition to Ma's success as a realtor, Junie's dad Raymond was a pediatrician with a thriving practice. Her parents worked hard and provided well for the family.

Then there was Patrick, 18 months younger than Junie.

Her brother was studying pre-med at Johns Hopkins University, with the aim of continuing his medical studies at either Johns Hopkins or Harvard. He hadn't come home for the summer because he was interning at a hospital in Baltimore. Patrick not only wanted to be a doctor, he wanted to be a surgeon. Because, Patrick being Patrick, he wanted to help people and save lives.

Not that she begrudged him his dreams. No—her brother was her best friend. He also was a decent guy, focused, crazy smart, and he worked his tail off. *And* he was funny, and loyal, and athletic to boot.

It was Junie who was the misfit, the proverbial square peg, a color among numerals. Where her family members were driven, she had no clue what she wanted to do. She had no BIG PLAN.

She drifted through school, being not particularly good at academics or sports. In senior year of high school, while her classmates were applying to four-year universities, she opted for the local community college. Even so, it had taken her more than three years to get her associate's degree in business administration.

After graduating, she had tried out a few dead-end jobs. It was a step up when Starbucks hired her. She was just settling into a comfortable, trance-like routine when Starbucks fired her.

Great. Washed up at 22. Her mother cried when she heard the news.

Stella had long despaired over her daughter's lack of ambition. After Junie's short career at Starbucks, Stella concluded that her daughter wouldn't get anywhere unless she built up her CONFIDENCE. If she could only start small, preferably doing something business-oriented because that was what she studied at community college, she would do alright. Maybe not stellar, but alright. So her mother somehow had found that job opening at Joe's feng shui practice. It was a sole proprietorship, so Junie shouldn't be overwhelmed.

Stella had found Joe himself while tracing her genealogy, one of her current crazes. It seemed he and Stella shared a grandfather, or was it great-grandfather? Joe was Stella's mother's first cousin once removed, or something along those lines.

Stella told Junie that because they were related, it would be unthinkable for him to refuse to hire her. After all, Chinese people have been hiring relatives for thousands of years.

Her mother meant to be reassuring when she said this. Junie, however, was thoroughly humiliated.

Okay, so maybe her mother was right about her low self-esteem. But her confidence was only part of the issue. The fact of the matter was that she couldn't seem to get excited about anything. The subjects taught in school were boring, and sports seemed like so much bother without any meaningful reward. And the jobs she managed to land with her paltry qualifications were less than inspiring.

Unfortunately, her mother now viewed her as a monumental challenge

—she was the ugly house with the one bathroom in an undesirable location between the railway tracks and the power lines that no one else could sell.

Junie flopped on her bed and buried her head under the pillow. After wallowing in self-pity for 10 minutes, she made herself get up. The only way to get Stella off her back was to actually succeed at something, or at least stick to it for longer than a few months. Her best bet right now was this job with Joe.

She couldn't deny that something had stirred within her when she saw the luopan. Could geomancy be the right course for her? If she was going to give it a chance, the least she could do was read up about it. She opened her backpack and took the feng shui book out.

Preparation is the gateway to success. Wasn't that what Pa always said? He had a saying for everything. He thought that gave him gravitas. Junie called it his Confucius Complex.

* * *

Joe found the events of the day racing through his mind as he tried to sleep.

He really hadn't been looking for an employee when Stella Soong called him from out of the blue a week ago. Before that, he had no idea she existed, or that he still had relatives in D.C. Somehow, after his conversation with her, he ended up agreeing to interview her daughter.

Still, he might have forgotten the incident had Stella not called yesterday to say her daughter was coming to the office to see him. Not to mention her two reminders this morning.

He decided that he liked Junie. She was quiet and seemed timid, but she hadn't panicked when they needed to rescue Dan. Except—the girl had looked so pale when she stood at the sinkhole, as if she had seen something truly dreadful. Oh well, as he had told her, it wasn't usually this exciting.

He sighed. Hiring Junie was probably a bad move. He was putting off the real decision—whether or not to shutter the business. The truth was, he had hardly any customers. But maybe, as Stella had so persuasively argued, Junie was exactly what he needed to attract new, younger clientele. New blood, as Stella had said. But could new blood compensate for what was missing?

Joe's father had been known as the Golden Dragon. His grandfather was the Iron Dragon. They, and their forefathers before them, had been more than feng shui practitioners. What the Tham Dragons did was as magical as you could get. He had seen it for himself, having accompanied his father on jobs until he was 10, when the Golden Dragon died.

By then, even though Joe was only a boy—and even though his Chinese name was Red Dragon—it was already evident that he lacked certain innate abilities. His father had known—Joe remembered the disappointment in his eyes.

It didn't help that after the Golden Dragon's death, his widow, Joe's mother, had hidden away all the tools of his trade, either because she blamed his demise on his occupation, or because she wanted to protect her son. It wasn't clear—Elsie Tham wasn't a woman who explained herself.

When Joe was in his 20s, Elsie had turned over to him all his father's things, including the luopan and the sword. Thinking to honor his father and ancestors' memories—and against his mother's wishes—Joe restarted the feng shui business and contacted his father's former clients.

In the beginning, the clients—remembering the old Tham name—had flocked to the practice. They quickly discovered that Joe Tham was not the next Golden Dragon. He didn't even know how his father's weapons worked.

Those clients soon disappeared. He eventually acquired new customers, mostly Chinese-Americans who wanted to reconnect with the old culture. Others, like Millie, were enamored with Eastern mysticism and traditions. A few clients just needed to fill a void.

Through word of mouth, Joe managed to build up a meager practice. Unfortunately, old-fashioned word of mouth didn't go so far today, in the social media age. He would be living on the streets if not for the wealth his father had accumulated.

Now, after more than 20 years of trying to make a go of it, he had all but given up. His father's money was almost all gone. Perhaps it was time to let the Tham name fade into the sunset. There was nobody left who would care.

Joe sighed again. He decided he would give Junie a month or two before letting her down gently. She was young—she could easily find another job.

Chapter 4

Junie was about to enter the stairwell for Joe's office when she spied the sign in the Laughing Buddha's window: "We serve bubble tea."

She had spent half the night reading the feng shui book. Bubble tea, or rather the caffeine in it, sounded like a good idea. She opened the cafe door and went in.

A tall guy stood behind the counter. He was about 25, with short, curly dark-blond hair and a neatly trimmed beard. His name tag identified him as Noah. His eyes were light blue, like the waters of the Mediterranean Sea at midday. Junie hadn't been to Europe, but she and her mother loved HGTV's *House Hunters International*.

"Hi," Noah said with a smile. "What can I get for you today?"

"You," she said to herself. But seriously, he was way, way, *way* out of her league. He probably spent most of his time fending off girls much prettier than she was. On the other hand, he worked the breakfast counter at an Asian cafe. Not a good prospect, her mother would say.

"Hello?" Noah sounded a little uneasy.

She realized he was still waiting for her to order. The eyes-like-the-waters-of-the-Mediterranean had turned quizzical. Had she been staring at him the whole time? Did she look spaced out? She adjusted her glasses, suddenly self-conscious.

"Do you need a minute?" he asked.

"Um, can I have the matcha milk tea?"

To her regret, Noah didn't take long to prepare the tea. "I'm Noah, by the way," he said as he handed her the order. "Are you just visiting our nation's glorious capital, or do you work around here?"

"I work on the third floor of this building," she said. "I just got hired."

"Oh." He looked surprised. "I didn't know Joe was hiring. Well, I guess I'll see you around."

She couldn't think of a response, so she turned around and left. As she climbed the stairs, it struck her that she hadn't told him her name. *Darn.*

Joe was engrossed in the *Washington Post* when she got to the office. "Good morning, Joe," she said politely. He mumbled something from behind the paper.

She went to the other desk and set her bubble tea down. From his lack of interest, she figured it was alright for her to sit there.

"So, what would you like me to do today?" she asked.

There was no response from behind the newspaper. The silence lengthened. Finally, he grudgingly pushed over the paper's Arts and Entertainment section. "Why don't you read that, see if anything catches your eye."

"Um, okay."

After about two hours, she had skimmed through every article in the *Post*. She wished she had brought her laptop. She couldn't sit still without anything to do. She cleared her throat.

She cleared it again, louder in case he didn't hear her the first time.

"*What?*" he barked.

"Say Joe, according to my feng shui book, the office isn't conducive to good energy flow." When he didn't reply, she added, "Can I take a shot at redecorating?"

He sighed heavily, picked up his paper and went through the kitchen to his apartment. She took that as a resounding "YES."

Junie, to her own surprise, had found the feng shui book extremely interesting. She couldn't put it down last night. The concept of qi made total sense to her, and she now was eager to apply the book's teachings. She trotted over to the front door, opened it and stood in the doorway. As suggested by the author, she visualized a pool of good fortune pouring like water into the office.

She was shaking her head before long. The way the furniture was positioned, Lady Fortune would collide with Joe's desk, get trapped in the corner between his desk and Junie's, and languish from lack of light and good air quality. No wonder the office felt so stagnant. She had to remedy the situation.

Her very first action was to prop the door open, so Lady Fortune *could* actually enter. Following that, she completely raised the blinds covering the three windows. Bright sunlight poured in. The light was a vast improvement, except for the fact that it revealed how very dusty the windows and the office were.

"Joe," she yelled, "do you have any cleaning supplies?"

Not receiving any answer, she went into the kitchen and helped herself to whatever she could find.

By the afternoon, Junie had washed the windows and polished the desks to a high shine. She started on the carpet after eating a late lunch, a sandwich she had brought from home. She whistled as she worked, thoroughly enjoying herself.

When Joe ventured out of his apartment in the early evening, he was greeted by an office so fresh and bright he had to blink. The front door was wide open. The two desks had been pushed to either side of the room to create a central walkway. The carpet was vacuumed, the newspapers cleared away.

But it wasn't just the neatness and cleanliness. The energy of the room was ... different.

"What do you think?" she asked shyly. When he grunted, she added, "If you give me money for paint, I can paint the walls. How about blue for serenity? Or maybe green for vitality?"

The phone rang, interrupting his indignant response. He took a deep breath before answering.

It was Millie, calling to say Dan twisted his ankle but hadn't broken any bones. He was back at the Kalorama house, waiting for an inspection. The building inspector was going to assess the sinkhole and review the structural integrity of the cellar and house.

Joe thanked her for filling him in. He told her how much she owed for his services, after which he ended the call.

"Well," he mumbled to himself. "That's that."

* * *

The next day, Junie brought an orchid and a painting to the office. If he didn't allow her to paint over the gray walls, she figured she would bring the color.

The painting was an abstract with bright red and orange swirls. It represented the fire element, and she hoped it would revitalize the office's limp energy. The orchid with its large white blooms represented wood, and would encourage growth and renewal.

The plant and art were Stella's. Junie knew she would never miss them. Her mother was always buying things at garage sales and discount stores to make the houses she was trying to sell more attractive.

Joe's face was sour when Junie lugged the items in. She ignored him. As Pa said, change is hard. And she had made a personal sacrifice—because her hands were full, she hadn't stopped by the Laughing Buddha to get bubble tea. So Joe could lump it.

She hung the art at the back wall, where it would be the first thing customers saw when they stepped in. She moved the orchid around her desk until she found the perfect spot for it. When she was satisfied with the plant's placement, she took her phone out and started snapping photographs of the office from various angles.

"Say Joe," she said when she was done with taking pictures.

He had gone back to hiding behind his paper. She heard a snort. Or maybe it was a growl.

"You know, because we're on the third floor, it's probably hard for walk-in clients to find us."

He growled again.

"So I'm thinking we should advertise. First of all, I'm going to ask my mother to post these photos on her Facebook page. It'll be great exposure —she knows everybody.

"We also should create a website for the company. What do you think? We can post photos of our work to the site and testimonials from satisfied customers. The photos can be posted on Instagram as well.

"And we should buy ads on Facebook. Here's a thought—what about offering discount packages through Groupon? And you know, right, that if we take Uber or Lyft, we could cut down on cab fare and keep better records of our expenses?"

A groan came from behind the paper. The groan was followed by a few hollow thumps, as if Joe was banging his forehead on the desk. *Was that a "no" to the Groupon discounts or to the ride-hailing services?* Junie decided it was more a "let's wait and see" on either suggestion.

At lunchtime, she walked down to the Laughing Buddha for her bubble tea. The cafe was almost filled with a young and diverse crowd, picking away at dim sum and noodles with disposable wooden chopsticks. There was a long line at the takeout counter. She caught sight of Noah in the kitchen, chatting with an Asian cook. He smiled and waved. She waved back, disappointed that she wouldn't get to speak with him.

The first call came after lunch. It was Mrs. Yang, a woman from Stella's mahjong circle. Mrs. Yang made an appointment on Monday for them to review the feng shui in her condominium.

The next call was Mrs. Zhui, one of Stella's oldest friends. She wanted Joe and Junie to bless her hairdressing salon. Mary Hudsen—one of Stella's new clients—called after that to arrange a blessing for the cake shop she was opening in Annandale.

By the end of the day, they had booked 10 appointments for the following two weeks, all connected in some way or other to Stella. It appeared Junie's mother wasn't taking any chances with her daughter's success.

It was Friday, so Junie didn't have to go to work for the next two days. She spent most of the weekend at the library, reading all the books and materials she could find on feng shui and qi.

Chapter 5

On Monday morning, Junie fielded a few more calls from people wanting appointments. Again, the callers were all related to Stella.

In the afternoon, she and Joe took a taxi to R Street Northwest to see Shirley Yang's condo.

Junie didn't know much about her mother's friend, except that she was an accountant for the federal government. Her husband was a researcher at the National Institutes of Health. The Yangs must be well compensated —their two-bedroom, two-bath home was located in a handsome brick building not too far from Logan Circle.

Shirley was waiting for them in the lobby. She was tall and thin, in her early 40s, dressed in a gray suit that was the virtual uniform of D.C.'s federal government employees. She smiled brightly and her handshake was firm; the color of her suit emphasized the faint dark circles around her eyes.

"Hi Junie, nice to see you again," she said. "And you must be Joseph Tham, Junie's boss."

The condo was located on the fourth floor. As she showed them around, Shirley explained that she and her husband bought the condo two years ago. The place was cool and spacious, and tastefully furnished with dark teak wood and leather seating. The walls were in shades of beige and peach, except for one accent wall that was deep red. The red color was picked up by lush carpets in the dining and sitting rooms. Chinese brush paintings of misty mountains and fishes hung on the walls.

"Well, what do you think?" Shirley asked when they returned to the living room. "How is our feng shui? Should we do anything to improve it?"

"Your home is lovely," Joe said politely, and truthfully. He made a show of taking the luopan out of his bag. "But beauty is only one measure of a harmonious home. You also need a beneficial environment, which in turn relies on the smooth flow of positive qi, or energy. My luopan will help us to assess the energy in here."

Shirley was impressed by the compass. "I've heard about luopans but have never actually seen one. It looks really complicated. What do the directions mean?"

While Joe showed the instrument to Shirley, Junie went to stand at the front door. Using the strategy from her book, she visualized qi pouring through the doorway as she had done at the office. She could see that unlike the office, there were no obstructions that would choke the energy or impede its passage. Just to be sure, she walked slowly through the condo, carefully tracing in her mind's eye the qi's probable pathways.

The flow in the Yangs' place seemed optimum. Junie looked over at Joe and Shirley, who were doing their own walk-through with the luopan. She moved behind the two and peeked over Joe's shoulder. Other than a slight quaver, the compass's needle wasn't doing anything.

"Why is it doing that?" Shirley tilted her head at the quivering needle. "Is that bad?"

Junie looked more carefully at the homeowner. She spoke before Joe could answer. "What is it about the condo that makes you feel uncomfortable? Are you having trouble sleeping at night?"

Shirley turned uncertainly to Junie, obviously startled by the questions. "I love my home, I truly do." She paused. "But now that you mention it, I always feel a little restless here. Restless and anxious. Sometimes my anxiety is so bad that it interferes with my sleep. But these issues may be due more to my job than this place. My work is pretty stressful. I just don't remember it being this bad at our previous apartment."

"You need to change the color scheme," Junie said impulsively. She was surprised at the depth of her own conviction. "Red isn't right for this place. It's too disruptive. It's at war with the natural harmony of the condo, given that it's north-facing. I think the color may also be incompatible with your internal rhythms."

She grew self-conscious when Shirley and Joe stared at her. "Change it to what color?" Shirley asked.

"Try painting the condo in shades of blue, gray and white. Change the carpets too. Think water. Think deep ocean. Deep, deep ocean. That'll help you relax."

Shirley looked thoughtful. "You know, I think I will try that. The condo was freshly painted when we bought it so we didn't see the sense in repainting." She suddenly smiled. "It's a *great* idea. Why did you suggest blue? That's my favorite color. How did you *know*?"

Shirley eagerly brought out her laptop and she and Junie spent the rest of the consultation comparing paint colors. Joe stayed tactfully on the sidelines. When they left, Shirley rode the elevator with them down to the lobby.

"Thanks again," she told them. "I can't wait to paint. I might even take a few days off to do it myself! The condo will look great. Junie, tell your mother I said 'hi'."

"I kinda liked the red myself," Joe said as he and Junie walked out to the curb. "But good call. She seems happy."

* * *

Business continued to pick up, given all the new clients that Stella sent their way. Junie began to think she actually might have a knack for feng shui.

Their work was mostly consultations and blessings. After their success with the Yangs' condo, Joe was more than happy to let her take the lead on jobs involving décor and/or furniture alignment.

She found that with practice, she was getting better at evaluating qi flow using her book's techniques. She was also developing her own instinctive feel for what the clients needed, and what they should do to get the results they wanted from their surroundings, be it to enhance vigor, induce peace and well-being, or invite good fortune.

For their part, the customers seemed satisfied with her suggestions on how they should rearrange their furniture, or add certain colors or items to their residences and workplaces. As proof of that, Stella reported back regularly with her friends' praises.

Joe generally didn't say anything while Junie was making her recommendations, nor did he criticize after the fact. On several occasions, after she moved a few items or after customers had adopted her suggested changes, she saw him looking around with a baffled expression on his face.

Junie got to see and assist in Joe's blessing ritual. Although he had a few variations, the ritual—as far as she could tell—consisted basically of radiating positive energy by thinking good thoughts, lighting candles with soothing aromas, playing relaxing music, and scattering red-dyed rice for extra good luck. He sometimes also chanted a mantra—"om mani padme hum"—that apparently was some kind of Sanskrit incantation.

Unfortunately, he couldn't answer her most pressing question: how did the luopan work?

"Most luopans are used to determine favorable and auspicious site conditions," he told her one evening after they finished blessing a customer's shop. "This luopan, however, is different."

"How so?"

He shrugged. "I'm afraid that's been lost to time."

"What does it mean when the needle spins around and around, like it did at Millie's cellar?"

Joe shrugged again. "That's the first time I've seen it do that. That must have been an anomaly. It usually just moves a little from side to side."

"If that's all it ever does, why do you bring it for every job?"

"Tradition," he said brusquely.

Chapter 6

Dan watched with a worried frown as his workers shoveled material into the sinkhole.

After several days of monitoring, the building inspector determined that the pit was safe to fill in. With the inspector's okay, Dan's crew had lined the bottom of the hole with a thick layer of wet concrete. The concrete plug ensured the hole wouldn't get any deeper. It also provided a solid base for the fill.

The mix of clay and sand they were using for fill should be dense enough to prevent water from seeping and collecting in the sinkhole. Now all they had to do was fill the rest of the hole with topsoil.

Dan was nonplussed when he found out during the inspection how shallow the hole actually was. When he fell in, it felt as though he dangled over a vast abyss. He had been terrified. If Tham hadn't been there …

Fortunately, the inspection hadn't turned up other sinkholes. The soil at that particular spot must have been undermined by the construction of the house, or maybe by the heavy rains they'd seen earlier in the year. As an extra precaution, a structural engineer was going to assess the cellar and the house again once the new topsoil had settled.

Matias Reyes, his site supervisor, stepped away from the other men. "Dan," he called. "We're done."

Dan mustered a smile and hobbled over to inspect the work. His ankle still throbbed, but not too much if he leaned on the cane. Under Matias's watchful eye, the laborers had done a good job tamping down the topsoil. You could hardly see where the hole had been.

"Looks good," he said. "Tell the guys they can leave for the day. We'll finish up tomorrow."

Matias nodded. He barked out a few orders and the workers started to store their gear. The supervisor's eyes drifted to the filled pit. He looked troubled.

"What's wrong?" Dan asked.

"We must have dumped in tons of material," Matias said in a low voice. "I thought it'd never be full."

"Well, it's done. Go home or I'll call Ana to come get you. How are the kids doing?"

Matias laughed even though it was clear his mind was somewhere else. "Alecia's in Puerto Rico visiting her *abuela* for the summer. Alex's baby is due next month. It's a girl; they're talking about naming her after Ana. I'm not sure that's a good idea, having two Anas in the family."

"Your first grandchild. Ana must be over the moon." Dan tried to catch Matias's eye, but the supervisor was still focused on the spot. He muttered something under his breath.

Extraño. Dan caught the word just before Matias stepped away to help the crew pack up. Puzzled, he stared at the burly man's retreating back. What was it about the sinkhole that had struck his supervisor as weird?

Matias left with the last of the men. Dan waited until everyone had departed before turning off the temporary lighting he had installed around the work site. The room's one light bulb would have been woefully inadequate. It had been a bitch to lug the lights, and the generators that powered them, down the cellar stairs and through the narrow tunnel. Not to mention his workers had to carry in the fill materials and mix the concrete by hand on polythene sheeting. To their credit, the guys hadn't complained too much about the trying conditions.

He glanced at the filled-in pit as he reached for the last light, and uttered a surprised expletive.

The dirt had been level when he looked it over with Matias. He was sure of it. Now, he could clearly see a slight depression. The fill must still be settling. He opened his mouth to call the crew back, then changed his mind.

It had to be almost night. He couldn't hear a sound from the main section of the cellar. His men probably were on their way home. It occurred to Dan how alone he was, and how much he hated it down here, especially this gloomy chamber. The construction lamp, bright as it was, couldn't penetrate the shadows crouching at the far corners.

He was still looking nervously over his shoulder when a furtive scratching noise came from under his feet. It made him jump; his bad ankle twinged at the sudden movement. In front of him, the depression in the dirt seemed to sink a little more.

Dan decided he couldn't bear to be in the chamber one second longer. He hurriedly turned off the lamp and limped out.

* * *

Three days later, Matias let himself into Millie's house. He didn't usually work on a Sunday, but there were specialized tools in the cellar that were needed at another job site early tomorrow.

Dan would have fetched the tools himself but the little league team he was coaching had a game today. He called this morning to ask if Matias could collect the tools for him.

Matias didn't mind, but Ana wasn't too happy. They were having dinner tonight with Alex and his very pregnant wife, and Ana wanted a few items from the grocery store for the chicken *asopao* she was cooking. The stew would be followed by *arroz con dulce* for dessert. Matias had assured her that it wouldn't take him long to pick up the tools, and there was plenty of time to stop by the store afterwards.

The foyer was bright from the afternoon sun. The house was quiet as he walked briskly to the cellar. He didn't expect to run into anybody. Millie wasn't moving in until the structural engineer gave the house a clean bill of health.

Down in the cellar, he turned on the light at the base of the staircase. The bag of tools was not too far away, exactly where Dan said it would be.

Matias was slightly ashamed at how relieved he was at not having to venture further into the cellar. There wasn't a hint of daylight down here. It might as well have been blackest night outside. He didn't like to think of himself alone in the tunnel or that uncanny room where the sinkhole was. An involuntary shudder shook his stocky frame. *Gracias a Dios for that small mercy.*

He had the bag in hand and had placed one foot on the steps when he heard the noise. It was a mixture of scratching and scrabbling, as if something was working away at the dirt.

He frowned and turned around. "Hello?" he called. "Who's there?"

The scrabbling became more frenzied at the sound of his voice. A brief silence after that, followed by a soft flop. Next came a series of thuds.

Footfalls. The word dropped like a pebble in his brain and his heart rate picked up. The thuds were footfalls. Something was coming toward him from the older part of the cellar. It—whatever it was—was moving through the tunnel now. The thuds were getting closer and closer together. Whatever it was, it was picking up its pace.

His heart was beating so fast and thundering so hard in his ear that he was surprised he could hear anything else. He dropped the bag of tools on the ground, opened it and grabbed up a large wrench. He dug the flashlight he had brought out of his pocket. He turned the flashlight on and shone it in the direction of the sounds. He raised the wrench in his other hand.

His beam stabbed through the darkness and lit up the tunnel's arched entryway. Something appeared in the light.

Matias blinked. He couldn't believe his own eyes. *Chupacabra.* The word burst involuntarily from his lips before his terrified brain could process what he was seeing. Chupacabra. Goat sucker. The creature from folklore that had scared Alex and Alecia when they were children. *But chupacabras weren't real.* The thing in front of him couldn't be real. THIS COULD NOT BE REAL.

He suddenly gasped. It felt as if someone had just punched him in the chest with a closed fist. His jaw clenched; massive pain surged through his left side and down his arm. The wrench and the flashlight fell from his hands. He was dead before he hit the ground.

The thing that Matias had seen dropped on all fours and crawled to his body. It leaned over him. It fed.

After it was done, it crept slowly up the stairs.

Chapter 7

Near the end of the month, Joe gave Junie her cut from the money they had made since she got hired. He saw her face fall when she opened the envelope into which he placed the cash.

"What's wrong?" He braced himself, sure she was about to demand a raise.

"It's not bad if we keep making this kind of money, but it won't be enough for me to move out of my parents' house anytime soon," she said despondently.

Joe initially had been alarmed by the sudden influx of business. He was even turning a profit! And it was all due to Junie's mother. If Junie left, he had no doubt the work would dry up. If it did, he would be back to the big decision—whether to close for good.

And the truth was, he enjoyed having something to do, and feeling useful. He also liked having someone around. Junie wasn't a bad kid. She worked hard, took instruction well and was good with the customers. And her feng shui knowledge was growing by leaps and bounds. Not to mention that after she was done with a place, he could swear he felt an actual shift in its energy. Not that he was the best judge.

He supposed he could raise Junie's take to 20 percent. Or perhaps there was a better solution. "Are you looking for a cheap place to rent?" he asked.

"I've looked at a few ads, but everything's been out of my reach. You know how expensive D.C. is." She loudly sucked up bubble tea through a straw. She couldn't seem to get enough of the infernal stuff, always running down to the Laughing Buddha to buy more.

"I've got a second bedroom in my apartment that has an attached bathroom," he said. "It used to be my parents' room. No one's using it now. I can let you move in there rent-free, but we'd be sharing the kitchen and living facilities."

Junie's face lit up.

"Don't get too excited yet," he warned. "The room's kind of cluttered. You'll have to clear it out and clean it. You also have to provide your own furniture."

"Can I see it?" she asked eagerly.

Joe already was regretting his hasty action. But it was too late to back out. He sighed and got to his feet. They trooped together through the kitchen into the apartment. When he opened the door of the bedroom, Junie looked daunted by all the newspapers, magazines, old clothes, cardboard boxes, broken knickknacks and plastic bags piled haphazardly on the floor.

"No need to decide now," he said. "Think it over, talk it over with your folks. It'll still be here Monday."

"Oh, I'm sure I want it," she said. "It's just I can't start on the cleaning now. My brother's coming home tonight, and my parents and I are meeting him for dinner.

"What about tomorrow? I know it's Saturday, but can I come over first thing in the morning? Can you let me in? I can't wait until Monday. Monday is *two days* away."

She finally stopped prattling. Joe stared at her for a minute. He shuffled over to a cabinet in the living room and took something from a drawer. He returned and handed her two keys.

"This is the spare key to the office," he told her. "This other one opens the stairwell door. The keys are yours while you work for me. You can let yourself in tomorrow."

Junie couldn't concentrate on work after that. Joe was relieved when she left for her dinner date with her family. He wished he hadn't mentioned his spare room. It had been a long, long time since he shared the apartment with anyone.

Maybe her parents won't allow her to be roomies with a middle-aged man, he thought hopefully. *And even if she moves in, I can always fire her if*

I can't take it any longer.

* * *

Junie was meeting Ma, Pa and Patrick at a Spanish restaurant in Penn Quarter that her mother wanted to try. The restaurant was only about a five-minute walk from the office.

It was Friday evening and the area was bustling with traffic and pedestrians. She hurried down 7th Street Northwest, trying not to run into raucous sports fans heading for some event at the Capital One Arena and the crowds thronging outside the restaurants and bars. At a cross street, she narrowly avoided being run over by a bike messenger who sailed through a red light.

She recalled on the way that her brother had something he wanted to discuss with their parents. She wondered what it was. She had been too busy with work to pester him. It was probably just another award or a new scholarship. As far as Patrick was concerned, the sky truly was the limit.

She decided she would slip in her own announcement about moving out while her parents were distracted by Patrick's news. How would Ma and Pa react? Surely they would be happy for her.

She imagined them turning to each other and smiling joyfully. Ma might have tears in her eyes. *Junie's finally found her feet,* she would say. *A kite soars highest when it is set free,* Pa would reply, reaching for Ma's hand.

When she got to the restaurant, Patrick and her parents already were seated. Her mother waved vigorously when she saw her at the door. "We're over here," she shouted, causing the other patrons to turn their heads.

Embarrassed, Junie tried not to catch anyone's eye as she threaded her way through the tables. She sat down beside her brother, who gave her a wide grin. He looked good. He had a healthy tan and his spiky hair stood up like freshly mowed grass.

"So what's the big news?" She fondly ruffled his hair. "I'm all agog."

"I'm saving it for after dinner," he said.

"Great." She raised her voice slightly. "I have news too."

"Okay," Stella said. She and Raymond exchanged fleeting glances.

Junie instantly felt defensive. She let out a soft sigh and hid her face behind the menu. *Did her parents think she got fired again?!* It was hard being the black sheep. Patrick must have heard the sigh because his foot nudged hers in sympathy.

"How's the new job going?" he asked.

She liked her work but didn't like talking about it. What could she say? *I moved two chairs and a table at a nail salon yesterday, and decluttered someone's living room this morning.* Not really impressive or interesting in the whole scheme of things.

"Swell," she told Patrick. "Just swell."

"Shirley *loves* the new colors in her condo," Stella interjected. "She can't stop raving about how good they look, and how restful the apartment now feels. And Connie claims she's doubled her orders since your visit."

"Like I said, just swell," Junie mumbled.

The restaurant served tapas. Stella ordered a variety of dishes, including calamari, fried potatoes and the eatery's specialty, steamed mussels. While they ate, Patrick entertained them with witty stories of his adventures at the Baltimore hospital where, as part of his internship, he followed surgeons around and performed lab work.

Shortly into dinner, Patrick told them he and the other interns had been examining the brains of patients with advanced Alzheimer's disease.

"You have no idea how much their brains shrink," he said with relish. He launched enthusiastically into more graphic detail about the differences between the brains of healthy people and those with Alzheimer's.

Junie looked sadly at the mussel on her fork. She no longer was hungry. Patrick seemed to have brains on his … brain. He couldn't stop talking about them. He had moved on to brain tumors. She pushed the half-eaten bivalve to the side of her plate and hid it under a piece of cabbage. She supposed she should be thankful that he wasn't pulling up photos of diseased brains on his phone to share with them.

While they were waiting for their coffee and dessert, Stella turned to her son and beamed. "So Patrick, tell us your news."

He leaned forward eagerly. "Our research on Alzheimer's patients was what got me thinking. You know I've always wanted to be a surgeon. I think I know what kind of surgery I want to specialize in. It's challenging, but that's what I want to do. I want to be a neurosurgeon."

After a breathless hush, Pa clapped Patrick heartily on the back. Ma clasped her hands together and positively cooed with pride.

Junie scowled. After all this anticipation ... "You couldn't tell them this over the phone?" she growled. They looked at her in bewilderment.

"No," Patrick said seriously. "I have a lot to discuss with Pa to make sure I'm on the right track. Everything I do now could impact my career path."

Raymond nodded in agreement. "A lot to discuss," he echoed.

She was a little envious of Patrick as he and Pa huddled together to ponder his future. The two male Soongs had so much in common, bonded by their mutual interest in medicine. It was an exclusive club to which she would never belong. It also struck her then how much alike her father and brother were. They both were pragmatic to a fault, constantly planning and calculating to get where they wanted. It wasn't in their nature to leave anything to chance. A life lived spontaneously was a life given over to chaos.

Wait. If Patrick took after Pa, did that mean that she took after Ma? Junie glanced surreptitiously at her mother. Stella was listening to Patrick and Raymond, her lips still pursed in the remnants of a proud smile. Could she possibly take after Ma?

Stella looked up and caught Junie's eye. Her brows drew together as if she had just remembered something. "Junie has news too," she said, interrupting her husband and son. "We haven't heard Junie's news."

Junie suddenly was the focus of three pairs of expectant eyes. She felt herself shrinking under all the attention, like the brains of Patrick's hapless Alzheimer subjects.

"Um," she said, "I'm moving out of the house."

"Oh," Stella and Raymond said simultaneously, both equally astonished.

"Oh," Stella said again, this time without Raymond. "Did you find an apartment? Where is it?"

Junie told them about Joe's spare bedroom. Her parents didn't appear to have any objections.

"Living on your own will be good for your confidence," Stella declared. "And Joe's practically your uncle anyway. He'll look out for you."

She resented her mother's remarks. She was moving out, which meant she was taking steps to look out for HERSELF. When Patrick went to college in Baltimore, he didn't get any lectures about other people looking out for him. And he was younger than her! But whatever.

Later that night, Patrick knocked on her bedroom door. "Hey," he said.

"Hey yourself."

"It looks like we're both moving onward and upward," he said. "Congrats, lousebutt. Good for you."

"Thanks, clamhead."

She grinned, appreciating her brother's gesture. Unlike him, she wasn't planning anything as ambitious as brain surgery. But he understood how important this was for her.

Chapter 8

When Junie stumbled out of her bedroom, Raymond was the only one at breakfast. Stella and Patrick were sleeping in.

"You're up early," he said, pushing some buttered toast in her direction.

She grabbed a slice and told him she was going to the office to clear out Joe's spare room. "I probably won't be back until late."

"Is the room furnished?"

When she shook her head, Pa said he would call Home Depot and rent a moving truck for tomorrow. "You can bring your bed and your bookshelf over. We should do it this weekend, while Patrick's around to help. If we collect the truck at 9 a.m., we should be able to drive back, load in the furniture and be at Joe's by about 11."

"I'll let him know."

"Your mother wants to take Joe out for lunch after we help you move. Are you okay with that?"

"Sure Pa."

"By the way." Raymond looked somberly at his daughter over the tops of his glasses. "If Joe tries anything funny, call me. I don't care whether it's day or night. I'll be there as soon as I can."

He paused for a beat and added, "Don't let your mother know I said this. She'll only worry."

Pa's medical practice, where he spent most of his time, was in a women and children's hospital on 23rd Street Northwest. He could be in Chinatown within 15 minutes if she needed him.

She almost laughed out loud at a sudden vision of Pa and Joe engaged in fisticuffs. It would be a hard fight. While Pa might have a few years—and a few pounds—on Joe, they weren't that different in terms of height and build. Joe had a few tricks up his sleeve, but Pa was tenacious.

Junie left for Chinatown, arriving at the office so early that the Laughing Buddha wasn't yet open. She galloped up to the third floor and let herself into the office. No sign of Joe. She tiptoed to the apartment. Still no sign of Joe. The door to his bedroom stayed firmly shut. She stopped in front of the door to the other bedroom and sighed.

Her own place. Independence. *FINALLY.*

She spent the next few hours hauling bag after bag to the trash and recycling bins behind the building. By late morning, all that was left in the room was an antique rattan rocking chair, which she hoped Joe would let her keep. There also was an old steamer trunk in the walk-in closet.

The trunk was covered with badly faded stickers that had Chinese characters on them. Perhaps Joe would let her keep the trunk as well. It would make a cute side table. If he let her empty it out, it would provide extra storage for her stuff.

Cleared of its mess, the room actually was quite spacious, with polished wood floors that were aged to a mellow gold-brown. The closet was bigger than the one in her old bedroom. There was only one window, but it was large. The view, granted, was of the alleyway below and the brick wall of the adjacent building, but she could think of several ways to keep the room's energy fresh and circulating.

Her stomach was growling by now. She went out to the living area. Joe was sitting at the small dining table eating a bowl of cereal. At her hopeful face, he rose silently, took out an extra bowl and retrieved the milk from the refrigerator. He gestured at the cereal box on the table. "Help yourself," he growled.

Fortified by two bowls of cereal, she went to work on the room's attached bathroom. The fixtures were old, but the floor was marble and the bathtub had claw feet. The shower curtain that went around the tub was fastened with antique fasteners shaped like dragons. At one time, real money had been spent on the apartment.

By late afternoon, Junie had cleaned everything in the bathroom. She had also swept and mopped the bedroom floor, wiped down the closet, washed the window, and dusted the rocking chair and steamer trunk. She was almost done, but she wasn't yet ready to go home. Sitting cross-legged on the floor, she thought about where she would place her furniture and belongings.

The closet could comfortably accommodate her clothes and shoes. Her twin bed could be placed against the wall opposite the bathroom door. She would mount her small TV on the wall that faced the foot of her bed, and there was enough space under the TV for her bookshelf. The rocking chair would go by the window. The steamer trunk would go by the chair.

She got up and carried the chair to the window. She pushed the trunk beside the chair. It wasn't very heavy. She raised the lid, curious to see what was inside.

There were two yellow robes in the trunk, neatly folded, as well as a bandanna with Chinese words on it. There also was a short wooden sword, a dented and tarnished bronze bell, a faded blue velvet bag, and a stack of yellow strips of paper about three inches wide and eight inches long. Red stylized symbols were painted on each one of the yellow rectangles. The symbols didn't look familiar, and Junie couldn't tell if they were meant to be Chinese characters.

She took out the velvet bag and brushed it vigorously with her hand. Like everything else in the trunk, the bag was grimy with age. Its contents were hard, like marbles, but irregularly shaped. She undid the drawstring, upended the bag and shook. Dust rose as several smooth stones of varying shapes, sizes and colors tumbled onto her lap.

Mixed in among the stones was an angular piece of white crystal that sparkled in the afternoon light. She picked up the crystal and quickly dropped it with a squeal. It was warm, and she could have sworn that it vibrated in her hand.

The shard now lay innocently still on the floorboards. But something seemed to move within its translucent depths.

Junie laughed nervously. She must be tired from all her hard work, or dehydrated, or something. She carefully returned the crystal and the stones to the bag. They might be valuable.

She next picked up the wooden sword. She wondered whether it was once part of someone's Halloween costume. It was surprisingly heavy for a cheap prop. The gilt on its handle was faded and chipped. Someone had carved Chinese words into its stubby blade—the characters were barely legible. She rose to her feet and brandished the sword as if it were a light saber from the *Star Wars* movies. It wasn't much to look at but it cleaved through the air with a satisfying swoosh. It felt just right in her hand.

She went to the door, opened it and looked out. Joe was watching a baseball game on TV.

"Hey Joe," she yelled. "Look what I found." She held up the sword.

"Those were my father's weap ... uh, things," he said. He came over and took the sword from her. "I'd forgotten about them. They've been lying in the trunk in the closet for close to two decades."

"What do those words say?" Junie pointed at the sword's blade. "Those are traditional Chinese characters, right?"

He muttered something that sounded like "chi qi." When she looked blank, he said, "The words, literally translated, mean 'eat energy'. My father named his sword 'Energy Devourer'."

"Oh, right." Junie took the sword back from Joe. For some reason, she'd grown a little possessive of it. Again, it felt right in her hand, almost *familiar*. She was having the oddest feeling of *deja vu*.

"Did you see an old stick in the closet as well?" he asked.

"About yea high"—she held a hand up to ear—"with a red cloth wrapped around its middle?"

"Yes. That was my father's old staff."

She confessed she'd thrown the stick out with the other garbage. "I'm so very sorry. Should I bring it back?"

Joe hesitated. "No," he finally said. "No, that's fine. Do you want me to take the sword and the other items away?"

"Actually, can I keep them for a little while? They're what your dad used for geomancy, right?"

He nodded cautiously.

"I'd like to examine them more carefully, maybe do some research," she said. "Who knows, we may be able to incorporate them in our practice. Don't you think they'd look cool?" She didn't tell the whole truth, which was that she was loath to give up the sword.

Joe nodded again. *What was the harm?* In his hands, the tools had only sentimental value. And he was the last of the line. "But please, these aren't toys," he said sourly as he went back to his TV. "Treat them with respect."

Junie placed the sword back in the trunk. "Sleep well, my Energy Devourer," she whispered, stroking its blade. It was like an old friend.

She left the apartment and dashed down to the trash bins. Thankfully, the staff was still there. So this wasn't just an old walking stick as she had assumed. She carried it back to her room and polished it with a rag. Like the sword, it was heavier than she would have expected. It was a little crooked, with small gnarls and bumps along its length. A knob at one end served as a natural handle. She supposed it also could be held in the middle. The rough fabric tied there with string ensured a secure grip.

The staff shone after her ministrations. Whoever made it had tried hard to preserve the pale wood's innate beauty. It really was quite lovely. When she was done admiring it, she propped it back in the closet.

Before she left for the night, Junie told Joe she was coming with her parents the next day to move her bed and a few other things into the room.

"We'll be here around 11 or so," she said. "I'm not bringing a lot, so we should be done in a couple of hours. My mother would like to bring you out for lunch afterwards."

"Surely that won't be necessary," he spluttered. But she was already gone.

Chapter 9

As promised, the Soongs arrived shortly after 11 in the morning. The family bustled up and down the two flights of stairs hauling furniture and bags of Junie's stuff to the spare bedroom. They were done by 1 p.m., as predicted.

"Where would you like to go for lunch, Joe?" Stella asked.

Joe didn't eat out very often. All he could think of was the Laughing Buddha. The Soongs trooped cheerfully downstairs with Joe in their tow. The cafe wasn't very busy. They were shown immediately to a table by the large front window.

Stella took charge, ordering the set meal of soup, three meat and three vegetable dishes, bowls of rice and dessert. When the waitress left, she turned to Joe and said, "So Joe, tell me about yourself."

Ma would have made an admirable detective, or CIA interrogator. By the time the food arrived, Junie found out that Joe was previously married—the wife walked out after five years. There were no children. His mother lived in Florida and rarely visited. He had an older half sister whom he hadn't seen in years.

"Well, please think of us as your family here in D.C.," Stella said. It was clear to Junie that her mother liked Joe. "We can't thank you enough for what you've done for Junie. We've never seen her so excited about anything."

Joe stared silently at Junie. She stared stoically back. He wasn't aware that he had done anything for her. Her hiring, and his decision now to let her stay in the apartment rent-free were largely motivated by his own self-interest, so he could further delay having to close the business for good.

Raymond and Patrick, sitting on either side of Stella, beamed at Joe as well. "Blood is thicker than water," Raymond intoned sagely.

Joe fought the urge to run from the table and flee back to his apartment. The Soongs' niceness and positivity were overwhelming. No wonder Junie was so eager to get away.

Noah brought the check while they were finishing dessert. "Hi Joe, nice to see you here, and ... um ... "

That's right. He didn't know her name. Despite her frequent visits to the cafe, she hadn't yet found the chance to introduce herself. "Junie," she said helpfully. She pushed her glasses higher, hoping she didn't have dust or debris in her hair or on her face.

Noah gave Junie a quick smile and addressed Stella, judging—correctly—that she was boss of the party. "My name is Noah, and I'm the manager here. Please let me know if there's anything else you need."

So Noah manages the Laughing Buddha. Junie looked at him with newfound respect while Stella was complimenting the cafe's food. He seemed young for the job, but she could tell he was good at getting customers to come back. Her mother looked quite taken with him.

After lunch, the Soongs and Joe traipsed back upstairs. Joe, exhausted, retreated to his room after mumbling something about giving them privacy to say their goodbyes.

Junie, to her own surprise, was a little sad to see her parents leave. She looped her arms around Ma and Pa and gave them a clumsy hug even though the Soongs generally weren't demonstrative people. "Thanks, you guys," she muttered. "Thank you for everything."

Her mother fiercely returned the hug. "Take care of yourself." She sniffed, her eyes suspiciously bright. "Make sure you eat well, and call us often to let us know how you're doing."

Raymond patted his daughter awkwardly on the back. "Don't be a stranger." He looked meaningfully at Joe's closed bedroom door. "Remember, any time, day or night."

She walked her family to the stairs. Patrick gave her a thumbs-up just before they rounded the bend and she couldn't see them anymore.

Still feeling slightly morose, she went back to her new room and started putting away her clothes and books.

The phone in the office rang in the late afternoon. Junie came out of her room, ran through the kitchen and picked it up. "Joseph Tham's office. Junie speaking."

"Hello Junie, this is Dan Groskind. I don't know if you remember me. We met at Millie Scarpini's place. Is Joe there?"

Joe didn't look pleased when Junie summoned him from his room. His rumpled clothes and creased face suggested he had been taking a nap. "It's *Sunday*," he complained. "Why are people calling us on *Sunday*?"

He rubbed his bleary eyes and held his hand out for the phone. "Joe speaking." His brow furrowed as he listened.

"Okay, let's meet," he finally said. "Do you know the Laughing Buddha in Chinatown? It's not far from the Gallery Place Metro Station. Say 6:30?"

"What's going on?" Junie asked after Joe hung up.

"It's Dan. He has something he wants to discuss. He says it concerns Millie and the sinkhole."

* * *

Junie glanced around after they were seated at one of the Laughing Buddha's tables. Noah was nowhere in sight, to her disappointment. Joe asked the waiter to bring a pot of Longjing green tea and three cups.

Dan came in just as the waiter left to fetch the tea. Junie and Joe didn't recognize him at first, not until he limped up to their table. The contractor looked like he had aged 10 years. There were dark smudges under his eyes, as if he hadn't slept in days. His hair was greasy, his clothes wrinkled. He leaned heavily on a cane.

When the tea arrived, Joe waved the waiter away and lifted the pot. As he filled their cups, a rich fragrance wafted up from the yellow-green brew. The aroma reminded Junie of roasted chestnuts and dried flowers.

There was a long silence while Dan sipped his tea. He wrapped both hands around the white porcelain cup. The hands trembled, sloshing the tea onto the white tablecloth. "Thanks for seeing me," he said at last.

There was another long silence. "I probably shouldn't even be here," he said. "But you both have been there from the very beginning. No one else will understand. And Millie seems to trust you."

Dan told his story slowly, in spurts interrupted by lengthy pauses. It seemed that Millie's sinkhole repair project had experienced a spate of very bad luck. It started with the death of Dan's site supervisor, who suffered a fatal heart attack in the cellar one weekend shortly after they thought they had filled the sinkhole.

"I worked with Matias for almost 30 years." Dan choked up. "I was the one who found him. I went to the house to look for him after Ana, his wife, called me in a panic. She said he hadn't come home and wasn't picking up his phone.

"He and Ana were expecting their first grandchild." His features contorted as he struggled for control. "He was strong as a bull. No one suspected he had heart problems, not even Ana."

After a brief investigation, the authorities decided Matias's death was not workplace-related. Dan and his men were allowed back on the work site. It wasn't long before more accidents occurred.

The engineer hired to inspect the house's foundation tripped in the cellar and broke his leg. The replacement engineer tumbled down the cellar stairs and suffered a concussion. Three workmen came down with blood poisoning after they scratched themselves on nails and had to be hospitalized.

"Furthermore, equipment keeps malfunctioning, including a set of temporary lights worth thousands of dollars," Dan said. "I know from experience that workplace accidents are depressingly frequent, but this all happened within the space of two weeks. Not only that—my ankle should have healed by now. It was a simple sprain. But it keeps hurting and the swelling hasn't gone down. The doctors can't tell me what's wrong.

"And that damn sinkhole—no matter how much we pour into it, it's never enough. The fill is sitting on a concrete plug so it should have stabilized by now. But it's still settling, and we keep having to haul in more topsoil to smooth it out. I swear that thing's bottomless."

Dan fiddled with his teacup. Noticing the cup was empty, Joe refilled it with more of the aromatic tea.

The contractor clutched the warm cup as if it were a lifeline. "There's more," he said in a low voice.

"Lately, a few of my crew have … uh … reported seeing things. One of my most reliable employees told me he saw a man in the cellar who was all burnt up and disfigured. The man was just standing there one minute, and gone the next.

"Another worker saw a man rushing down the cellar stairs, shouting about a fire. He said the man was dressed like a union soldier. Others said they've heard screaming and moans.

"I myself have seen—" Dan had to take a deep breath before he could continue. "I saw two men in that narrow bit between the main cellar and that spooky room where the sinkhole's at. They were on fire, writhing in pain. It was so real I even smelled smoke and burning flesh. I ran toward them thinking they were my workers, but they … they disappeared when I got close.

"Then on Thursday—" He gulped. "On Thursday, as I was leaving for the day, I glanced back as I was rounding the bend in the cellar stairs. I … I thought I saw Matias standing at the bottom. It was dark and it was just a glimpse, but … "

Dan's face was ashen; his Adam's apple twitched as he inhaled and exhaled harshly. "I'm sorry," he finally said. "The sight scared the hell out of me, but this isn't why I wanted to meet up. I … I wanted to talk about Millie."

"What about Millie?" Joe asked.

"For starters, she hasn't been herself since the day she summoned both of us to the house," Dan said. "She's been … I don't know … preoccupied … vague. Then Matias died, and it was a major blow. She was very upset. When the authorities let us go back to work, she told me that once we were done with the sinkhole, she was going to nail the cellar door shut and never open it again in her lifetime.

"On Friday, the day after I thought I saw Matias, she told me to stop work altogether. She asked—no, *ordered*—me to take my men and go. She said she'd had enough. She said she didn't want anyone else dying in her house.

"Don't get me wrong. It's no problem for me to end the job. Most of my crew are refusing anyway to return to the site. I'm not too eager myself, to tell the truth. And Millie's not in any physical danger. Despite the fact that the soil hasn't finished settling over the old sinkhole, the inspectors and engineers seem to think it's safe. They've signed off on everything.

"What I can't get over is how Millie looked when we last spoke. Something had frightened her badly. She was shaking, and white as a sheet. Maybe she saw the same things my men and I did. But ... I don't think so—she hasn't been down to the cellar.

"Anyway, I'm hoping that you can check on her. Like I said, she trusts you. Surely you can come up with some excuse or other to visit? Isn't this what you specialize in? I'm really worried about her. I don't feel good about leaving her alone in that house, even if she stays away from the cellar. I don't think she should have moved in at all."

Joe took pity on the contractor, who looked thoroughly miserable. "I'll be happy to drop in on Millie, and examine the cellar as well," he said.

He turned to Junie. "Do we have anything scheduled for tomorrow?"

"No."

"In that case, I'll call Millie in the morning and set up an appointment."

On the way upstairs, Junie asked Joe what he thought of Dan's revelations. "What do you think is going on?"

"Who knows?" He shrugged. "You take an eerie place, a series of accidents and an unfortunate death. Imaginations are likely to be working overtime. It's human nature to try to impose order on chaos. We can't help rationalizing everything. It's never just simple, random bad luck."

"But why would Dan and his workers imagine fire and people burning up? What has that got to do with the heart attack and the other workplace incidents?"

He shrugged again. "It's best not to speculate until we talk to Millie and see the cellar for ourselves."

"Could the cellar be cursed? I haven't seen you tackle one of those yet."

He shook his head at her hopeful expression. "Sadly, the few curses I've been asked to remediate all had prosaic, not to mention extremely dull, explanations."

* * *

Junie found it difficult to fall asleep, still unsettled by what Dan had told them. On the other hand, her wakefulness could be due to her first night in an unfamiliar place. After tossing and turning for what felt like hours, she finally slipped into a fitful doze, only to jerk awake.

A little boy sat cross-legged at the foot of her bed. The room was completely dark, yet she could see him clearly, even without her glasses. She wasn't very good at judging children's ages, but he seemed very young, perhaps slightly older than a toddler. He would have been cherubic if not for the sickly pallor of his skin.

When he saw her eyes open, he crawled up to her. "Junie, open your eye," he said.

"My eyes *are* open." She scowled, a little cranky at being so rudely awakened.

"No, your eye." He raised his hand and smacked her quite painfully on the forehead with the heel of his palm. "Your eye, Junie, open your EYE. Your THIRD EYE. Use the crystal. Millie needs your help."

"Newsflash, nimrod," she grumbled. "I have four eyes, not three."

But the little monster had disappeared. She fell back to sleep wondering why she was dreaming about bad-tempered little blond boys.

Chapter 10

In the morning, Junie looked in the mirror and was surprised to find a faint bruise on her forehead. The blemish was barely noticeable, and it didn't hurt much when she pressed on it. She must have knocked her head in her sleep, probably at the same time she dreamed about the boy.

When she walked into the office, Joe was in the middle of the call to Millie. "It's just a courtesy follow-up visit," she heard him say. "Is today convenient?"

It must have been, because he added, "See you then."

They arrived at the house shortly after noon. It was as beautiful as before, its glass surfaces and metal planes and girders glinting in the sun. Millie opened the door before Joe could knock. "Come in, come in," she said.

She was dressed in another expensive pantsuit. She looked rested and vibrant, nothing like what Dan had suggested. Junie followed Joe into the house and immediately was chilled.

The imposing two-story foyer *felt* different. It was cold and dark, as if it were a drizzly fall day outside instead of summer. Junie could see the sun, but its rays weren't penetrating the glass.

Joe didn't appear to notice. He was telling Millie that they bumped into Dan. "He says you've had quite a bit of excitement over the last month, ever since we discovered the sinkhole."

"Oh, *that*." Millie's tone was casual. "I hope Dan isn't hurt by the way I terminated his services. I *was* feeling pretty depressed about the accidents, especially the death of that nice man, the supervisor. I couldn't help thinking he would still be alive if he hadn't been here that day." She sighed heavily.

"How are you feeling now?" Joe asked solicitously.

"So *much* better, and thanks for asking." Millie smiled brightly. "My sister, knowing I was upset, is staying with me temporarily. You might see her—she's around here somewhere. It was she who set me straight. That man's death was *not* my fault, and agonizing about it won't bring him back. Honestly, she's been *such* a comfort."

"Well, I'm glad you're fine," Joe said. "And I see you've done some decorating." He gestured at a new addition to the foyer: a large and pointy copper sculpture.

Millie beamed. "Do you like it? It's by an up-and-coming young artist from Detroit."

Junie could tell Joe didn't, but he nodded anyway. As he had observed on their prior visit, there were too many poison arrows in the house. Good feng shui is all about rounded shapes and graceful curves. Sharp corners and angles, on the other hand, generate sha qi, which is "murderous," or negative, energy.

"My decorator isn't done yet—she wants to add more pieces," Millie said as she led them to the cellar. "I told her the house must be finished by next Friday, at the very latest. I'm hosting a housewarming party the day after. You're both invited, if you can make it. I'm inviting Dan as well."

The decorator seemed already to have accomplished a lot since Joe and Junie last saw the residence. The place was now tastefully furnished. In addition, there were other new artwork and accessories scattered about, including tall Chinese vases and contorted statuettes that sat on polished black pedestals. Junie knew only one reason to place something on a pedestal—it cost a lot of money. She nervously kept both elbows and her backpack close to her body for fear of knocking something off its stand.

They passed a large cased opening, and Junie's eyes were drawn to the gleaming appliances inside. She poked her head in. Millie's newly installed state-of-the-art kitchen looked as expensive as the rest of the house. A woman stood at the sink with her back to the opening. She didn't turn around. That must be Millie's sister—she had similar chestnut-brown hair.

They were at the cellar door. Millie frowned. "So Joe, what is it that you want to do again?"

"We normally do a follow-up visit after we bless a place, but we didn't actually get the chance to perform a full blessing the last time we were here. Since you paid for a blessing ritual, I can do it now."

"Oh." She looked uncertain. "I guess that'll be fine. I'll leave you to it—Dan showed you around the last time. You know where everything is. I have to return to the foyer to wait for the decorator. She's due any minute and she doesn't have her own key.

"When you're done, just let yourselves out," she added. "Holler if you need me. I'll be around. Don't forget my housewarming party. I'll email the invitation sometime this week."

Frigid air tickled their faces when Joe opened the cellar door. He went in, turned on the landing light and started down the stairs. Junie stepped onto the landing after him and froze. She was paralyzed by the sight of a man crawling up the steps. He emerged from the gloom, his eyes bulging amid flesh that was red and blistered. His white shirt was blackened and smoldering. "Fire," he croaked. "Fire."

Joe brushed by him as if he wasn't there. The crawling man disappeared when Joe turned on the light at the base of the stairs.

* * *

"Junie," Joe called up impatiently. "What's keeping you?"

She made her way down on legs that trembled. Her heart was still hammering from shock. Joe was standing by the stairs, a flashlight in his hands. When she reached the cellar floor, he handed her the flashlight. He stooped and took the geomancer's compass from his bag, blissfully ignorant all the while of the shadows around him.

No, not shadows. They were definitely men, albeit gray and insubstantial, with black hollows where their eyes and mouths should be. They were almost invisible in the dark. They clustered silently around the stairs, standing just beyond the circle of light cast by the overhead bulb. Some were clad in union uniforms; others were clothed in soiled white shirts and dark pants. Some were bandaged; some had amputated limbs. They all wore expressions of terror. The stench of smoke clung to them, thick and acrid.

This was far, far worse than what Dan had described. It wasn't just one or two disembodied spirits.

There was a man standing right beside Joe who was more substantial than the others. He was short and broad, and dressed in modern work clothes. He saw her looking at him and tried to catch her arm. "Chupacabra," he whispered. "Beware the chupacabra."

She winced and reared back.

"What's the matter?" Joe asked, glancing curiously at her. He turned his head and gazed over his shoulder. "Did you see something?"

Not waiting for her answer, he walked into the crowd of men. He walked THROUGH them, as if they were nothing more than the smoke that clogged her lungs.

She somehow found the courage to move her legs. She felt cold when she scurried between the men, as if invisible damp spiderwebs trailed along her skin.

Joe had turned on another bulb. He blinked hard as he peered at the compass in the weak light.

"Well, the luopan isn't acting up this time," he said when she joined him. "Can you find the rest of the light bulbs and turn them on? If all seems well, we can just perform the blessing and go. I'll call Dan and tell him he's overreacting. Millie is fine, and the cellar looks just the same."

"Joe." Junie's teeth chattered so hard she could barely speak. "Joe, don't you see the shadow men?"

Bewildered, he stared at her. He scanned the dark cellar. "Where? *What* men?"

"All around. They're standing all around. I can even smell and hear them."

He gaped at the fear on her face. "Are you seeing what Dan and his people saw?"

"Yes, except there are more of them. Many, many more."

"What are they doing?"

"Nothing. They're just standing."

"Show me." He nodded at the flashlight in her shaking hands. "Point them out."

She pushed the flashlight's "on" button, then wished she hadn't. The phantoms looked even more horrific in her jittering beam. To her, at least. Joe obviously was blind to them.

Joe's expression was now grave. He tucked the luopan under his arm. "Junie, I want to check the extent of the problem," he said. "I need you to tell me, with as much detail as possible, what you're seeing and hearing here and in the rest of the cellar. Are you up for it?"

She took a deep breath and nodded. Her shaking was subsiding. They proceeded slowly, turning on the overhead bulbs as they went. When she saw, heard or smelled something, she shone the flashlight at the spot and described to Joe what she was experiencing. The phantom activity seemed to be centered around the stairs. She encountered fewer and fewer ghosts as they walked deeper into the cellar.

The specters she had seen so far were all men, which was why Junie was startled to find a woman at the far end of the main cellar. The female ghost wore a white cap over her hair and a white apron over her long black dress. She hid in the shadows but the fury she radiated was white-hot and blazing. Junie made sure to keep herself and Joe well clear of the angry apparition. Her baleful and accusing eyes followed the two of them as they sidled past her.

The spectral activity was picking up again. In the passageway leading to the chamber, Junie saw two men writhing on the ground. They were on fire, like Dan said, the flesh melting off their bodies. Their screams bounced off the walls.

The chamber was colder and darker than she remembered it to be. Her flashlight revealed huddled shapes, some little more than mounds of smoking and charred flesh. One of the mounds moaned and lifted something that must have been its head. It was impossible to tell whether it was a man or a woman, a young person or old. It had no features—its face had been burned off.

She decided to skip telling Joe about the thing with no face. She wouldn't have been able to find the words. The smell was overwhelming. Her head pounded and her vision swam. She was afraid she was about to pass out.

Joe headed toward the chamber's single light bulb. Before he had gone more than a few paces, Junie shouted, "Joe, STOP." She aimed the flashlight at the ground beneath the bulb.

Her beam showed a slight depression in the earth, in the middle of which was a small round hole about a foot or so in diameter. Joe stepped gingerly around the hole and pulled on the bulb's string. The weak glow that emanated did little to improve the situation.

He craned his neck to get a better view of the shaft. "Is this *new*?" He tested the ground with his foot to make sure it was firm before stepping closer. "Dan said the sinkhole was impossible to fill, but he didn't mention anything about a new hole."

Junie obligingly shone her light into the cavity. It was deep, deeper than her beam could travel. Unlike the previous pit, which had sloping, friable sides, the new hole was smooth except where chunks had been dug out. She moved a little nearer and extended her arm and flashlight into the aperture. As far as she could see, the missing chunks were regularly spaced. It was as if something had gripped the clayey sand at regular intervals to pull itself up.

"Junie, step aside. Let's see how deep this thing is."

Joe tossed a rock into the shaft. They waited, but couldn't hear a thud indicating that the rock had found the bottom of the cavity.

He turned his attention to the luopan. The compass's needle was wobbling slightly. After a moment of silent contemplation, he handed the instrument to her. "*You* hold it."

The needle skittered the instant the luopan touched her hand. Then it spun around and around. Joe sucked in his breath. He appeared to be deep in thought.

"Joe, can we leave?" she asked after a while. "I think I've had about as much as I can take." She gazed around the chamber in trepidation. The humped figures were still there, and they were still smoldering and twitching. She was proud that there was only a slight tremor in her voice.

He nodded reluctantly, reached up and switched off the light. They picked their way out of the chamber with the aid of the flashlight.

Their return to the staircase was excruciatingly slow because Junie insisted on going around, rather than through, the phantoms. As Joe turned off the bulbs, she couldn't decide which was worse—having the spirits ahead of her in the light, or behind her in the dark. She was profoundly grateful when they walked out of the cellar. Millie wasn't there but they could hear voices coming from some other part of the house. They found their way back to the front door and let themselves out.

The warm day had gotten even warmer. Junie felt as though she had spent a lifetime in the cellar, but it was only three in the afternoon. She lifted her head to the sun, reveling in its fierce, wholesome rays.

Chapter 11

When they got back to Chinatown, Joe treated Junie to a very late lunch—or an early dinner—at the Laughing Buddha. She was shell-shocked by what she had gone through, and didn't say much while they ate. She retired to her room for a nap after the meal.

While she napped, Joe called Dan to tell him he was right and that the situation *was* dire. "I don't want to say too much until I've done more research, but there definitely is something wrong with the cellar."

"But what about Millie?" the contractor asked.

"I think she's fine. She seems to be doing a lot better since you last saw her. It's the cellar I'm worried about."

"Well, thanks for checking it out. Is there anything I can do?"

"I'll let you know," Joe said. "By the way, when you and your men were clearing out the cellar, did you notice any weird symbols or bits of yellow paper in the vicinity of the sinkhole? The symbols or the paper would have been embedded or buried in the dirt, or attached in some way to the ground."

"No. But Matias was in charge of the clearing operation. I wasn't there myself. If he saw anything strange, he didn't mention it. Why? Is this important?"

"I'm not sure yet."

After hanging up, Joe went into his room and started searching. Finally, he located his father's old map under a pile of insurance documents. He brought the map to the dining table where he carefully unfolded and spread out the large sheet of paper.

The map was of D.C. and it was crisscrossed with red lines. The Golden Dragon had used a red marker to denote all the dragon, or ley, lines he discovered. Joe's heart sank when he confirmed that Millie's residence was situated where several dragon lines converged. In other words, her new home was built over a vortex.

That was bad news. *Very* bad news.

He groaned and clutched his hair. He chastised himself for not consulting the map sooner. It should have been a requirement before the start of any job. He had grown careless. Who knew how many incidents he had missed, how many he might have prevented? Take the unprecedented toxic political atmosphere, for example. How about the spike in homicides in the District?

And what else? He wasn't even very good nowadays at keeping up with current events. The Golden Dragon must be turning in his grave in shame.

He would have overlooked this one as well, if not for Junie. She had seen what he couldn't. *And the way the luopan had responded to her.* It was as though the instrument had confused her with the Golden Dragon.

Well, now that he knew better, he was going to make sure that his apprentice stayed away from the house. As far away as possible. The things that a vortex unleashed were not only dangerous, they were vicious.

But Joe himself had to do something. He would be letting down the venerable Tham lineage if he didn't. He could live with his conscience when he ignored the things that go bump in the night, as long as he wasn't aware of them. However, now that he knew they were there, he had to fulfill his duty. The question was: what *could* he do?

Having him fight a Dragon warrior's battles was like asking a blind man to make it on foot across one of Los Angeles's freeways. Except, in Joe's case, the stakes were higher and the chance of success lower. He was doomed to failure.

He heard Junie's door open. She came over to the table before he had time to put the map away. "Why are you consulting this?" she asked sleepily. "Did we get a new assignment?"

Before he could answer, she pointed at a spot on the map. "Hey, look. Isn't this where Millie's house is? What are all these red lines?"

Joe hesitated. *How much should he tell her?* She had been

extraordinarily brave in the cellar. Surely she deserved to know. "Those are dragon lines, otherwise known as ley lines," he explained.

"The lines are known by many other names," he continued when she looked interested rather than skeptical. "The ancient Peruvians called them 'spirit lines', the Irish 'fairy paths'. The Chinese and other cultures believe these are spiritual passageways that draw on the earth's energies. In olden times, houses of worship, burial sites and other mystical structures were built on or near such routes because of their power."

"Did you draw the lines on the map?" she asked.

"My father did. He traveled all over D.C. with the luopan to find and chart the pathways."

"What does it mean when the lines meet?"

"Trouble," he said grimly.

* * *

Junie couldn't believe what she was hearing. Millie's mansion was sited over a vortex of energy created by intersecting dragon lines. That wasn't the worst part. According to Joe, something had come through the sinkhole.

"Something?" she asked.

"Something really, really bad," he said.

"Malevolent supernatural entities are drawn to the vortices, which essentially are whirlpools of energy," he explained. "Sometimes, these monsters find or create a portal and break through to our world."

"*Monsters*? What are you talking about?"

"The Chinese call them 'yaoguai'; in Arabia they are known as 'jinn'. The Church labels them 'demons' and 'devils'. In non-religious parlance, they are 'elementals'. They existed long before humankind. I'm not exaggerating when I say they're evil personified. They come into our world to wreak havoc because ... well, that's what fuels them. It's what they do."

"You're telling me that a yaoguai climbed through the sinkhole into Millie's cellar?"

He nodded. "And you know this ... how?" she asked.

"When these monsters break through, they create gateways that may allow some of the vortex's power to leak into our realm," he said patiently. "If the vortex is in a place where wrongful death or suffering occurred, the excess energy can lead to ghosts suddenly manifesting. An abrupt increase in spectral activity was one way my father tracked yaoguai."

Junie's head was reeling from Joe's mystical mumbo jumbo. She didn't even believe in the existence of ghosts until today. She would have questioned his sanity if not for her experience in the cellar. "What do you mean he 'tracked' them?"

"He hunted them down and either killed them or returned them to the void, after which he sealed the portals," he said. "My father was the Golden Dragon. It was part of his responsibility as a Dragon warrior to help restore the balance of the universe, the yin and the yang, so to speak."

"Dragon *warrior*? Is that like some kind of superhero, like Spider-Man or Batman?"

"Um, yes, I suppose. Except Spider-Man and Batman are make-believe."

"The items that I found in the steamer trunk—they were what your dad used to track and hunt down the monsters?"

"Yes."

"Is that what you do as well?"

"No," he said sadly. "I am not worthy."

"So let's say the yaoguai holes up in Millie's cellar. Is that a problem? Dan said she's going to nail the door shut."

"These creatures aren't pests that you can just *ignore*." His tone was a little snippy. "When it comes to yaoguai, there's no such thing as peaceful co-existence. Most of them desire only one thing: human suffering. They feed on it. It's nectar to them; it prolongs their existence. Millie's yaoguai is up to something, you can count on it."

"How long do these monsters stay up here? Don't they have to go home sometime?"

"Yaoguai usually return quickly to their netherworlds after they've eaten their fill from mayhem or a disaster of their causing. They don't stay long because that can have unpleasant consequences for them. They're more vulnerable here. That's their Catch-22."

"Huh?" She knitted her brow. "What do you mean?"

"By feeding, these creatures can stretch out their existence, maybe even live forever, which is to become immortal. Basically, yaoguai desire immortality. That's why their hunger for human suffering is infinite. To feed, however, they must enter our plane, where it's easier to kill them, where it's easier for them to die. They have to risk dying so they can live forever. See the irony?"

Junie's brain was threatening to go into overload. She decided she needed some time to process all the information he was throwing at her. It was getting late anyway. He suggested that they both get some rest.

She returned to her room, but found she was too agitated to go back to bed. She turned on her laptop and typed in Millie's address.

* * *

Junie showed Joe the results of her research in the morning.

In the early 1800s, when the Kalorama neighborhood was untamed countryside, a wealthy merchant by the name of Thomas Montgomery Hobart built a brick manor on the site now occupied by Millie's new home.

Hobart lived and died at the house, after which it passed to his son Samuel in the 1840s. In late 1864, when Samuel was an old man, he moved out and turned the residence and its grounds into a hospital for union soldiers who had been wounded in battles nearby, in areas that would later become the Washington suburbs.

The manor caught fire in late March 1865, just before the Civil War ended. At the time, it housed about 150 wounded men. The manor burned for two days and was gutted. When fire officials finally entered the smoking ruins, they found 43 bodies in the cellar.

According to a survivor, the men and one woman—a nurse by the name of Sally Kinde—had been driven into the cellar by the inferno. By the time they realized the cellar had no exits, it was too late. Witnesses said they could hear cries of agony coming from the depths of the house, but were helpless to do anything.

Fifteen of the deceased who had holed up in an older part of the cellar were burned to death and/or crushed when the ceiling above them collapsed. The rest died of smoke inhalation.

Another five soldiers were listed as missing.

"I think it's safe to say we know who the ghosts in the cellar are," Junie said. She glared at Joe, her eyes bright with unshed tears. "When you say yaoguai like nothing better than human suffering, is this what you mean?"

He sighed and nodded.

"The article says the cause of the fire was never determined. Could it have been set by a yaoguai?"

"Perhaps," he said. "The yaoguai—maybe even the same yaoguai that we're dealing with now—could have assumed the shape of a soldier or a nurse and done the deed. Or it could have whispered in someone's ear. Or it might even have turned into a cat or a dog and knocked a candle over."

"They're *shape-shifters*?" She was horrified.

"Yes."

"If your dad knew about the vortex under Millie's house, why didn't he seal the portal?"

"A vortex doesn't automatically mean there's a portal," he said. "Such gateways have to be created, and it takes a fair amount of energy to punch through from one world to the next. My father tried to seal any portal of which he was aware. And he may well have sealed the one in Millie's cellar, but the seals can be broken or weakened. The Golden Dragon is gone so he can't tell us."

There was a long silence. "The yaoguai that's come through the sinkhole—what do you think it will do?" she asked at last.

"It's already created problems for Dan and his men. But that won't be enough. These things crave chaos. They're like Bond villains—nothing would make them happier than calamity on a large scale. The sooner the better. The bigger the better. The more people hurt or killed the merrier."

Joe and Junie eyed each other. "Millie's party," they said simultaneously.

"That's the biggest event on the horizon, so far as we know," he observed. "Large groups of people will be milling about the house. Some of them may be inebriated. Give one of them a gun. Throw in a grudge, or maybe some jealousy … "

"What's our game plan?" she asked.

"First, I need to get back into the cellar." Joe's forehead wrinkled as he concentrated. "I have to free those poor, trapped souls. They're only residual energy, but their continued suffering is grist to the yaoguai's mill. Their pain only makes it stronger. Think of a cow regurgitating its last meal and ingesting it again."

He ignored the face Junie made. "I should also get Millie to tell me more about the party so I know what I'm dealing with. After that, I have to somehow find out what the yaoguai is planning so I can foil it. Last but not least, I have to root out the yaoguai and vanquish it."

He looked slightly aghast at the uphill tasks ahead of him. Fortunately, he had some time. The party was one and a half weeks away.

"What about me?" she asked impatiently. "What do you want me to do?"

"You are not going near the house again. Needless to say, yaoguai are dangerous. Once this one knows it's been discovered, it'll fight tooth and claw."

"Joe, I hate to remind you, but you couldn't see or sense the ghosts in the cellar. You'll have no idea whether or not you've successfully released them."

He gulped. She was right.

"Face it, Joe. You. Need. My. Help," she said emphatically. "The creature has to be stopped. We can't allow it to cause another catastrophe, if it's the same one that surfaced in 1865. I'm coming with you to the cellar to free the souls, and I'm going to the party."

He opened his mouth, about to demur, when his face suddenly blanched. He looked queasy.

"What?" she asked in alarm.

"I'm assuming at this point that it's only a yaoguai," he said. "Those are lower-level entities. In Chinese culture they are frequently viewed as evil or spiteful animal spirits. But what if Millie's monster is a mogui?"

"*Mogui.* What's that?"

"Mogui are far rarer, but also far more deadly. They aren't just monsters —they're major league demons."

The expression on Joe's face grew even more somber. "Let me give you an idea of scale. There is a vortex similar to the vortex under Millie's house in the Brigittenau district of Vienna, Austria. That vortex, more specifically, is under a building that once was a public dormitory for men.

"Adolf Hitler lived in that dormitory from 1910 to 1913, during a very formative phase of his life," he said. "My father believed Hitler wasn't human, or fully human, by the time he became Germany's chancellor in 1933. He was either possessed by a mogui, or he had been killed and a mogui was wearing his skin like a coat. How else could a talentless artist and a school dropout achieve so much power and infamy?

"Think about it." He stared at Junie, whose reaction was an appalled silence. "Hitler's invasion of Poland in 1939 led to World War II. Tens of millions of soldiers and civilians were killed in the war. Not to mention the six million Jewish men, women and children that Hitler and his cohorts wiped off the face of the earth."

Holy cow. She could feel the blood draining from her own face. "If it's a mogui, what are we going to do?" she whispered.

"You can't kill a mogui," Joe said miserably. "Mogui aren't like yaoguai. They're indestructible. If it's a mogui, the best I can do is send it back to Diyu, the Chinese version of hell."

"Wait a minute," she exclaimed. "Hitler committed suicide! If he was taken over by a mogui, how could he die?"

"Did he die?" He raised his eyebrows. "All we have are bits of bone and teeth closely guarded by the Russians.

"Some people believe that Hitler didn't die, that the Russians are keeping him prisoner still. They're holding the Führer in an underground cell somewhere deep under Moscow because he simply refuses to die."

Chapter 12

Joe wasn't eager to talk to Millie so soon after they supposedly had finished blessing her cellar. But it had to be done. He picked up the phone and punched in her number. Junie offered moral support in the form of a thumbs-up and an encouraging grin.

"We only managed to conduct an evaluation yesterday," he told Millie. "Based on that evaluation, I've decided the cellar needs a thorough, full-scale blessing. I know, I know … and I apologize about that, but it's best not to delay or postpone such things."

She must not have been convinced, because he spent the next few minutes explaining the merits of a fully blessed and positively charged home environment. He looked exhausted when he hung up.

"What did Millie say?" Junie asked.

"She says we can come Thursday morning, but we better not expect to be paid extra. She says she's wasted enough time on our—and I quote —'claptrap'."

"Are we still invited to the party?"

"I think so. The only thing I could learn about the housewarming is that about 70 guests or so are expected."

Since they didn't have any appointments, Junie wanted to spend the rest of the day familiarizing herself with the Golden Dragon's weapons. She dragged the steamer trunk out to the living room and fetched the staff from her closet.

"Tell me exactly how each one works. If I'm going to be helping you, I need to know."

"Well, you've seen the luopan in action," Joe said. "My father considered the compass one of his most important tools, because it detects the presence of unnatural and supernatural energies. At least, it does so in the right hands."

"Why doesn't it react when *you* hold it?"

He shrugged. "I'm not as sensitive as he was. Or as you are, or even Dan and his workmen. I don't have the ability to see beyond the material plane."

"Is that why you're not a Dragon warrior?"

He nodded curtly and hurriedly picked up the wooden sword. "Next," he said crisply.

"The Energy Devourer was my father's primary weapon, because it can pierce the flesh of monsters. The sword absorbs their energy when you stab them through the heart. For minor yaoguai, that's enough to kill them.

"And that's an important point to remember," he stressed. "At the core, these monsters are pure, negative energy. I'm not sure what they look like in their worlds, but they can't enter ours without assuming a tangible, physical shape. And that presents both a pro and a con for us.

"Remember what I told you yesterday about yaoguai being vulnerable while they're in our realm? That's because they are easiest to destroy when they are in their physical forms. That's the pro. The con is that the creatures can alter their looks and take on disguises very easily. They frequently adopt frightful appearances to intimidate their victims. Fear is one of their strongest weapons."

As Joe spoke, he could almost hear his father's voice alongside his, like a faint echo. All those decades ago, when he was a little boy, his father had explained the same things to him, using almost the exact words. He felt a sudden tightness in his chest.

Junie, unaware of the detour down memory lane that he was taking, asked whether he could see yaoguai. "Or are they like ghosts, and only certain people can sense them?"

"Anyone, including myself, can see the creatures when they're in their physical incarnations. Although, come to think of it, I honestly can't say I've ever seen one."

Well, that was reassuring. She had a sinking feeling that the odds were stacked against Joe and herself.

He moved on to the wooden staff. It was for fighting, like the sword. However, he wasn't clear what magical powers it had, if any. It was a weapon that the Golden Dragon seldom used.

The bronze bell was for freeing restless and trapped spirits. According to Joe's father, the instrument was forged in ancient times by Tibetan monks who shunned the material world in favor of meditation and prayer. The monks honed the bell's peals to the exact timbre of their sacred chants, which were so powerful it was said they could heal human sorrow. When the bell was rung vigorously, the sonic vibrations from its resonance scattered and dispelled residual energy.

"We're bringing the bell when we revisit Millie's cellar," he said. "We'll use it to lay the spirits of the soldiers, and whatever else is there, to rest. Another advantage is that its clangs annoy the heck out of yaoguai and mogui. It has something to do with the low frequency of the creatures' auditory range."

The strips of yellow paper were talismans. Their power derived from the symbols painted on them. "The talismans have several purposes," he said. "You can use them to seal portals. You can also immobilize the undead by pinning the talismans to their foreheads."

Joe next shook out the yellow robes. They had big sleeves and black markings.

"These are Taoist vestments," he said. "The smaller garment was my father's. It was what he wore for his geomancy work. He told me the robe helped him to tap into his Dragon powers and connect with his lineage. I guess for him it was like putting on your power suit before an important meeting. It helped him bring his A game."

"Who's the other robe for?"

"That's mine. I had it made when I restarted the business."

"Are you Taoist?"

"Nah," he said. "Unitarian. I haven't worn the robe for quite some time. I decided I didn't want my geomantic practice linked to any particular religion."

He looked thoughtfully at Junie. "What about yourself, if you don't mind me asking? Are you religious?"

"Agnostic."

There was a brief silence. She broke it by pointing to the bandanna in the trunk. "What's that for?"

"My father tied it around his head when he went into battle." He explained that the Chinese words on the bandanna were "lung ping," meaning "Dragon soldier."

Finally, they came to the stones. He touched each one with his index finger before picking up the clear quartz crystal. "I'm not sure what the other stones do, but the Golden Dragon used this to center and amplify his energy. It helped him to access his third eye, he used to say."

Junie's mouth fell open. "Did you say 'third eye'?"

* * *

She told him about the little blond boy in her dream. "He told me to open my third eye, Joe. Do you know what that means?"

"The third eye, also known as the inner eye, allows you to see the spiritual plane."

He pointed at the center of her forehead. "That's where the eye is supposed to be located. The Golden Dragon used his eye to look behind yaoguai masks. The monsters are so good at shape-shifting that sometimes, the only way to spot them is by their aura, which is completely black. The third eye can also see their spoor."

"Show me how to use the crystal."

Joe picked up the crystal and held it in his right palm. He shut his eyes. "That's what my father did, but other than that, I'm not sure what else needs to happen. It's not as if the third eye is an actual eye that I could see opening in the middle of the Golden Dragon's forehead. And he got so good at it that eventually, he didn't need the crystal."

She took the shard from him and closed her eyes. As before, it was warm to the touch and vibrated ever so gently. The heat slowly intensified in her palm. Just when she felt the crystal was getting too hot to hold, its warmth seeped into her fingers and shot up her arm.

"I think I can feel the crystal's energy," she whispered.

"Try moving that energy into your head. When you can feel it between your eyes"—he lightly tapped her forehead—"shoot it out as if aiming a spotlight."

Odd as the instruction was, she understood what he meant. She shut her eyes for a few minutes. The crystal's heat filled her. She imagined the heat as a laser beam shooting from her forehead. When she opened her eyes, the living room was hazy. Joe's entire body was suffused with a brownish glow.

It wasn't just him. Everything, including the furniture, was luminescent. "Something's happening," she said. "I'm seeing colors."

"Those colors are auras, or energy fields, that surround all things, whether animate or inanimate," he said. "I think you've successfully opened your eye."

Junie practiced a few more times. It was tiring—she had to really focus—but she got quicker at opening her eye. The auras became brighter and more distinct every time she did it. She also found that they went away after a while if she didn't need her third eye.

When she became comfortable at opening and using her eye, she insisted that Joe teach her how to wield the sword.

"You do understand that you're not going to be fighting the yaoguai, right?" His tone was severe. "If I wasn't clear before, let me clarify now: I do the fighting. You're a mere spectator. Your role is limited to letting me know whether the ghosts in the cellar are still around. And if you do spot the yaoguai, tell me immediately, then hightail it out of there."

"Even if I don't expect to fight it, I should know how in case I have to," she said stubbornly.

He sighed. He grudgingly demonstrated some simple exercises with the sword. When she could execute the exercises to his satisfaction, he showed her how to thrust the weapon without losing her balance. "It's all a matter of where you place your feet and how you shift your weight."

She asked to see more. Joe had to admit that was all he knew. "I was only 10 when the Golden Dragon died," he said in his own defense. "I didn't get the chance to learn more."

Chapter 13

On Wednesday morning, Joe and Junie traveled to a client's new coffee shop to perform a blessing. After they returned to the office, he announced he had a personal matter to attend to and disappeared.

Left to her own devices, Junie happily retrieved the Energy Devourer from the trunk. She also picked up the bandanna on impulse and tied it around her head. She went into the office—where there was more space—and tried out the exercises Joe had taught her.

Her motions became more and more fluid, until the sword felt like an extension of her arm. She started mixing in other actions she had seen from kung fu movies and the *Star Wars* franchise. She was so engrossed she didn't hear the rapping on the door.

"Wow," someone said from behind her. "That's pretty awesome."

She whirled around, almost dropping the sword. Noah stood at the door, an envelope in his hand. "I hope I'm not interrupting anything," he said apologetically. "I did knock, but I was afraid Joe didn't hear me."

"No, that's fine." She pushed her glasses higher. Her mind had gone totally blank and she couldn't think of anything else to say. Unlike other times when she had seen him, there wasn't a counter or a menu between them, or anyone else with them.

He came a little closer. "Um, I have the rent check for Joe." He still sounded slightly apologetic.

She nodded and held out her hand for the envelope. That explained another mystery—how Joe, despite his lack of customers, could afford operating in D.C., and in such a high-rent area. He *owned* the building. The Laughing Buddha was his tenant. The cafe probably was his main source of income.

"So what was that anyhow?" Noah looked intrigued. "Are you trained in martial arts?"

Junie shrugged and blushed at the same time. "No. I hope I didn't look too stupid. I was just kind of fooling around."

"No, you looked pretty *badass*." He smiled, seeming to be genuinely impressed. "Do you mind if I watch?"

She hesitated, not sure that she wanted him to see her practicing. She was too self-conscious in his presence. *What if she smacked herself with the sword? Worse—what if she slipped and fell on her ass?*

Sensing her discomfort, he took a step back. "I should probably go. Sorry again for disturbing. The office looks great, by the way. Knowing Joe, he had nothing to do with it."

She didn't want him to go. But she was too tongue-tied to stop him.

Noah was already out the door when he suddenly turned back. "Um, it's Junie, right?" When she nodded, he asked, "Would you like to hang out sometime?"

She was astounded, but in enough control of her body to nod again.

"The Smithsonian Institution's annual Culture on the Mall festival starts next week," he said quickly. "They're screening outdoor movies in the evening as part of the festival. They're scheduled to show old Jackie Chan and Jet Li period movies a week from Sunday. Would you like to go?"

He paused, his face reddening. "I mean, I don't want to assume that just because you're Asian, you automatically like kung fu movies ... "

She had to laugh. "Actually, I *love* kung fu movies. I'd love to go."

"Great." He relaxed. "I work at the cafe until 5 o'clock on Sundays. We could meet outside around that time and maybe grab something to eat before walking to the Mall. The movies start around 7:30."

"Sounds like a plan." She tried not to appear too eager. "I live here now so meeting at the cafe is perfect."

"Great," he repeated. "Uh, I'm going now, but, um ... great." He flashed her a quick smile and left.

The smile on Junie's face remained long after Noah was gone. He hadn't made it sound like a date—more like something two friends could enjoy in the company of other geeks—but it was a start. Didn't Pa always say there had to be a seedling before a mighty oak?

She picked up the sword and resumed her practice. Now, more than ever, she had to make sure she could protect herself.

Her "date" with Noah was a day after Millie's party. She planned on surviving until then.

* * *

Joe walked down a cement path, a bouquet of flowers in his hand. Stone and metal monuments sprouted from the verdant grass around him. While some of the monuments were modest, little more than slabs in the ground, others were impressive works of art. Not that he noticed.

He came to a familiar bend in the path, at which point he stepped onto the grass. He walked up a little hill until he came to a copse of trees. He stopped in front of a simple headstone under the dappled shade of a tall, graceful ginkgo tree. The grave marker was inscribed with the words: "Tham Jing Lung. 1934 – 1981. Beloved Husband, Loving Father."

Every year on August 1st, Joe came to Rock Creek Cemetery to pay homage to his father. The Golden Dragon had died on that date, 38 years ago, when he was only 47.

He placed his flowers by the headstone. "Hello Father," he murmured. "It's me, your son." He smiled wryly. "I hope you're resting well."

He sat down on the cool grass beside the slab of granite. He tried to picture his father's face, but no matter how hard he tried, he couldn't recall what the Golden Dragon looked like. The man in his mother's photographs was a stranger, too stiff and serious to be reconciled with what he *did* remember: patient smiles, gentle fingers that corrected him when his sword positions were wrong, strong arms that embraced him when he cried. And the pungent smell of tobacco.

His father had smoked like a chimney. If his heart hadn't given out, his lungs probably would have.

Joe sighed. The Golden Dragon had been so happy when he was born

—he was the male heir, the chosen one, the one who would carry on the Tham traditions. What Joe didn't want to remember—but would never forget—was the look on his father's face when he discovered the cruel trick that genetics had played.

Still, he hadn't given up on his son. He had tried to inculcate, through constant teaching and demonstration, what Joe couldn't pick up instinctively. Who knew how successful that might have been, given enough time? Mercifully, the Golden Dragon hadn't lived long enough to find out his son was a total failure.

The looming fight with the yaoguai from Millie's cellar might be Joe's one chance at redemption. Even if he didn't survive the encounter, his father would be proud that he had tried.

"Father, you deserved better," he whispered wretchedly. "Who knows? You might get the chance to tell me so real soon."

Unless, of course, the yaoguai not only killed him but dragged his soul down into the depths with it. In which case he was well, and truly, screwed.

While he knew ghosts existed, Joe had only a vague notion of what happened to a person after death. Unitarianism wasn't exactly clear on the subject. Most Unitarians didn't believe in hell, or the devil, for that matter.

In truth, he hadn't been a practicing Unitarian for a long time. He couldn't remember the last time he stepped into a church. He adopted the faith in his youth, at a time when he yearned to be seen as "more" American, even though he, and his father before him, were born in the U.S.

Perhaps Taoism, the religion of his forefathers, had a better answer about life after death. In Taoist lore, hell—Diyu—was a frightening, multitiered subterranean maze in which souls were trapped, judged and tortured for their sins. There was no way out short of reincarnation.

Personally, he found it easier to believe in eternal damnation than in reincarnation. He was certain that once dead, a person stayed dead.

You only had one shot at life. Why else would ghosts cling so hard to what they had lost?

Chapter 14

Instead of Millie, they were greeted by a trim woman of indeterminate age, her years probably closer to Joe's than Junie's. Her pleasant features were framed by a smooth bob of mousy brown hair. Her air of competence was enhanced by her fitted black suit and the clipboard that she hugged to her chest.

"Hi," she said briskly. "I'm Emma Frankel, Millie's personal assistant. She's very busy today so she asked me to help out."

Emma escorted them to the cellar, telling them on the way that the decorator was almost finished with the house. "Everything is right on schedule," she said.

"Will you be at the party?" Joe asked.

She nodded as she opened the cellar door. "I'll come by in an hour's time. You should be done by then, right?" She left without waiting for their answer.

"Looks like we don't have a lot of time," Junie whispered as they trudged down the stairs. He nodded glumly.

She hung back when she neared the end of the staircase. The shadow men were still there, crowding around the base of the steps. Their terror was as palpable as before, as was the pall of smoke that hung over them. The phantom that used to be Matias Reyes stood with his back to the others, staring wide-eyed into the dark.

Joe cut blithely through the specters and set his bag on the ground. He pulled the chain to turn on the bulb. The light shone oddly through the men's gray translucence, making them look like eerie photo negatives.

By the time Junie mustered the courage to step off the last tread, Joe had taken out the luopan, the bell, two flashlights and a few candles in glass containers. He passed the luopan to Junie. The device's needle started its frenetic circling.

He fished a lighter out of his bag, lit one of the candles and handed that to her as well. The scent of lavender drifted up to her nose, faint against the pervasive odor of smoke.

"Are they here?" he asked in a low voice.

She gritted her teeth. "Yep."

"This is what we're going to do," he said. "The releasing of spirits is a lot like a blessing ritual, except it includes the bell. We're going to walk clockwise along the walls of the cellar in a continuous circuit. I'll ring the bell. You follow behind holding the candle and the luopan. Turn on any bulb we come across. We want the ritual to be conducted in bright light. We will check the luopan when we complete one circuit. If the needle is still spinning, we will do another circuit. Basically, we repeat the process until the needle goes still."

"What's the candle for?" she asked.

"It's a calming medium." His nostrils flared as he breathed in deeply. "I brought it for me."

He nodded to signal that the ritual was about to begin. He tucked one of the flashlights in his jacket pocket. He turned the other one on and held it in his left hand. He grasped the bell in his right hand and shook it hard.

The clangs were deep and rich, startlingly loud in the confined space. The nape of Junie's neck tingled and her eardrums buzzed. The peals had a droning after-note—sounding somewhat like a swarm of angry bees—that lingered in the air.

"Om mani padme hum." Joe started chanting in a sonorous voice. "Om mani padme hum, om mani padme hum, om mani padme hum."

The bell's rings and his chants wove together until they formed a hypnotic susurration that resounded throughout the cellar.

Junie eyed the shadow men to see if there was any effect on them. Nothing happened at first. She was about to alert Joe that the bell wasn't working when the men quivered almost imperceptibly. The quivering became a flickering, as if they were flames about to die out. Their features and clothes grew more and more indistinct, like smoke dispersed by a light breeze.

She had a sudden crisis of conscience when the soldiers were reduced to mere wisps. *By banishing them, were she and Joe killing the men twice? Were they casting the men into eternal darkness?* But she happened to see Matias's face before he completely disappeared. He looked relieved, happy even. The ritual had freed him from the terror that held him captive in his last moments of life, and after death. She hoped that was true of the union soldiers as well.

Matias was the last one by the stairs to go. "Joe, there are no more ghosts here," she whispered.

He nodded without pausing his chanting and ringing. He pointed the flashlight so she could see the route he planned to take. Staying close to the walls, they headed slowly toward the passageway to the chamber.

He released more shadow men, followed by the two soldiers on fire in the tunnel. When they entered the chamber, he and Junie were careful not to venture too close to the hole in the center. The bell's peals and his chants bounced off the walls, the echoes making it sound as though he had backup bell ringers and chanters. The smoking corpses, as well as the thing with no face, quickly faded away.

They returned to the main cellar. Junie blew the candle out and set it on the floor. She looked all around, after which she took the spare flashlight from Joe and probed the dark spaces. She couldn't see any other phantoms.

"I think we're done."

"Check the luopan," he cautioned.

"The needle's still turning," she told him, "but not as quickly as before."

"That means we've missed something."

Junie recalled the angry nurse, especially memorable because she was the only woman haunting the cellar. Had they missed her? "Hey Joe, let's backtrack a little. There's something I want to check out."

They traipsed back to where Junie previously had seen the woman. "There was a ghost here the last time," she said. "She looked really furious. I don't think I saw her when we did the circuit."

The light was still on from when they came through the first time. It was a particularly cluttered corner of the cellar. Discarded and broken furniture was stacked on the floor, some of the pieces shrouded by dust covers. Dan's workmen must not have gotten to this area.

"Do you see her?" Joe asked.

She deposited the luopan on a rickety table. Holding the spare flashlight high, she searched behind and around the furniture, even going so far as to lift some of the dust covers. Nothing. Finally, she got down on her hands and knees and looked under the furniture. A sudden movement caught her eye.

She jumped to her feet and sprinted to where she had seen the movement. She got there in time to see the edge of a black dress sliding behind a cupboard. When she aimed her flashlight behind the cupboard, a bone-white face snarled at her. The figure slipped out the other side of the cupboard before she could call Joe over.

"This one seems to be hiding from us," she shouted.

"*What?*" He ran to her. "Did you say it was *hiding*?" He scowled. "This must be an active haunting rather than residual energy. Active, sentient ghosts are much more problematic. They have their own agendas. Let's see if we can smoke it out." He raised the bell.

While Joe rang the bell, Junie swept her beam around in wide arcs. She glimpsed furtive stirring at the edge of her light. She directed her beam at the spot and saw something crawl under an old bedstead. She opened her mouth but before she could get Joe's attention, she heard the door of the cellar open.

"Aren't you done yet?" Emma's voice floated down from the head of the stairs, tight with impatience. "It's been well over an hour. And do you mind not ringing? I can hardly hear myself."

Joe plodded over to the staircase. "Can we have a bit more time?" he yelled.

They heard footsteps on the stairs and Emma appeared at the lower landing. "Afraid not," she said firmly. "Millie was clear that you have only an hour for the blessing. Your time is up."

She stood watch while Joe and Junie collected their things. She wouldn't even allow them to turn off the lights.

When they were back upstairs, she marched the two of them to the front door. She told them to email Millie regarding any extra charges and shut the door in their faces.

* * *

Joe had hoped to see more of Millie's home after the blessing ceremony. His plan had been to sneak up after they performed the ritual and learn as much as they could of the mansion's layout. They would claim to be lost if Millie or anyone else accosted them.

The efficient Emma had nixed that plan by hustling them out of the house. Unfortunately, he had no Plan B.

"If we're going to run the yaoguai to ground, we need to know where the house's entrances and exits are, at the very least." Joe paced up and down while Junie tried to hail a cab. "We can't wait until the day of the party. We have to be prepared. I can't let the yaoguai escape or trap us in a corner."

"How about we walk around now and take a look?" she suggested. "That might give us some idea of how the house is laid out. We can take a look at the neighborhood too."

He decided that wasn't a bad idea. Trying to act casual, they strolled along the perimeter of the property. After that, they explored a few of the side streets surrounding the house.

Millie's exclusive neighborhood consisted mostly of grand brick mansions set in well-kept grounds. Her corner lot was extensive compared to some of her neighbors' premises, but narrow and deep. A high stone wall girded the back part of the residence. Unfortunately, the wall was too high for them to see over, which was probably why it was there.

From what they *could* see, there was, in addition to the front entrance, another entrance located at the side of the house near a detached two-car garage. People leaving through the side entrance had easy access to the street via a flagstone path that cut across the paved driveway in front of the garage.

When they finished reconnoitering, they walked down a lane that wasn't visible from Millie's place to get to the main road. They didn't want Emma to glance out a window and find them still loitering in the vicinity.

"Well, that was somewhat helpful," Joe said. "There must be at least one more exit that leads into whatever's behind the wall. That's the problem with rich people—their homes are so damn BIG." He huffed in exasperation. "I'll have to call Dan after all. He probably has blueprints for the house. I was hoping to avoid that."

"What's wrong with calling him?"

"Because, Junie, I'll have to explain what a yaoguai is to yet another person." His expression was sour. "My father was so successful precisely because he operated in relative secrecy. People aren't so ready to believe, not like you. And I, personally, don't want to be hauled off in a straitjacket and confined to a padded cell."

"I don't think Dan will be a problem."

"Let's hope you're right."

Joe tried to contact Dan when they were back at the office. He wasn't available, but the person who answered the phone promised the contractor would return the call sometime in the afternoon.

Chapter 15

Dan didn't call until the next morning. Yes, he did have the blueprints for the house. However, he couldn't meet them until Wednesday.

"That's five days away!" Joe spluttered. "Couldn't we do this any earlier? It's kind of urgent. How about emailing the blueprints to me?"

"I'm afraid I won't be available for the next few days." Dan sounded strained. "And I'm not handing anything over until you give me a good explanation as to why you need those plans, and what you intend to do with them."

Joe envisaged telling the contractor about otherworldly monsters over the phone. Like Junie said, Dan was bound to be open-minded given what he and his men had experienced, but still … "It's a little difficult to explain over the phone," he said at last.

"Well, I'll see you Wednesday then."

"Wednesday is better than nothing," Joe said gloomily.

He brooded in his room for the rest of the morning. Fortunately, they had back-to-back consultations in the afternoon to take his mind off the yaoguai situation.

Business was still quite good, although it wasn't as busy as it had been in the early days, when Stella was actively promoting the practice. They were now relying on satisfied customers to refer them to other people.

Junie was at loose ends after an early dinner. Joe was still grumpy, so she decided it was a good time to go out and shop for something to wear to

Millie's party. Their invitations had arrived, as promised. The dress code for the party was "cocktail attire."

Joe hadn't said anything more about whether she was attending the party. She, for her part, was determined to be there. She was confident she could help in whatever he was planning. Of course, he hadn't yet discussed how they would handle the monster. She suspected he didn't yet have a plan.

She took a leisurely stroll to the department stores near Metro Center Station. It was a pleasant evening, a cool breeze temporarily easing D.C.'s legendary summer steaminess. The streets teemed with harried suit-clad office workers who couldn't wait to start their weekends, mingled with tourists who had all the time in the world. A man with a megaphone hurled a stream of invective at passersby from his soapbox at a street corner.

She spent the next two hours trying on dresses and tops. In the end, she bought a silk blouse with sequined straps. The blouse would pair nicely with her dressy black trousers and black ankle boots. Her pants had large pockets that could hold at least a small flashlight. They also were loose enough that she could run and jump, if necessary.

And swing the sword, if necessary. No matter what Joe said, she wanted to be ready to defend herself against a yaoguai assault.

Walking back, she saw Noah standing outside the Laughing Buddha. He was talking to a tall, pretty blonde about Junie's age or a little older. The woman's hair was so pale it was flaxen. She was laughing at something he said, her face tilted up toward his. Her body language suggested that she knew him well, and wanted to know him even better.

Junie tried not to stare as she sauntered past the pair. She stopped reluctantly when she heard her name.

Noah came up to her. "We haven't had much chance to talk. I wanted to check that we're still on for next Sunday." His light eyes crinkled at the corners and his smile was warm.

"You bet." Nothing could stop Junie from going, not even monsters. *But who the heck was this woman?* She tried to muster a smile.

"Were you shopping?" He looked at the bag in her hand.

Before she could answer, the blonde asked, "Aren't you going to introduce us?"

Her voice, of course, was low-pitched and sexy. And of course she had a face and body that matched the voice. Her full lips were like pincushions.

"Uh, Greta, meet Junie. Junie, this is Greta. Greta and I went to the same hospitality management school in Providence, Rhode Island. She just landed a job in D.C."

"Gosh, congratulations," Junie said.

"Thank you."

Junie found herself eyed up and down. She pushed her glasses higher, wishing she had worn something more glamorous than shorts and a T-shirt. Her makeup comprised only eyeliner and sunscreen.

"Noah was a little ahead of me in school." Greta smiled at him and linked her arm possessively—or so it seemed to Junie—with his. "How do you two know each other?"

"Junie lives and works upstairs," Noah said, pointing above the Laughing Buddha.

"Oh." Greta eyed Junie again. "How ... convenient."

"By the way, Greta and I are going out for drinks later, after the Laughing Buddha closes, to celebrate her new job. Would you like to join us?"

Greta glared at her, daring her to tag along. Junie didn't particularly want to be a fifth wheel so she pleaded a prior engagement.

"Um, sure." Noah smiled again. "I'll see you later."

Behind his back, Greta shot her a glance that wasn't at all nice.

Junie reflected on her way upstairs that the yaoguai might be the lesser of the scary monsters she faced. To take her mind off Noah and Greta, she ensconced herself in her room where she practiced opening her third eye.

*　*　*

Joe was too filled with anxiety to be good company. He spent most of his waking hours either watching TV or reading the paper, during which he would sigh a lot and mumble to himself.

Junie was tired of practicing with the sword and crystal. She impulsively invited her parents to brunch on Sunday, seeing it as a good excuse to get out of the apartment.

She was a little apprehensive as she entered the restaurant. She wondered how the conversation would go. Patrick wasn't around to help take up the slack if she ran out of things to say. She steeled herself against Stella's inevitable grilling.

Mindful of Joe's warning to be discreet, she reminded herself not to mention Millie or the yaoguai. She was quite sure her parents wouldn't believe her anyway. Her father, in particular, had a difficult time with anything not grounded in hard science.

To her surprise, her mother kept persistent questions to a minimum and let her take the lead in the conversation. She relaxed before long and began talking about her work and about the complexities of feng shui and ensuring her clients got good value for their money. It took careful calibrating of what they needed and what their resources or the location could offer, she told her parents.

Stella knew quite a few of the clients, so she and her mother had fun gossiping about them. Raymond was content to mostly listen, interrupting now and then with random observations. She found—again, to her surprise—that she was enjoying herself. It was nice having her parents to herself. Though she loved Patrick with all her heart, he tended to hog the limelight. And what he had to say always seemed so much more important.

Near the end of the meal, she caught a glimpse of a young woman in one of the restaurant's many mirrors. The woman's face was slightly flushed, and she was laughing animatedly and obviously having fun. It was a shock when she realized she was gazing at her own reflection.

Could that really be her? The woman in the mirror looked *confident*, like someone in control of her life. She looked like someone who knew where she was going.

"Is anything the matter?" her mother asked curiously.

"No." Junie smiled. "I saw someone who looked familiar."

When the check came, she reached for it before her mother could. "My invite, my treat," she said firmly.

"Are you sure?" Stella asked.

"Yes, Ma. I'm sure."

"Well, your dad and I sure had a great time." Stella looked at Raymond, who beamed. "We're so happy you found something you can be passionate about. We've got to do this again. We like to hear about all the things you're doing. You're usually so quiet. It's hard to get you to open up."

A warm glow enveloped her at her mother's words. It was gratifying to hear that her parents genuinely were interested in her and in what she did, even if—in her own mind, at least—it paled in comparison to what Patrick accomplished.

Perhaps she was in the right family after all.

Chapter 16

Noah waved from the counter when they entered the Laughing Buddha. Junie hadn't seen him since Friday. She wondered how his night out with Greta had gone.

Dan already was seated at a booth near the kitchen, where the other diners couldn't overhear what they discussed. They were disconcerted to find him looking much worse than before.

He had lost weight and his skin had acquired a grayish pallor in the 10 days since they last saw him. The smudges under his eyes now resembled bruises. Deep grooves were etched across his forehead and on either side of his mouth. His injured foot was heavily bandaged. Instead of a walking stick, a pair of crutches leaned against the table.

"Dan, how are you doing?" Joe asked after he and Junie were seated across from the contractor. "You seem … um … how's the ankle?"

"No need to tiptoe around the truth." The corners of Dan's mouth lifted slightly in a grimace of a smile. "I look terrible. And I feel terrible." His gravelly voice had a new brittle quality akin to the crunching of dry leaves underfoot.

"In answer to your question, the swelling and pain have increased. I couldn't see you any sooner because I was at a hospital over the last few days undergoing tests. I got the preliminary results earlier today." He cleared his throat. "They think I may have a rare form of malignant bone cancer. The bad—or I should say, even worse—news is it's metastasized."

Joe and Junie were stunned into silence.

"But we're not here to talk about my health. I have a copy of the blueprints with me." He patted a bag by his side. "Before I give them to you, I'd like you to tell me why you want them."

A waiter came to take their order. Joe requested a pot of Longjing green tea—the same tea they had had before—and a selection of dim sum dishes.

"Well?" Dan rapped the table impatiently after the waiter left. "Out with it. You said this was urgent. My doctors tell me I may not have a lot of time. So *please*. Don't. Waste. My. Time."

Joe did his best to abide by Dan's instruction. He was interrupted halfway through his recital by the arrival of the tea and food, but all in all, Junie thought he did a good job explaining the situation. Succinct, yet clear. There was a long silence after he finished.

"Let me see if I have this right," Dan said at last. "You're saying this supernatural entity, this yaoguai or whatever, caused our bad luck, including Matias's heart attack. You think it may be planning something worse for Millie's party, so you and this young lady here are going to stop it and banish it back to the pit from which it slithered. In order to do that, you need to have a sense of the house's layout."

"Basically," Joe said.

"In a nutshell," Junie added.

Another long silence. "That's good enough for me." Dan leaned over his bag and pulled out a sheaf of papers. He was taking it far better than Joe had anticipated. He saw their faces as he pushed the blueprints toward them.

"*What?* You thought I wouldn't believe you?" His laugh was hollow. "Don't forget, I was the one who told you something strange was going on. I *know* my cancer is tied somehow to Millie and the cellar. You're not exactly dealing with a skeptic here."

Joe nodded gratefully. He cleared a space by his plate and spread out the house plans so Junie could see them as well.

According to the plans, Millie's house was a sizable 6,000 square feet. The first level consisted of the foyer, a large eat-in kitchen, a formal dining room, a sitting room with a fireplace, a bathroom, a powder room, a library, a music/movie room, and a small utility room.

The second floor could be accessed via the stairs in the foyer, or through another set of stairs at the back. There were four bedrooms on the upper level, the largest of which was Millie's. Each bedroom had its own bathroom.

Millie's master bedroom also had a private sitting room with a spacious balcony. The balcony overlooked the back garden and a swimming pool. The stone wall that Junie and Joe had seen was set on a slight slope, which elevated it so that it provided maximum privacy for the compound and pool.

The house had three means of egress, as Joe had surmised. In addition to the front and side entrances, there were sliding doors at the back of the house leading to the backyard and pool.

"So what exactly do you plan to do?" Dan asked.

"The yaoguai has to still be in the residence," Joe said. "These monsters tend to stay near their portals so they can make a quick escape if necessary. On the day of the housewarming, Junie and I will sneak into the house earlier, say around 6 p.m., and hunt it down. The party doesn't start until 7 so we have some time before the other guests arrive."

Junie was glad that Joe was resigned to her coming along, but she couldn't say she was impressed by the plan. "If we get caught, what's our excuse for turning up so early?" she asked.

"Tell them we forgot the time?" Joe's smile was weak. "Or we could say we were in the area and it was convenient."

He looked at Dan. "Will you be at the party? Millie said you were invited."

"Doubtful," Dan said. "My health is deteriorating fast. I'd like to spend what time I have left with my wife and kids."

His face contorted with sudden emotion and he turned away to hide it from the other two. "So," he said, struggling to sound casual, "the yaoguai could be in its original form, or assume the shape of something else, like an animal or a person?"

"It won't be in its original form, which is pure, negative energy," Joe clarified. "It's likely to assume a human shape. On the other hand, it could adopt a monstrous appearance to scare us. It employs fear and intimidation the way humans use knives and guns."

"If it assumes a human shape, how will you be able to identify it?"

"Junie can. She has special talents."

Dan regarded her with respect. She blushed.

"We'll start by searching the bedrooms first." Joe jabbed his index finger at the plan of the second floor. "If we can't find it there, we'll have to look among the guests. At the same time, we have to keep an eye out for anything unusual that could signal what the creature's going to do."

Junie's brow wrinkled. "If we're right that it's planning something awful at the party, the yaoguai probably talked Millie into throwing the party, right? We're looking for someone close to her that appeared right around the time of the sinkhole. Could it be the sister, or the decorator?"

"What sister?" Dan looked confused.

"Millie's sister," Joe explained. "The one who's now staying with her."

The contractor shook his head. "Millie doesn't have a sister. I've done work for her and her husband before. She told me previously that she's an only child."

Junie and Joe eyed each other. "Well then, that makes our job easier," he said. "We'll search for the so-called sister."

"And what happens when you find it, the yaoguai?" Dan asked.

"We have special tools that will drain its power and kill it," Joe said. "Failing that, we have to chase it back into the sinkhole. We also have to seal the sinkhole so no others can come through."

"Boy, I sure hope you know what you're doing." Dan looked worried. *Very* worried. "I don't like this talk of killing. If I hadn't had firsthand experience of what's happening at Millie's place, I would be reporting you to the police. As it is … "

He stared at the barely touched food that Joe had heaped on his plate. He sighed softly and looked up. "Good luck," he said.

"You too," Joe said sincerely.

After Dan left, Joe paid the check and he and Junie trooped upstairs. They spent the rest of the evening poring over the blueprints.

* * *

Joe grew visibly more agitated as the day of the housewarming approached. Junie continued practicing with the sword and crystal.

On the night before the party, Stella called while she was preparing for bed. Her mother wanted to chat. Junie, distracted by what was coming, only listened to half of what she said. It was a mishmash involving Patrick's latest triumphs, Raymond's most problematic patients, and Stella's newest listings.

Just as her mother was about to ring off, Junie impulsively said, "Ma, I love you. Tell Pa I love him too."

"We love you too, Junie," Stella said warmly. "We're so proud of you and your brother."

She felt a lump in her throat and hung up before she blabbed everything to her mother. Would this be the last time they spoke? Her heart quickened at the thought of what lay ahead. She wondered whether she should be more afraid.

Frankly, she was confused by her own emotions. Joe's warnings about the yaoguai were dire, but it was difficult to contemplate the possibility that she might die. She *was* nervous, but excited at the same time.

She even *looked forward* to the confrontation. The yaoguai might fight tooth and claw, but so would she.

* * *

Joe heard Junie talking on the phone in her room. He turned off the TV, went to his own room and shut the door. He hemmed and he hawed, but his sense of duty forced him to make the call.

The phone rang twice before it was answered. "Joseph, what is it? *Is anything the matter?*"

Elsie's voice was strident with panic. Why was she always so *afraid*? After his father's death, her fear and her negativity had ruled Joe's childhood and shaped his life. He became the boy who had to leave early from any and every activity because his mother wanted him home. He was the boy with few friends because his mother was suspicious of everyone.

And that boy, raised in fear, eventually became the man who was afraid to talk to his mother. It was kind of ironic, really.

The silence lengthened. He realized Elsie was still waiting for him to tell her what was wrong. "Nothing, Mother," he said quickly. "I just wanted to say I'm thinking of you."

She didn't immediately reply, but he could hear her breathing. Finally, she said, "That's nice Joseph. I'm thinking of you too." They both lapsed again into uneasy silence.

He wanted to tell her about the yaoguai, and that he might not make it past tomorrow. He wanted to say he was grateful for all she had done for him. But he didn't, because he could anticipate her response. First, she would plead with him not to do it, then she would rebuke him for carrying on his father's work. To Elsie, his choices never were the right ones.

He decided he didn't have the energy to put up with another of her lectures. He already was regretting the phone call. "Well, Mother," he said awkwardly, "I hope you have a nice weekend."

"It's good to hear from you, Joseph. You have a nice weekend too." She didn't hang up, as if she thought he might have something else to add. He ended the suspense by hanging up first.

As always, Joe was depressed after communicating with Elsie. He went to bed. He told himself he needed to make sure he was well rested for tomorrow.

However, sleep eluded him. He tossed and turned; his brain went over scenario after scenario of his looming confrontation with the yaoguai. Every scenario ended with him stone cold dead.

He wondered, yet again, whether he should leave Junie out of it. What right did he have to put her in danger?

But what choice did he have? She could be the difference between thwarting the yaoguai's plan, or letting it run amok. And there was no way he was going to let it run amok. She was right—the creature had to be stopped.

At what cost though? Junie was way too young to die. His own probable demise didn't trouble him as much. He'd already lived one year longer than the Golden Dragon. And he would meet his end doing what he'd done for most of his life—trying to be the man his father wanted him to be.

He sighed. Even after all these years, there still were times he missed his father so much that his heart ached. "Father, I sure could use your counsel right now," he whispered.

The Golden Dragon didn't answer, of course.

And even if he did, Joe had no ability to hear him.

Chapter 17

Joe dragged himself out of bed in the morning, exhausted from his restless night.

He spent most of the day "meditating." For him, that meant plonking himself in front of the TV and watching major league baseball. He told Junie in strict terms not to disturb him, saying he was mentally preparing for the night's work.

She obediently steered clear of him. She stayed in her room and diligently practiced with the sword and crystal. She was getting good at opening her third eye, but she wasn't sure if she was improving with the sword.

At 5:30 in the afternoon, she had applied makeup and put on her new blouse and black trousers. The crystal was snug in the trousers' right-hand pocket. The other pocket held paper talismans. She also carried a flashlight, her phone, her lipstick and some cash in her black leather purse. The bag had a shoulder strap she could sling across her chest.

She wished she could bring more. She fretted over their lack of weapons. But how could they smuggle them into the house? Millie's invitation specified "no gifts," so they couldn't even bear presents in which they could hide the Energy Devourer or the staff.

Joe wore his usual attire of sports coat, button-down shirt and pants. She passed him a few talismans, after which he asked for the sword.

"But where are we going to put it?" she asked. "It's not some accessory we can casually carry around."

"I can slip it down the back of my shirt."

Fortunately, the Energy Devourer's blade was short. Joe's gait was a little stiff with the sword down his back, but his coat concealed any telltale bulges.

He forced her to meet his eyes just before they left the apartment. "Remember what I said." He looked steadily at her, his expression grave. "The yaoguai is extremely dangerous. It will kill you—I repeat—KILL YOU, in a heartbeat. Do not engage with it under any circumstances. Your role is limited to helping me deal with it."

She took a deep breath and nodded solemnly. The show—maybe the last show of her life—was about to begin.

They arrived at Millie's home a little past 6 o'clock. Joe asked the cab driver to stop across the street. When the taxi departed, they ducked behind a screen of privet bushes in the yard of a house with a "For Sale" sign out front.

They had seen the sign—and verified that the house was vacant—during their walk around the neighborhood. Joe was counting on the fact that no potential buyers likely would ask to see the house on a Saturday night. The privet hedge offered cover from which they could monitor Millie's front and side entrances without being seen.

From their vantage point, it seemed that preparations for the party were well underway. A group of people wearing white shirts and black pants milled about in front of the garage, obviously the caterers and their waitstaff. They were unloading covered platters from a van parked in the driveway and bringing them into the house through the side entrance. The door was propped open to facilitate their coming and going.

A few minutes later, a sedan cruised to a stop in the street. Two women and two men got out. The men were clad in black suits while the women wore long black dresses. The four retrieved musical instruments from the car's trunk, after which the vehicle pulled away. The string quartet members carried their instruments—two violins, a viola and a cello—down Millie's flagstone path and disappeared through the open doorway.

"How about we sneak in through the side entrance?" Junie suggested. "Everyone's using it. It's so busy it's unlikely anyone will stop or challenge us, or even notice us."

Joe checked his watch. It was already 6:20. They were running out of time. "Let's do it."

They stepped out from behind the hedge. They were about to cross the street when Emma, armed with her trusty clipboard, trotted out through the open door. She approached one of the caterers and they started talking. Joe and Junie hastily ducked back behind the privet. There was no way they could get past Millie's conscientious assistant.

Emma's conversation didn't look like it was going to end anytime soon. They shifted their attention to the front door. Before long, the door opened and a woman came out. She lugged a large tote bag in one hand and empty grocery bags in the other. She walked quickly down the front path and got into a car parked on the street. The car's engine started. The vehicle executed a neat three-point turn and drove away.

"How much do you want to bet the front door is unlocked?" Joe whispered. Junie nodded. When they were sure Emma wasn't looking in their direction, they scurried across the street and down the front path. Fortunately, Emma couldn't see the front door from where she was.

They had almost made it to the door when two young men wearing matching red polo shirts and beige pants sauntered around the side of the house. Joe and Junie froze. The men greeted them cordially but didn't seem particularly interested in what they were doing.

As the men continued down the path, Junie saw the word "VALET" printed on the back of their shirts. Millie must have hired a valet service for the night. She let out the breath she didn't even know she was holding and pushed Joe toward the door. "Quick, before more people come by."

Mercifully, the door opened when he tried it.

The foyer was empty, but they could hear voices carrying from other parts of the first floor. They raced up the stairs as quietly as they could.

* * *

At the top of the stairs, they found themselves in a wide hallway with doors on either side. The second set of stairs was at the other end of the hallway.

The doors were open. Joe sneaked through the first doorway on his right, followed closely by Junie. They were in a large bedroom, sumptuously furnished. One entire wall was made of glass. Floor-to-ceiling vertical blinds kept out the evening sun.

On first sight, the room appeared empty. Joe quickly closed the door behind them. He opened the bathroom door and peeked in while Junie got down on her hands and knees to check under the king-size bed. Joe went next to the built-in closet and slid the doors open. The empty closet confirmed that the room wasn't occupied.

They crossed the hall and entered a second bedroom, also expensively furnished. It was empty as well, as was the third bedroom.

While they were in the third bedroom, they heard footsteps ascending the foyer stairs and traveling along the hallway. The footsteps were accompanied by faint bangs. Whoever it was was pulling the bedroom doors shut. The footsteps continued past their door, paused and doubled back.

Junie looked at Joe. Had their closed door raised suspicion? He put his index finger to his lips, warning her not to make a sound. The footsteps stopped in front of their door. The handle started to turn.

The two of them were standing on either side of the bed. Like a well-coordinated stunt team, they dropped as one onto the luxuriously carpeted floor and rolled under the bed. Just in time. The door opened. Peeping from under the bed skirt, all they could see was a pair of legs shod in elegant high heels.

The heels stood in the doorway for a few seconds. Their owner must have been satisfied with what she saw because she didn't bother to enter the room. To their relief, she closed the door and the sound of her heels receded as she went down the back stairs.

Joe slowly released his pent-up breath. He clambered out from under the bed, hampered slightly by the sword under his shirt. He crept to the door and pressed his ear against it. When he didn't hear anything outside, he opened the door slowly and peered out. He signaled to Junie that the coast was clear.

They tiptoed down the hall toward the last room—the master bedroom. Laughter and the murmur of conversation drifted up from downstairs. The string quartet was playing music by Johann Sebastian Bach. By some acoustical feat, the notes were as crisp as if they were standing right beside the musicians. Junie glanced at her watch. It was past 7 o'clock. The party had begun.

Joe paused with his hand on the door's handle. "Get your third eye ready," he growled. His and Junie's nerves were taut with tension—if the yaoguai was upstairs at all, it had to be in this room.

She slipped her hand in her pocket and grasped the crystal. The shard buzzed. Its familiar heat tingled up her arm and filled her body. Her vision blurred and soft colors bloomed around her. She nodded to Joe. He opened the door gingerly, ready for a surprise attack.

Millie's room was bigger and grander than the other bedrooms. In addition to the bathroom and closet doors, there was a set of French doors through which Junie could see the balcony. She also glimpsed a four-poster bed, a large flat-screen TV, a desk and a love seat, before Joe drew her attention to the woman at the dressing table.

The woman sat very still with her back to the door. She appeared wholly captivated by her own reflection. From the back, she looked like the woman Junie had spied in the kitchen.

"Check her aura," Joe mouthed silently. He shut the bedroom door as quietly as he could. He reached behind him for the sword.

Junie was surprised to find the woman's aura wasn't black but a dull gray. Despite her absorption, the woman must have become aware of them because she was turning around slowly. Her profile came into view, then her full face.

Junie gaped; Joe almost lost his grip on the sword. It was Millie. The woman was Millie, but a Millie so haggard and hunched, so gripped by terror that she was barely recognizable. Her lips moved; nothing issued except a tortured mewling.

The door opened softly behind them and someone entered. They were so riveted by the sight of Millie that the sounds didn't register until they heard the door click shut and the lock engage. They whirled around and their jaws dropped again.

"Well, well, well," Millie said. "Did I forget to mention the upstairs is out-of-bounds?"

Chapter 18

The new Millie smiled. "Fortunately, the bedrooms are soundproof, so what happens here stays here."

Joe and Junie's eyes scooted back and forth between the terrified Millie and the one who had just entered. They were the same woman, yet a study in contrasts. One was pinched and drawn; the other was robust and radiant with health.

To Junie's third eye, Robust Millie was sheathed in an aura so dark it looked like oily black smoke. And she seemed to be growing. Correction—she *was* growing, *and* changing at the same time. Junie's insides shriveled with fear.

Robust Millie was now almost seven feet tall. She towered over them, her arms lengthening and growing thick and ropy with muscles before their very eyes. Her cocktail dress transformed into skin that was coarse and gray, like the trunk of a tree. Her features shifted, compressing in some places and swelling in others until her eyes were red pinpricks set in deep hollows, her nose snout-like. Her mouth stretched impossibly wide from ear to ear; her parted lips revealed jutting teeth.

Joe made a choking sound. He raised the Energy Devourer and pushed Junie behind him. "Stay back," he warned the thing that used to be Robust Millie.

The yaoguai stared at the sword in his hand. Its beady orbs flattened, becoming slits. "What is this, geomancer?" Its voice was soft and sibilant.

From the sword's trembling, Junie could tell Joe was as scared as she was. Nonetheless, he took a step forward and jabbed the Energy Devourer at the monster. The yaoguai skipped back, its eyes glued to the sword.

Joe took another brave step forward. This time he slashed sideways, catching the yaoguai on the side.

The creature yowled and backed away. It looked down its side, where the skin was blistering from contact with the sword. "Only wood cut from the sacred groves of the Shen Ting Mountains can do that," it hissed. "And I know of only one sword made from that wood."

Its eyes crawled over Joe's face. "I thought the Tham Dragons died out," it said nastily. "Who are you?"

A snarl came from deep within Joe's throat. He held the Energy Devourer aloft and lunged at the yaoguai.

The monster was taken by surprise, yet it still managed to parry the sword's blow with its arm. At the same time, its other hand swiped viciously.

The creature's three-inch talons would have torn into Joe's belly and ripped out his entrails if he hadn't stepped back in time. It swiped again, almost tearing the sword from his hand. He retreated, his breathing loud and ragged.

The yaoguai advanced. He took another step back. The real Millie began to whimper.

If Joe continued backing up, Junie knew the yaoguai would trap all three of them—him, her and the real Millie—in a corner. Her eyes desperately roved the room. The bed was beside them. The love seat and a small coffee table covered in newspapers and other items were on the other side of the bed. The creature, meanwhile, was focused on Joe and the sword.

She flung herself across the bed without thinking twice. She landed on her feet on the other side, took three steps to the coffee table and snatched up a large mug. She wound back her arm and pitched the heavy cup at the yaoguai's head.

Joe and the yaoguai had turned at Junie's sudden movement. The stoneware flew through the air and smacked the creature squarely between the eyes, causing it to stagger backwards. Joe immediately raised the Energy Devourer and rammed it into the yaoguai's heart.

Except—the sword couldn't penetrate the monster's thick hide. The blade bounced off its chest; the impact made Joe lose his balance. Before he could recover, the yaoguai knocked the sword out of his hand. It grabbed him by the throat and lifted him four feet off the ground.

Joe's face turned purple as he gasped for air. He beat futilely at the creature's sinewy arm; his legs kicked and thrashed.

It chuckled, amused by his weakening struggles. "Geomancer," it taunted, "the sword's full power can only be called forth by a *Dragon*. The rumors *are* true—the Tham Dragons are no more."

Its head swiveled to Junie, its expression venomous. "After him, you," it hissed. "Little girl, I can taste you already."

The yaoguai's jaws split open like a steel trap. Joe's eyes bugged with horror and his struggles grew frantic as it forced his head closer to its jagged teeth. Millie's whimpering became a full-blown screech.

Junie eyed the Energy Devourer on the bed, where it had fallen. She knew she didn't have a second to spare. She sprinted around the bed and picked up the sword. The yaoguai was about to chomp down on Joe's face when she stabbed it in the back, angling the weapon upward toward its heart. She felt an initial resistance before the sword slid smoothly in, like a knife slicing through warm butter.

The monster bellowed in shock and pain. It dropped Joe and reached behind with both arms, raking its own back with its talons as it tried to yank the sword out. Junie ducked under the flailing nails, managing somehow to keep her hold on the sword. The Energy Devourer was growing warm—she could feel waves of energy pulsing up its blade even as the yaoguai rapidly deflated.

It wrapped its arms and legs tightly about itself as it shrank, looking as though it was collapsing in on itself. When it was no more than a basketball-sized blob speared through the middle by the sword, Junie relaxed slightly and tried to shift her posture. Her arms ached from hanging onto the sword. The blob was small but heavy.

Suddenly, slender legs sprouted from what remained of the yaoguai, catching her off-guard. The segmented limbs lashed about, whipping her in the face and almost dislodging her glasses. She lost her grip on the Energy Devourer while trying to protect her eyes.

That gave the yaoguai the break it needed. It sprang up to the ceiling and clung there like a giant spider. Without Junie to hold it in, the sword slipped out of its body and fell to the floor with a dull thud.

She stared up in amazement, her face twitching with disgust at the creature's latest permutation. Its spidery limbs had shortened and it had grown a new head—it now looked like an immensely ugly black dog the size of a pug. It had a rat-like snout and beady red eyes; razor-sharp fangs peeped out of its snapping jaws.

"Don't let it get away," Joe rasped. "We have to kill it while it's enervated and vulnerable."

The yaoguai had other ideas. It scuttled upside down on the ceiling. Junie was reaching for the sword when she heard a crash. She turned and saw a large hole in the door, where the thing had busted through.

Chapter 19

Sword in hand, Junie raced to the door, unlocked it and thrust it open. The hallway was empty. She stepped outside and was about to rush down the back stairs when Joe called her back. She gritted her teeth and returned to the room.

"Use your third eye," he said as she helped him to his feet. He leaned heavily against the wall, panting and wiping gooey streaks of saliva from his face with his sleeve.

The excitement had been too much for Millie. She was slumped over the dressing table in a dead faint.

"Use your third eye now, quickly, while the yaoguai's tracks are still fresh!" Joe prompted when Junie didn't move fast enough. "And hand me that sword."

While he slipped the Energy Devourer under his sports coat, she groped in her pocket for the crystal, suddenly fearful she had lost it in the fight. She heaved a sigh of relief when her fingers closed around the rock. Her sight became blurry; the colorful auras appeared. She stepped back into the hallway.

There were black paw-like prints on the floor heading toward the back stairs. The prints were beginning to disappear, seeming to dissolve into the hall's white marble tiles.

She and Joe followed the trail down the stairs. They found themselves in Millie's sitting room, or perhaps it was a reception room. Well-dressed guests milled about clutching drinks and little plates filled with appetizers. The string quartet, playing in one corner, had moved on to a Beethoven symphony. They wound through the crowd, searching under the partygoers' feet for the creature's spoor.

The trail led out the sliding glass doors onto a porch whose roof was the floor of Millie's balcony. The rectangular swimming pool was close to the porch. Millie must be a serious swimmer because the pool was not only large, there was a diving platform at one end. The yaoguai had loped around the pool's deck, then headed into the garden beyond the pool area.

It was a beautiful evening and many guests were outside, either sitting by the pool or strolling about the compound. They tried not to attract undue attention while doing a quick circuit of the grounds. The dense plantings and thick shrubs offered myriad hiding places, especially for a small animal. It didn't help that the yaoguai's prints were difficult to discern on grass and mulch. Even worse, the natural light was fading, but it wasn't dark enough yet for the garden's artificial lights to come on.

Junie kept searching, trying to find some sign of the creature. A woman approached them while they were poking under some bushes.

"Are you looking for that dog?" she asked.

When Junie nodded, she pointed at the sliding doors. "It came out here, then ran back into the house. I hope you catch it. It's ferocious. Somebody tried to pet it, and it almost took his hand off."

They hurried inside, where Junie managed to pick up the yaoguai's trail again. They were following its tracks along a corridor when she heard her name. Startled, she turned—and saw her mother and father, drinks in hand, wearing their nicest outfits.

"Junie, what are you doing here?" Stella asked in astonishment.

"Ma, Pa, what are *you* doing here?" Junie stammered.

"Millicent Scarpini is a board member in Pa's hospital," Stella explained. "I had no idea you knew her. You should have told me you were coming to the party. We could have driven by and picked you and Joe up."

Stella's voice faltered and she stared, her eyes growing wide. Junie glanced at Joe. In the heat of the chase, she hadn't noticed how disheveled he was. His hair stood up in tufts. His neck was red and blotchy from the yaoguai's stranglehold. He wasn't the world's most immaculate dresser but his clothes were even more creased than usual, and one of his coat sleeves was damp and slimy.

He looked like he had been fighting. She herself probably looked only slightly better.

Joe, blissfully unaware of his appearance, plucked nervously at Junie's arm. "We gotta go," he mumbled.

"Um, Millie is our client," Junie told her parents. "Joe and I must hurry—urgent feng shui business. We're actually on the clock right now."

"Oh, have you seen Millie?" Stella asked. "Where is she? We wanted to say hello. I just talked to a woman with a clipboard who says she's looking for her as well."

Junie looked at her father in desperation. Pa got the message. He touched his wife's elbow. "Let Junie do her job."

"Alright, alright," Stella grumbled.

Junie flashed her father a grateful smile and she and Joe hastened down the corridor. But it was too late. The trail had gone cold.

"I can't see any more prints," she said.

"Let's just keep looking. We might get lucky again, like with that woman in the garden."

Weaving between groups of laughing, chatting people, they hunted throughout the house for more of the yaoguai's tracks. They came eventually to the kitchen, where the caterers were busy prepping food and filling trays and platters. A few of the staff looked up when they entered but soon went back to what they were doing.

To the caterers' annoyance, Junie walked around the kitchen with her eyes glued to the floor. When she was done, she left the kitchen through a different entryway. She found herself in a new hallway and paused to get her bearings. It dawned on her that the entryway was the cased opening through which she thought she had glimpsed Millie's sister.

That meant that the side entrance was close by. There it was, although the door was no longer propped open. The cellar should be … She stopped so abruptly that Joe ran into her.

"What is it?" he asked in confusion. "Why are we stopping? Did you find something? If not, I think we should try the foyer. We haven't searched there yet."

She pulled him farther away from the kitchen so the caterers couldn't overhear them. "The yaoguai is in the cellar," she said in a low voice.

"What? How do you know? Did you pick up its trail again?"

"No, but the little blond boy from my dream is standing in front of the cellar door. He's pointing at it."

"*What* boy?" Joe's eyes darted to the cellar door before swinging back to her. He obviously couldn't see the child.

* * *

The little tyke was as pale as he had been in Junie's dream. He turned his head and looked at her as she and Joe approached the cellar door.

"Stop the monster, Junie," he said. "Get it." He abruptly vanished.

She took the Energy Devourer from Joe. She held the sword in her right hand and cautiously opened the cellar door with her left. A strong stench hit her and she wrinkled her nose. "Joe, I smell gas."

She stepped onto the landing and reached for the chain of the bulb overhead. Before she could grasp it, Joe grabbed the back of her blouse. He hauled her out of the cellar and slammed the door shut.

"Don't turn anything electrical on or off," he said frantically. "That could cause a spark, which in turn could set off an explosion if there is enough gas in the cellar to be combustible. An explosion in the cellar could bring the whole house down."

Junie swallowed hard. She should have remembered how dangerous electrical devices can be during a natural gas leak. Her insides turned to ice as the full implication of what he was saying sank in.

"That's the yaoguai's plan, isn't it?" she whispered. "While Millie's home is full of people."

A vein throbbed at the side of Joe's forehead. He looked as horrified as she felt. "The monster's original plan may have been to simply toss a lit match down the cellar stairs, once it judged there was enough gas to burn," he said. "Or it may have planned to open the cellar door and let the gas fill the corridor while the caterers were heating food in the kitchen.

"Now, who knows what it will do?" He shrugged helplessly. "We interrupted Plan A. I don't know if there's a Plan B. And we don't know at this point how much gas has leaked."

"Surely it won't blow up the house while it's still in it!"

He shook his head. "Junie, it's a *monster,* an otherworldly entity. When it enters our realm, it has to obey our laws of physics, chemistry and biology to some extent, but not like we do. I assure you—not only will it be unscathed, it thrives on exactly this kind of havoc."

Junie had some knowledge of gas explosions. A residence not too far from her parents' Springfield, Virginia, neighborhood had blown up last year due to a gas leak. She was home at the time and heard the thunderous blast.

The explosion obliterated the residence and hurled debris hundreds of yards. Two people were killed, scores injured. It made the national news. She and her parents drove by the explosion site a week after the incident. All that was left of the building was half a wall and a whole lot of rubble.

Through the media coverage, she learned that natural gas consists mainly of methane. She also learned that methane has to reach a certain concentration before it can burn in air.

How much time did they have before the methane in the cellar was within its explosive limits? They probably didn't have long. The party was still in its early stages, but most of the guests would have arrived. If she were the yaoguai, she would plan for the explosion to occur anytime now.

And should Millie's house explode … Junie's stomach not only dropped, it went into free fall when she imagined all the glass raining down on the partygoers, on the waitstaff, on the neighboring homes and streets.

"Joe, you need to get everyone out." Her voice was strident with urgency. "Then call the fire department and the gas company."

Joe held her back when she tried to open the cellar door. "I'm not letting you down there!" he exclaimed. "We're both staying up here. *You* can call the fire department while I get the people out."

She shook his arm off. "I have to make sure the yaoguai doesn't find an ignition source before everyone can evacuate." Her breath suddenly hitched. "Joe, MY PARENTS. My mom and dad are in the house. We have to hurry. Please get them to safety. I can't let anything happen to them." She looked away, but not before he saw the tears spilling from her eyes.

He was conflicted. Nonetheless he knew, as she did, that she was the only one with a chance against the yaoguai. "Take this," he said finally, pulling a flashlight from one of his pockets.

She wiped her tears on the back of her hand and gratefully accepted the tool. She had left her purse—and her own flashlight—in Millie's bedroom. Joe's eyes bored into hers, then he took off running for the kitchen.

Junie threaded the sword between her waistband and belt and turned on the flashlight. She opened the door, went in and shut it behind her to ensure the gas remained in the cellar.

She placed one foot on the first tread of the steps.

Chapter 20

Junie's legs shook so hard she didn't think she would make it to the bottom of the stairs. She had never been so frightened in her life. She expected at any moment to be engulfed in a giant fireball.

Or grabbed by a fearsome supernatural monster.

Her heart stopped racing when she reached the cellar floor in one piece. She exhaled through chattering teeth, then took a deep breath to calm herself. Methane was lighter than air so it was easier to breathe down here than it had been on the stairs. As the fog of fear eased its grip on her brain, she remembered another helpful nugget of information from the news reports about the gas explosion near her parents' home. She risked asphyxiating if she breathed in high concentrations of natural gas. *Great. Just ... great.*

Hearing hissing, she directed her flashlight at the joists above her, where the gas and water lines were. One pipe was broken and hanging loose. It was from this that the hissing issued.

Should she try to stem the leak? Unfortunately, the joists were out of her reach. It would take too long to search for something to stand on. She hadn't seen a ladder during her previous visits to the cellar. Even if she could get her hands on a ladder, how would she be able to join the pipes together so the gas couldn't escape? She hadn't brought any tools or duct tape. No, her best bet was to find the yaoguai and prevent it—or at least delay it—from igniting anything while Joe evacuated the premises and alerted the authorities.

Where could the creature be hiding? It could be sheltering anywhere amid the uncompromising gloom. She hadn't realized how very dark the cellar was when the door upstairs was shut and all the lights were off. Good thing Joe had thought to give her a flashlight. Without it, she wouldn't have been able to see her hand in front of her face. Even with a flashlight, there were *way* too many shadows and murky recesses.

Peering into the dark, she again got the sense that the cellar was far more expansive than its walls suggested. *How many worlds did it harbor?*

She swept her beam over her surroundings. The shadows were the only things that moved, wavering in and fleeing from her light. At least she and Joe had gotten rid of the spectral soldiers. It was one less problem to fret over. She listened intently but heard nothing other than the soft hissing of the gas.

She tensed her muscles and inched slowly forward, stopping every now and then to listen. The smell of gas became fainter the further she traveled from the leaking pipe.

She had no particular strategy in mind other than to ramble around the cellar. She had a feeling that the yaoguai would come for her.

* * *

Joe heard the cellar door slam behind him as he ran. Junie was on her way down to confront the yaoguai.

He broke out in a cold sweat at the enormity of what they had to do. Lives were depending on them. On HIM.

The waitstaff stared when he skidded to a stop in the kitchen. "Everyone!" he shouted. "I need your attention. There is a gas leak in the cellar. You must leave the house immediately! Alert everybody!"

No one moved. A few gaped. One youngster giggled as if she thought he was playing some kind of prank.

An older woman detached herself from the kitchen's large island. She eyed him from head to toe as she warily approached. She didn't appear impressed by what she saw. "Sir, have you been drinking?" she asked. "This is the kitchen. We're the caterers. Do you need assistance finding your way back to the party?"

She grasped his elbow firmly and tried to steer him out of the kitchen.

The others lost interest and went back to what they were doing.

"This is NOT a joke!" he yelled desperately. "You all need to get out NOW."

He tried to pull away from the woman but she was surprisingly strong. Her fingers gripped his arm like a steel clamp. Thankfully, Emma with the clipboard rushed in to see what all the shouting was about.

"Mr. Tham?" She gawked at his rumpled state. "What's going on?"

"There's a gas leak," he said urgently. "You have to get everyone out of the house NOW."

Emma looked at the woman, who was still keeping a firm hold on his elbow. The woman released him and shrugged. "I think he's had a little too much to drink," she said, which elicited a snort from the teenager who had giggled.

Joe threw up his hands in frustration. "Come with me," he said to Emma.

Fortunately, she followed quite willingly. He dashed to the cellar door and tugged it slightly open. The odor of gas wafted out.

"Oh *crap*." Emma's face drained of color.

He quickly closed the door before more gas could escape. "Get everyone out of the house," he told her. "I'll call the fire department now."

Emma was sprinting back to the kitchen before he finished talking. "OUT, OUT, OUT!" she screamed. "Marcia, get everyone OUT!"

Emma, unlike Joe, was a born leader and communicator. People listened to her. Joe was speaking with the 911 operator when the waitstaff started streaming from the kitchen and out the side entrance.

After hanging up, he wondered briefly whether he should help with the evacuation or join Junie in the cellar. He decided the efficient Emma could cope on her own. Junie needed him more. He raced back to the cellar and was about to open the door when something occurred to him.

Hadn't Dan's blueprints shown the location of the main shutoff valve for the house's gas supply? If he could shut the gas off, that surely would lessen the chance of anybody getting blown to bits while he and Junie tackled the yaoguai. The only problem was—where was the valve?

He started to panic when he drew a blank. He took a deep breath and forced himself to visualize the mansion's layout. He had gone over the blueprints many times. He reviewed them just this afternoon, right before he left the apartment.

It was coming back to him. The valve was located outside, where the gas line entered the house. If he recalled correctly, it wasn't far from the side entrance. That, at least, was a lucky break.

A few dawdlers were still making their way out. He squeezed among them and ran outside. It was chaos and pandemonium everywhere—partygoers and party staff were stampeding across Millie's manicured garden to get to the street. On and across the street, more people wandered about in confusion. Cars were beeping their horns, flashing their headlights and traveling very slowly to avoid hitting anyone. Puzzled neighbors stood on their front lawns wondering what was going on.

Joe had a moment to enjoy the refreshing night breeze on his hot skin before he ducked into the graveled alleyway between the house and the garage. It was dark here—too dark to see. He brought out his spare flashlight and turned it on. It didn't take him long to spot the gas meter and the valve.

He'd turned off a main shutoff valve once before, when there was a gas scare at the Laughing Buddha. Thankfully, that turned out to be a false alarm. Unfortunately, he hadn't remembered that he needed a wrench or a pair of pliers to do it. *Damn.* He was conscious of the clock ticking away. Every second counted. Where could he get his hands on a wrench?

He ran back up the alley and found the door into Millie's garage. He went in and flipped the light switch. Bright energy-saving LEDs lit up the large space and reflected off a gleaming BMW sedan and Mercedes-Benz sport utility vehicle. He ran to the back where there was shelving. He rifled through Millie's belongings—carelessly sweeping and tossing things off the shelves—until he found what he was looking for, nestled inside a box of tools.

He returned to the alley with a large wrench in hand. Hurrying to the gas meter, he mentally reviewed what he had to do. Should he turn the valve clockwise or counterclockwise to shut it off?

Too long. He was taking too long. Joe's anxiety level ratcheted up with every second that elapsed. He hoped Junie was okay. *Please Junie, please, please be okay.* He forced visions of her mangled corpse from his mind and bent over the valve.

Sweat dripped into his eyes. He heard the wail of sirens in the distance. The emergency responders were on their way.

Chapter 21

The monster attacked when Junie was at the far end of the main cellar. Hearing a faint scratching above, she aimed her beam upward, in time to see something come at her with red eyes and razor teeth.

In her panic, she reflexively raised her flashlight and batted. By sheer luck, she hit the creature and sent it sailing into some chairs stacked on top of each other.

The chairs fell over with a loud bang. The monster—still the size of a small dog but now with six pointed crab-like legs—scrambled to its feet and scurried under some dust covers. Shining her flashlight after it, Junie recognized where she was from the jumble around her. She had arrived at the area where the ghost nurse eluded her and Joe.

Double drats. The discarded furniture provided ample hiding spots for the yaoguai.

She switched the flashlight to her left hand and slid the Energy Devourer from her waistband. She crept up to the dust cover under which the yaoguai had crawled and slipped the sword underneath. She cautiously raised the fabric. When nothing jumped out at her, she yanked the cover completely off the leather armchair it protected. The yaoguai, of course, was no longer there.

Next to the armchair was a heavy armoire backed up against the cellar wall. The antique wardrobe was divided into three vertical sections. The door of the middle section was ajar and swinging. Hoping to surprise the creature, she gripped the knob of the partially open door and flung it wide. It was she who was surprised.

The door to her left suddenly slammed open. The yaoguai leaped at her, its two front legs raised and aiming for her eyes. She barely had time to move her arm in front of her face before the creature was on her. Its teeth bit down on her left elbow while its six legs—each ending in a sharp nail—tore at her flesh.

She screamed in pain and rammed her elbow hard against the armoire. The impact jarred her arm and caused the yaoguai to clench its jaws, but now the creature was pinned against the wardrobe's only closed door. Unfortunately, she had dropped both the sword and the flashlight. She couldn't retrieve either item without relaxing her hold on the yaoguai.

With the flashlight on the ground and pointing away from her, the creature was an amorphous black blob that was barely discernible in the dark. It growled and squirmed, its glowing eyes less than a foot from her face.

Still pinning it firmly in place with her left elbow, Junie moved her right hand to where she judged the yaoguai's neck to be. She wrapped her fingers around its throat and squeezed. At the same time, she dug her feet into the ground and pressed even harder against the armoire. The growling stopped and the creature gagged. It writhed desperately as she both choked and crushed it. The vice around her elbow loosened.

The instant she felt the pressure ease, she tore her elbow from the monster's jaws, screaming again at the hot flare of pain. She wrapped her left hand around the creature's throat as well. Now she had both hands around its neck. Its teeth snapped viciously and its nails slashed at her arms, but it was trapped.

She took a deep breath and braced her feet. She shoved the yaoguai forcefully into the armoire's middle section, quickly kneed the door shut and leaned her shoulder against it. The creature yowled, the eerie keening raising gooseflesh on the nape of her neck and upper arms, as it threw itself frenziedly against the door. The sturdy wood creaked in protest, but it held.

She took another deep breath. She rotated her body until her back was jammed against the door, keeping it shut. She slowly slid her feet apart, bent her knees and lowered herself to the ground. Her fingers reached for the Energy Devourer.

Her fingertips were touching the sword when something crept out from beneath the armoire.

* * *

Junie felt a cold sensation just before something grabbed the back of her blouse. She yelped and twisted aside; her blouse ripped. The wardrobe door crashed open a split second later, narrowly missing her head. The yaoguai hurtled out and scampered into the murk.

Swearing, she snatched up the sword and the flashlight and jumped to her feet. She looked under the armoire—and almost lost the flashlight again at the sight of the pallid face glaring back at her. The ghost nurse's eyes were filled with malice; a corner of her black lips lifted in a triumphant sneer.

Junie momentarily wondered how Sally Kinde managed to huddle under so tight a space. The wardrobe's curved legs—ending in claw-and-ball feet—had to be less than eight inches high. There wasn't much room, even for a ghost. A rattling sound alerted her to the fact that the heavy piece of furniture was rocking. She threw herself sideways just as the armoire toppled to the ground with a loud crash.

The nurse was trying to kill her. Perhaps Sally held a grudge from Junie and Joe's attempt to evict her. And the murderous apparition wasn't done yet. The old bedstead shot across the floor, nearly knocking Junie off her feet. A bottle whizzed by Junie's ear, so close she could feel the wind from its passage.

Sally wasn't a mere ghost—she was a *poltergeist*. A chair came next, tumbling through the air. If June hadn't skipped aside, it would have smacked right into her. It hit the wall with such force that it smashed into pieces. She grunted as sharp splinters dug into her exposed skin. Her eyes, luckily, were protected by her glasses.

Junie shone the flashlight wildly around, wondering what else was in store. Her beam skittered to a stop on the nurse, now standing upright about 15 feet away.

Sally was dressed as before, in a long black gown, white apron and white cap. Her gown billowed, making her look like some kind of grotesque bat. She raised her hands and her face twisted with rage. She suddenly rushed at Junie, moving fast despite the broken furniture in her way. Her skirt blew up, and Junie's insides turned to ice when she saw the nurse's feet *weren't touching the ground.*

Junie stumbled backwards until she could go no further. Too late, she realized her fatal mistake—she was trapped against the wall. Large furniture on either side of her prevented any escape. She cowered as the nurse's gelid, skeletal fingers reached for her.

Something dropped onto Sally's head, squishing her cap and causing the specter to stop short less than two feet from Junie. The object sat on the ghost's head, looking for all the world like an ugly black hat, before it flowed down like viscid oil and covered her face. The nurse screeched and cried and clawed at the oily tar-like substance, her muffled screams sounding more spectral than actual to Junie's ears.

In the meantime, Junie's feet were moving of their own accord. She barreled past the beleaguered ghost, stopping only when she was a safe distance from Sally and her mysterious assailant. Junie's brain took a little longer to kick into gear. Watching the nurse blunder about trying to dislodge the thing on her head, it slowly dawned on Junie that the thing was none other than the yaoguai. The creature had ambushed Sally and now was gorging on her negative energy.

The monster was growing rapidly, even as Sally's cries became weaker. The nurse was visibly fading, growing more and more insubstantial until she was completely gone. In her place stood the yaoguai. Whoever and whatever Sally had been in life, her apparition had possessed a lot of negativity. That negativity had helped the yaoguai to regain some of its former stature. It was now almost as tall as Junie.

The creature resembled what it had transformed into in Millie's room —ropy muscles, rough gray skin and jaws hinged at the ears—except shorter and squatter. If anything, that made it look even scarier. Its wide grin broadened even more at the revulsion on Junie's face; its long tongue flicked playfully over its jagged teeth as though savoring the taste of her flesh.

However, she wasn't intimidated. Poltergeists—Joe hadn't told her how to deal with those. Yaoguai, on the other hand, could be vanquished with her sword. And she knew enough by now not to feed it with her fear.

She decided to instill some fear on her part. Channeling Wonder Woman, former First Lady Michelle Obama and Viking berserker, she raised the Energy Devourer, uttered a feral battle cry and charged.

The yaoguai grabbed a piece of wood—part of the chair that had smashed against the wall—just as she fell on it with the sword. Though it was stronger than the pug-like creature it had been, it was still relatively weak. It deflected the Energy Devourer's first thrust but soon was retreating in the face of her ferocious onslaught.

She rained blow after blow, trying to find the right moment to ram her sword into the monster's heart. She knew she held the upper hand—for now. She had to strike before the yaoguai could tap into more negative energy. It must have known too.

Without warning, the yaoguai chucked its weapon at her head. When she ducked, it crouched and leaped upward. It hit the ceiling with its four limbs and clung upside down above her. It started crawling, heading rapidly for the chamber from which it had sprung.

She trained her flashlight on the fleeing figure and gave chase. As her heart, arms and legs pumped, she had an epiphany. She knew exactly what she had to do. She knew exactly why she had to do it. She knew what was at stake. For the first time in her young life, she experienced absolute clarity. There were no doubts; there was no insecurity.

Some people were born to be poets. Some were born to be statesmen, or teachers, or saints, or martyrs. She was born to fight yaoguai and other supernatural horrors.

Come what may, she was NOT going to let this particular horror escape.

Chapter 22

She arrived at the chamber just in time to see the yaoguai wriggling headfirst into the new sinkhole. It was quick, but she was quicker. She dropped the flashlight—but not the sword—and grabbed one of the creature's thick ankles. It yowled in pain when the sword touched its skin. It raised its other foot and kicked at her.

She dodged the foot while still maintaining her grip on the yaoguai's ankle. She pulled. Amazingly, the yaoguai felt weightless in her hands. It slid smoothly out of the hole.

The creature kicked again, this time with both feet. One of the feet slammed into her chin, causing her to bite her tongue. She inadvertently let go and the yaoguai scooted out of reach.

The blood in her mouth tasted metallic. She spat it out and retrieved her flashlight from the ground. Standing at the chamber's entrance to ensure the yaoguai couldn't get away, she combed the shadows with her beam until she located the monster. It crouched in a corner, blending in with the dark except for its red eyes. She raised her sword and walked toward it, making sure she came between it and the portal.

"Wait!" The yaoguai's voice—sibilant and nasal—hadn't changed despite its smaller size. "At least tell me who you are before you kill me. Why do you command the sword of the Tham Dragons?"

"I'm just an apprentice," she said cautiously. Joe had warned her that these creatures were deceptive. *Was it trying to buy time?* "I work for the

Golden Dragon's son."

"Are you the next Tham Dragon?" the monster asked.

She paused. *Could she be a Tham Dragon?* She and Joe were blood relations, if Stella's genealogical research was accurate. "Maybe," she finally said.

The creature smiled malevolently. "I'm surprised that anyone wants the job. Didn't you hear what happened to the last Dragon?"

She was confused. "Yeah. He died of a heart attack."

The creature's beady eyes glowed with spite. "The Golden Dragon didn't die of a heart attack. He was murdered."

"By *yaoguai*?"

"No, he was hunted down and murdered by another Dragon." The yaoguai sniggered at her expression. "You didn't know? The Golden Dragon was stabbed, then gutted like a pig. He whimpered like a child as he bled to death."

The monster cocked its head all of a sudden. Its bat-like ears twitched, as if it had heard something. It stared over her shoulder at the tunnel's black maw.

Despite herself, she turned and looked as well. The yaoguai took advantage of her momentary distraction. It bowled her over and knocked her to the ground in its headlong rush for the sinkhole.

Fortunately for her, the creature was too intent on escaping to try and kill her while she was disoriented. It scurried to the sinkhole on all fours and jumped in, this time feet first. Despite its thick girth, it didn't seem to have any problem fitting into the foot-wide aperture. The crown of its head was disappearing into the cavity by the time she picked herself up.

She ran to the sinkhole and shone her flashlight inside. There was no sign of the monster or its eyes within the hole's tubular depths. She was debating what to do when her ears caught a soft sound in the tunnel. She whirled around.

Facing the passageway, she failed to see the thing that snaked out of the sinkhole until it was too late. It grasped her ankle and yanked. She fell prone; the wind was knocked out of her and the Energy Devourer and the flashlight flew out of her hands. Another powerful tug and she was hauled inexorably into the hole.

She tumbled down to her waist before she managed to slow her descent by pressing her knees against the sides of the narrow cavity. She clawed at the dirt, trying to keep her upper body above the hole's lip, but her fingers couldn't gain a purchase in the topsoil that Dan's men had piled on and around the former sinkhole. She felt a third tug on her ankle; she sank up to her armpits.

Her shoulders now were jammed tightly in the hole like a cork in a bottle. The narrow aperture was constricting her chest, making it hard to breathe. Was she going to die slowly and painfully of compressive asphyxia, struggling to draw every precious breath as the cruel earth crushed her lungs and other vital organs? *If she was dragged deep enough, would they even find her body?*

It took her a second to realize that something was happening beneath her. The restraint around her ankle was gone and the soil was loosening up and falling away from her body. Her knees no longer were wedged against the hole's sides. She thrashed her legs, but that only loosened the soil even more. She sank rapidly, this time pulled down by her own weight, until only her arms stuck out of the hole.

With her head below the surface, all she could see was black, black earth. More soil fell away—it seemed as though a chasm was opening up under her—and she slid several inches lower. Her hands clung desperately to the hole's rim; her arms strained to bear her weight.

Clods dropped on her head—the soil was crumbling under her fingers. She started to free fall.

* * *

Her descent was halted abruptly by a vise-like grip on her wrists. The pressure on her wrists increased, making her wince, as she was hauled slowly upward.

She knew who her rescuer was even before she saw his face. Joe was swearing loudly and profusely. When her head surfaced above the hole's brim, she saw his sweat-stained face and terrified eyes in the beam of the flashlight poking out of his breast pocket. Veins bulged in his arms and forehead as he hoisted her up and out of the cavity.

When her feet were back on firm ground, she tried to stand but couldn't

—her legs were shaking too much to support her. She crawled on her hands and knees away from the hole and collapsed. She lay spread eagle, her chest heaving with exhaustion.

"Joe," she suddenly croaked. "JOE."

His anxious face hovered over her. "What is it, Junie? Are you badly hurt? Are you in pain?"

"Put the sword in my hand so I'll be ready if the yaoguai climbs back up."

He quickly found the Energy Devourer and placed it in her hand. Her fingers closed around the hilt and she felt much better.

"My parents—"

"Emma got everyone out. I'm sure they're fine."

"You came back for me." She sniffled, getting a little teary. Her adrenaline had dissipated and her emotions now threatened to overwhelm her. "I thought I was going to be stuck forever in the sinkhole. I thought I was going to die in there."

He dropped down heavily beside her, his eyes and flashlight fixed on the cavity in case the yaoguai made an appearance. "I'm sorry I didn't return immediately," he said. "This was too close a call. If I'd been just a second later … "

He shook his head, his face bleak. "By the way," he added, "you're bleeding."

Junie had almost forgotten that she was injured. She sat up and wiped her glasses, which were a little smeary from her travails and her tears, on the front of her blouse. When her glasses were reasonably clean, she put them on, retrieved the flashlight she had dropped and inspected her wounds.

There were cuts and scratches on her face and arms, and bites on her left elbow. The knees of her trousers were torn, the skin below scraped raw. None of it looked too serious, even the puncture wounds left by the yaoguai's teeth. The bleeding had mostly stopped and the injuries were starting to scab over.

"Can yaoguai bites and scratches get infected?" she wondered aloud. "Is it too late to get a tetanus shot? Or should I be treated for rabies?"

"You'll heal quickly," he reassured her. "That's your magic, the magic of a Dragon." His eyes flicked to hers. He seemed at peace with the revelation.

She was as well.

"I'm sorry I lost the yaoguai," she said. "It escaped back through the portal."

"Don't worry about that for now. You did well just by surviving. And by the fact the house didn't blow up."

"Are we out of danger?"

"I think so," he said. "While Emma was evacuating the house, I alerted the fire department and shut off the gas supply. That's why I took so long."

He caught sight of the rips at the back of her blouse. "What happened there? Did the monster spring at you from behind?"

"No. It was a poltergeist. You have to give me pointers on how to handle those."

Poltergeist? He nodded speechlessly, deciding he was too tired for the time being to ask for details.

"Um ... I have something else to tell you." Junie bit her lip, not sure how he would react to what she had to say. "The yaoguai mentioned your father, the Golden Dragon."

"I know," he said. "I heard while I was in the tunnel."

"Do we—?"

He cut her off. "I'll deal with that later," he said brusquely. "Right now, we have important things left to do."

"Like what?"

"We have to seal the portal so the yaoguai and its brethren can't use it for another visit."

"How do we do that?"

"I'll show you. Are you ready? We have to hurry. I don't know when the firefighters will find us and make us leave."

The trembling in her legs was mostly gone. They went to stand at the sinkhole's edge. When Joe aimed his beam into the cavity, she was disconcerted to see the hole was as narrow as before. *Had she imagined the loosening soil? Had it all been in her head?*

He cleared his throat to get her attention. "I'm a little hazy about the sealing process," he confessed awkwardly. "My father explained it to me, but I've only seen him perform it once. It involves two main measures, the first of which is closing the portal. You do that by utilizing the energy absorbed by the sword."

She passed the sword to him so he could show her how. He dipped the blade into the hole. "Try to harness the sword's energy when you do this," he said. "Then you compel the hole to close."

He saw the doubt on her face when he returned the Energy Devourer to her. "How about this?" he suggested. "Visualize energy flowing from your arm into the sword and pushing down and outward. And visualize the hole as a … a cardboard box. When you compel it to close, picture the box's flaps closing and you taping them shut."

Junie tried her best to follow his instructions. She pushed the Energy Devourer into the aperture. When a wave of heat transferred from her arm into the sword, she conjured up an image of herself closing the lid of an empty pizza box.

Nothing happened. She opened her mouth, about to ask for more guidance, when the sinkhole shivered at the margins. The movement was so slight that she blinked, wondering if her eyes were deceiving her. The hole suddenly emitted a low, grinding sound and the movement at its lip became more pronounced. The edges were inching forward, as if they were growing in brief spurts. It was like watching shaky time-lapse photography. The cavity became smaller and smaller until its edges finally touched and fused together.

The hole was gone. Not just the hole—there also was no sign of the sunken area that marked the outlines of the first sinkhole. The compacted soil looked as if it had lain undisturbed for hundreds of years. Junie could easily imagine there never was a sinkhole, except for the fact that half the Energy Devourer was buried in the dirt.

She tugged on the sword and it slid out easily. "Is that it?"

"The portal is closed, but that's only half the job. Remember I said there were two measures. The second measure involves the talismans. We must use one of them to seal the—"

Joe stopped in mid-sentence and his eyes shot to the tunnel. "*Damn,*" he muttered. "We're out of time."

Junie heard it too—voices, and more than one. People were coming through the passageway. He hastily took the sword from her and slipped it down the back of his coat. Not a moment too soon. They were brightly spotlit by a ray of light from the tunnel.

"What are you doing here?" The voice was muffled but the speaker clearly was irritated. "Do you know the house has been evacuated because of leaking gas?"

A strapping fireman stepped into the chamber. He was wearing a self-contained breathing apparatus, which explained why his voice was muffled. He clutched a small, oblong object in his hand, which Joe surmised was a gas detection monitor. He was followed by another firefighter who was shorter but similarly clad in bulky protective gear.

"Sorry," Joe said glibly. "We mistook the cellar door for the way out. Then we got lost."

Chapter 23

The second firefighter turned out to be a woman. She hustled Joe and Junie out while her colleague continued checking the chamber for gas.

"Are we still in danger?" Joe asked.

"No, sir. The gas level never got to the lower explosive limit. Apparently someone shut off the gas supply in time." She pointed to her SCBA. "This is a precaution until we can reduce the levels to zero percent. In the meantime, I have to make sure the two of you are out of here as quickly as possible."

"Did everyone make it out safely?"

"I think the homeowner was transported by ambulance to a hospital. There were a few other injuries, including one gentleman who tripped and broke his wrist while trying to vault over a chair." She paused for a beat. "Hopefully, you two are the last of the stragglers."

The firefighter had a friendly voice but a no-nonsense manner. Joe didn't dare ask if they could stay a little longer in the cellar.

The firefighter gestured at Junie's bleeding arm. "You should ask the paramedics to check that out. What happened?"

"I ... um ... tripped in the dark," Junie mumbled.

At the main cellar, a group of firemen conferred under the broken gas pipe. Their masked faces swung toward Joe, Junie and their escort as they passed by. Two men wearing T-shirts with the Washington Gas emblem were making their way down the stairs.

"Where did these two come from?" one of the firemen asked, nodding at

Joe and Junie.

"They said they got lost," their friendly firefighter responded.

Upstairs, the three of them ran into more firefighters, some of whom were opening windows to ventilate the house. The guests were all gone and the electricity was turned off.

Their feet crunched on broken glassware and crockery. Their escort's powerful flashlight also revealed mashed food, pools of spilled drinks and abandoned belongings scattered on the once-pristine floors. Millie's expensive furniture and artwork were upturned, knocked aside or pushed askew. Everything probably was insured, but her cleaning crew had serious work ahead of it once the authorities deemed the house safe to enter.

Finally, they stepped outside. Fire trucks, police cars and ambulances were parked a little distance away. The vehicles' strobing lights lit up the night and reflected off the house's many panes of glass. Junie had to shield her eyes—sensitive after so long in the dark—from the frenetic lighting. She tried to find her parents' faces in the crowd gathered outside the authorities' barricade.

Joe tugged at her uninjured arm. "Come on, we have to get you some medical attention, like the firefighter said. You can look for your parents afterwards."

He brought her outside the restricted area to a spot where emergency medical technicians were attending to people injured in the evacuation. A paramedic examined her elbow.

"What's this?" He frowned. "It looks like something bit you. Was it a dog? You may need rabies shots."

Junie smiled and shook her head at the same time, which confused the man. He stared at her a little longer, then shrugged and began cleaning and bandaging her arm. He was about finished when she heard familiar voices. She turned. Her mother and father ran toward her waving frantically.

The paramedic nodded to tell her he was done. She stood up and sprinted to Stella and Raymond, who enveloped her in their arms.

"Junie, I'm so glad you're safe," Stella sobbed. "I told the firemen not to come back out until they found you." She fingered her daughter's bandages. "Are you hurt?"

"It's just a scratch," Junie said hurriedly. Her own face was wet with tears of relief. "And I'm glad you and Pa are safe too."

"Where's Joe?" Stella looked around.

"I'm here." He rose to his feet from the curb, where he had been waiting for Junie's wounds to be treated.

Stella insisted that Junie come home with her and Raymond. As a rule, Pa parked in the first spot he found, even if it was far from his destination. His embrace of the "bird in hand" maxim had saved the Soongs from having their car temporarily impounded within the cordoned-off area.

Joe assured Stella that he could find his own way home. He was walking away when Junie pulled him aside.

"Joe, what about—?" She wiggled her eyebrows, hoping he understood she was referring to the sealing of the portal.

"You go home with your parents tonight and rest up," he said. "We'll deal with that later. No one will let us back in the house anyway. In the meantime, I have a few things to sort out. I'll be in touch."

He looked so tired and somber. "Are you sure you're okay?" she asked tentatively.

He waved his hand to indicate he was fine, but his smile was forced.

* * *

He decided to walk back to his apartment. Although it was almost two miles, he thought the hike might help him think, or at least help clear his head.

Millie lived not far from Dupont Circle, a popular destination for locals and tourists alike because of its many coffee shops, restaurants and bars. Given that it was a Saturday night, the walkways were busy, especially around the metro station. Joe, buried in his thoughts, barely noticed the people around him as he trudged along Massachusetts Avenue.

He hoped Junie wasn't worrying about sealing the portal. He hadn't had the chance to reassure her that while it was a concern, it wasn't an immediate one. With the portal closed, the yaoguai couldn't surface again, at least not in its weakened state. Nevertheless, they shouldn't wait too long, in case the monster found another source from which to replenish its energy.

The talisman seal was the final guarantee in keeping out the yaoguai and its ilk. Once sealed, a portal couldn't be reopened from the nether dimensions except with the Energy Devourer. Of course, the seal could still be physically tampered with or broken on the human side, but Joe had an idea of how to deal with that.

Right now though, all he could think about was the yaoguai's revelations regarding his father. They weighed heavily on his heart and mind. *Could what it told Junie be true?* The creatures lied, of course. They couldn't help it. It was part and parcel of their nefarious natures. *But what if it hadn't been lying?* Why did he believe all these years that the Golden Dragon died of a heart attack?

He was at school when his father set out on his last job. Joe still remembered the day clearly, as if the memory were seared into his mind. It was hot, the sun a scorching disk in a blue, blue sky. His shirt stuck to his back and sweat stains grew under his arms as he walked home from school. He was disappointed to find he had just missed his half sister, Pearl. She didn't visit very often but when she did, she played with him. She teased him and made him laugh, sometimes so hard it felt as if his belly would burst.

However, he couldn't be upset for long. His father would be home soon. Joe was watching TV when he heard a knock on the front door. The raps were not loud, but they sounded urgent. He jumped up but his mother got to the door first. Whatever she saw there caused her to scream at him to go to his room. Her body blocked the doorway so he couldn't see who, or what, it was. Elsie screamed at him again and he ran to his room.

His curiosity eventually overcame his fear of his mother. He put his ear to the wall that separated his room from the living room. Elsie was crying and in the middle of a phone call. She spoke so softly that he couldn't make out her words. A little later, he heard her open the front door. Judging from the voices, she admitted at least three men into the apartment. There were dragging sounds and furtive conversation, after which she left with the men. When he tried to come out of his room, he discovered that Elsie had locked him in.

He crawled into bed, bewildered and scared. He knew something important was happening, but *what?* Why didn't his father come home and tell him everything was okay?

He fell asleep. Hours later, his mother returned and let him out. She told him the Golden Dragon died from a heart attack and his body had been taken away. He never even got the chance to see his father one last time—she refused to let him view the body.

Joe breathed in slowly. It was painful to relive that day. He had no choice but to call his mother if he wanted to verify what the yaoguai said. He couldn't rest until he knew the truth. He glanced at his watch—it was too late now, she would be in bed. He would call her in the morning. It would be a difficult conversation, but he was determined to make Elsie talk.

The yaoguai told Junie that the Golden Dragon was murdered by another Dragon. That part surely was a lie. There were no other Dragons after his father's death, until Junie came along.

He had no doubt that she was his father's natural heir. He was certain the minute she thrust the Energy Devourer into the yaoguai and sapped its strength. The sword would have killed the creature if it had stayed in any longer.

So she—a distant relation who didn't even bear the name—somehow had inherited the genes that created the Tham Dragons. It also explained why the luopan and the crystal responded to her.

These—the sword, the luopan and the crystal—were not mere tools. They were one-of-a-kind weapons with magic of their own. In the right hands they could level mountains, part oceans ... even smash worlds if necessary.

And look at the way she had pursued the yaoguai back to its realm. Despite her youth, she was quick-thinking, single-minded, courageous, *relentless*. She was everything a Dragon should be.

Now that he knew, could he handle this? How did he feel about her taking what should have been his?

He discovered, to his own surprise, that he didn't resent her. Not at all. Indeed, he was filled with a new sense of purpose. Now, after so long, he knew his place. His years of strife made sense—he had kept the business running, waiting all this time for Junie to find him. He had a calling, an important one. He wasn't a Dragon, but neither was he a mere sidekick. His role was to nurture and guide the latest Dragon.

Joe was to Junie what Yoda was to Luke Skywalker, what Splinter was to the Teenage Mutant Ninja Turtles, what Albus Dumbledore was to Harry Potter. If not for the teachers, where would the students be? His chest swelled with pride.

"Father, rest assured, I will do my best," he vowed. "I will not let you and our honorable name down."

He felt an unexpected burst of joy when something occurred to him. His father hadn't died, not really. The Golden Dragon, the Iron Dragon and all the Dragons who preceded them would never die, not as long as there were others who could carry on the fight. The Dragons lived on in Junie. And it was Joe, the Red Dragon, who would ensure she understood her responsibilities and reached her full potential. Through Junie, he could be close to his father again.

But what if he failed in this as well? A needling whisper reminded him that he wasn't all that familiar with the Tham Dragons himself. His education in his heritage ended at the age of 10. Was he qualified to help Junie fulfill her destiny?

He pushed the troublesome thought away. He had enough problems without having to deal with ones that hadn't yet transpired.

Chapter 24

" … well-known philanthropist Millicent Jenks Scarpini was hospitalized following an emergency evacuation at her Kalorama—"

Joe blearily opened his eyes as a news reader from the local radio station described last night's harrowing events. He had set the alarm on his clock radio for 8 a.m. so he could catch Elsie, an early riser, before she got busy with whatever it was that she did during the day.

He got up, hurried out to the living room and turned on the TV. The local news stations were covering the story as well.

He retrieved his cell phone from his bedside table and called Dan. Hopefully, Dan hadn't yet heard, seen or read the media reports about the gas leak. The contractor didn't need a coronary on top of his other health problems.

In any case, Dan had taken a big risk by passing them the blueprints—he deserved to know what happened at the party, and that his actions were instrumental in heading off the yaoguai and averting what could have been a real disaster.

The call went directly to voice mail. Joe left a message, but he couldn't help a twinge of disquiet at not being able to reach Dan. He reminded himself that it was Sunday, and Dan might be sleeping in. He also was entitled to not answer calls—even personal ones—during the weekend. *But surely he was expecting Joe's call?*

By the time he rang Elsie, it was almost 9 o'clock.

"Hello Joseph." A brief hesitation, as if she was expecting some kind of a verbal blow.

"Um, hello Mother."

He always sounded so stiff when talking to her! And now that he actually had her on the line, he found he wasn't quite sure how to proceed. When he rehearsed the words in his head last night, it had seemed so simple and straightforward. He was going to be direct and firm. *Did you lie about Father's heart attack?* And he wouldn't allow her to prevaricate or give her time to come up with any excuses.

"You're calling twice in three days. What's wrong?"

"Nothing! No, that is … um … did you … can you tell me again how Father died?"

"Why?"

"Uh, I've come across something that might, um, suggest it *wasn't* a heart attack."

There was a long silence. "I'm in the middle of something," she said abruptly. "Let me call you back."

Joe stared at his phone in disbelief after Elsie hung up on him. No. *No way.* He wasn't going to let her avoid the question. He ground his teeth and was about to redial her number when he heard a phone ringing. It took him a second to catch on that it was the office's landline rather than the cell phone in his hand. He hurried out of the apartment and snatched up the handset on his desk. The caller ID showed an unfamiliar number.

"Hello?" he said. "Joseph Tham speaking."

"Mr. Tham? It's Emma Frankel, Millie's personal assistant."

"Yes, hi." He was ashamed that he hadn't tried to contact Millie, after all she had been through. "How is Millie?"

"You must have heard by now that she was taken to a hospital. The doctors here are a little worried about her and want to keep her under observation."

"What are they worried about?"

"I'd rather not discuss her condition over the phone," Emma said. "She can tell you about it herself. And that's why I'm calling. I know it's Sunday, but Millie would like to meet with you and your colleague today. Are you both available to see her at the hospital?"

Joe's self-reproach eased slightly. Millie couldn't be in too bad a shape if her doctors were allowing her to have visitors. "Um, I can't answer for Junie, but I'm definitely available," he said. "Do you know why she wants to see us?"

"Well, I told her it was you who discovered the gas leak and called 911. I think she wants to express her gratitude in person."

"I see. I have a few things to discuss with her as well. What would be a convenient time?"

"Wonderful! Say around 2 in the afternoon?" She told him which hospital it was and Millie's room number.

The appointment couldn't have come at a better time. He and Junie had to get back into the cellar to finish sealing the portal. He would broach the subject with Millie this afternoon.

He texted Junie to ask whether she could make the meeting. After that he tried calling Dan again. His call to the contractor was transferred to voice mail, again.

He tried calling his mother. That call went straight to voice mail too.

* * *

Junie got Joe's text while she was eating breakfast with her parents. As a special treat, Stella made bacon and pancakes.

"Millie wants to see us today at 2 p.m. Can you make it?" According to the text, Millie was recuperating at the hospital whose board she sat on, and where Junie's dad practiced.

"I have to work today," Junie announced after she texted Joe that she would be there.

"But it's *Sunday*," Stella protested. "And *one day* after our collective near-death experience."

"You guys work weekends too, right?" Junie pointed out.

Stella looked chagrined; Raymond nodded in commiseration. It was true. The Soongs worked whenever it was necessary.

After breakfast, Junie peeled off the bandages covering her injured left arm. The paramedic had recommended that she swab the wounds with antiseptic and replace the dressings daily. She was startled to find that the bites and cuts had scabbed over. In fact, there was nothing left of them except for patches of skin that were pinker than the rest.

She flexed her fingers experimentally and jiggled her elbow. The arm felt as good as new. *Talk about Dragon magic!* She couldn't wait to tell Joe.

She was glad they were seeing Millie at the hospital. Today was the day she and Noah were going to the Culture on the Mall outdoor showing of Jackie Chan and Jet Li movies. She was really looking forward to it—she would be pacing or climbing the walls if she didn't have something else to occupy her mind.

She kept her fingers crossed that Noah hadn't forgotten about their "date." Unfortunately, she didn't have his phone number so she couldn't call him to confirm. She caught a glimpse of him on Friday in the Laughing Buddha's kitchen but he had been too busy to talk.

Her mother could tell something was up. "So what are you doing tonight, after that meeting with Millie? Do you want to come back here for dinner?"

"Uh, I'm going somewhere tonight."

"Is it with somebody special?" Stella teased.

She didn't answer the question, but her blush said enough. Stella beamed. She had hopes that her daughter's life finally was coming together. A steady job and a ... possible *love interest?*

Junie spent a lazy morning with her parents. Raymond gave her a lift to the hospital after lunch. Millie had a private room on the fourth floor. She took the elevator and walked along the tiled corridors until she found the room.

The door was open. Even from the outside she could see the room was filled with bouquets of flowers. Her parents had sent flowers too. She entered the room and her nose immediately was assailed by a dozen floral aromas mingled with the sharp smell of disinfectant.

Joe already was there. His shirt was buttoned all the way to the top to hide the ugly bruises on his neck.

She was surprised to also see Emma. She didn't recognize Millie's assistant at first. Emma wasn't as formally dressed as she usually was, perhaps because it was Sunday. Her business attire was replaced by comfortable jeans and a plaid shirt with the sleeves rolled up. Her severe bob was held back by a slim hairband. She carried a notebook instead of a clipboard.

Junie wondered whether Joe knew beforehand that the assistant would be at the meeting. Her presence was going to hamper their ability to converse freely with Millie.

Emma's casual appearance didn't diminish her air of efficiency. "Hello there," she said to Junie. "I was just telling Mr. Tham that it'd be best to keep the visit short. Millie needs her rest."

Junie glanced at the bed. Millie was hooked up to numerous medical devices, including a heart monitor and a pulse oximeter. She looked frail and shrunken against the white sheets and pillows. And no wonder. She had been enthralled by an otherworldly entity that borrowed her guise while feeding on her fear and confusion. She was lucky to be alive, all things considered. Her recovery probably would be long and slow.

"I'm glad you're both here." Millie spoke laboriously in a voice that was little more than a hoarse whisper.

Joe drew up a chair and sat by her bed. He gently took her hand as if afraid he might break her bones. "How are you feeling?" he asked with genuine concern.

"I've been better." Her face lit up with a flash of her old vitality, but it was short-lived.

"Emma said you wanted to see us?"

"She told me what you did at the party. I wanted to thank you and Junie."

"We did what anyone would have. It was Emma who took charge of getting the guests out." He smiled at the assistant. "I'm relieved no one was seriously injured. Where were you when Emma sounded the alarm?"

His body tensed as he awaited Millie's response. *How much did she remember of their confrontation with the yaoguai?*

"I was upstairs," she said at last after a long silence. She told them she awoke and found herself at her dressing table. She could hear emergency sirens approaching the house. She stumbled downstairs and joined the partygoers who were filing out. She fainted again when she got outside. A guest who also was a doctor stayed with her until the paramedics strapped her onto a gurney and rushed her to the hospital.

"Everything before that is a blur." She shook her head. "I don't remember what I was doing at the dressing table. I don't even remember planning the housewarming. That's why they're keeping me here."

"What do the doctors say about the gap in your memory?"

"They think I'm having some kind of breakdown, exacerbated by fatigue and the shock of the gas leak. They're running some tests, including a full physical."

Joe's stomach clenched when Millie mentioned tests. It was unsettlingly close to what was happening with Dan. Two innocent people stricken with inexplicable, life-threatening maladies. He had hoped that with the portal closed and the yaoguai gone, their symptoms would vanish. Was it too late for them? Perhaps they just needed more time.

"Meanwhile, the doctors are insisting I take it easy," Millie said. "They think rest will help to calm my nerves."

Right on cue, Emma cleared her throat and made a show of looking at her watch. "It's getting late," she announced. She picked up an envelope from the table beside Millie's bed. "Before you go, Millie wants you to have this." She placed the envelope in Joe's hand.

He opened it and took out a check. It must have had quite a few zeros because his jaw dropped.

"This is to thank you both for all your trouble on my behalf." Millie closed her eyes, looking drained. "I hope it's enough," she whispered. "Thank you again."

Joe slipped the envelope and check into his pocket. There was a note of finality in Millie's tone. She apparently thought there was no further need for their services. Emma must have picked up on that as well. The assistant raised her arms, as if preparing to shoo out a gaggle of wayward geese. Before she threw them out, he had to come up—quickly—with an excuse for why he and Junie needed to return to the house.

"Um, before we go," he said hurriedly, "what do the authorities say about the gas leak?"

Emma lowered her arms. "A representative from the utility company told me this morning he thinks the gas pipe was accidentally dislodged during the construction work. The pipe must have finally come apart last night in time for the party."

"Is the house safe to enter?"

"I'm not sure." Emma glanced at Millie, who seemed to have fallen asleep. "They brought in fans in the morning to speed up the ventilation, so the electricity must be restored and it's okay to use electrical devices in the house. The gas, however, is still shut off. The representative said they won't turn the gas back on until the pipe's fixed and they've made sure that everything is in good working order. That might take a few days."

Joe decided to take the bold approach. "Junie and I must get back into the house," he declared with as much authority as he could muster. "The sooner the better."

"Why?" Emma's eyes narrowed.

How much could they tell her? She didn't look like the sort to believe in supernatural entities. "Uh, I've been talking with Dan Groskind, Millie's contractor, about some structural changes that might improve the house's feng shui and counteract the recent run of bad luck," he said. "All Junie and I need is about half an hour in the cellar to take some measurements before I issue my recommendations."

"*Really?*" Emma's eyes narrowed even more. "Surely the measurements can wait a few days." Her chin lifted slightly and her nostrils flared. It was a weak excuse, even to his own ears, and she clearly wasn't buying it.

He scratched his ear and cleared his throat, taking his time to respond. Emma was an uncompromising control freak and a zealous guardian of Millie's time and assets. He had to tread carefully if he didn't want his request immediately shot down. Even worse, she looked like she was about to have him and Junie arrested for fleecing the gullible.

He was still thinking when Millie spoke from the bed. "It's okay. They can do whatever it is that they need to. They have my permission."

Joe stared triumphantly at Emma. *You heard her*, his expression said.

A muscle twitched beneath the assistant's right eye. "Fine," she said grudgingly. "But let me make a few phone calls first to ensure the house is no longer off-limits. After all, we won't want anything to happen to you and your apprentice. I'm also going to contact Mr. Groskind. I'll be in touch to let you know what I find out."

"Have you spoken to Dan recently?" he asked hopefully.

Emma shook her head. They both turned to look at Millie but a soft snore confirmed that she now was sound asleep.

Emma held her index finger to her lips, like a stern librarian reprimanding noisy kids. Taking that as their signal to leave, Joe and Junie tiptoed out of the room.

When they were at the elevators—and safely out of Emma's earshot—Junie asked unhappily, "Are we going to the house tonight?"

"I'm not sure. It all depends on Emma's phone calls. Why?"

"I've got plans for this evening."

He thought it over and shrugged. "No point ruining your evening. Go out and have fun. We probably won't hear back from Emma until tomorrow, if then."

"Thanks Joe."

He looked at her carefully. "By the way, how do you feel after last night?"

"Pretty good. The bites and scratches are mostly healed."

"No lingering aches or pain, or even just plain fatigue ... ?"

"No. No, I feel fine."

Joe's fingers crept to his own tender neck. And he had wrenched something in his back from having saved her from plummeting down into God knows where. He envied her ability to recover so quickly and easily from her night of peril.

They walked out into the street. He phoned Dan once more while they were waiting for a cab to take them back to the office. All he got was voice mail.

Chapter 25

Junie dated occasionally but never had a serious boyfriend. Unless you counted the guy she went out with during her first year of community college. He broke up with her after two months.

He was nice about it. It wasn't about her, he said. He explained that he needed a girlfriend with more drive and passion, someone who *cared* about things. Which was a kind way of saying she was bland and lacked ambition.

The last time she saw him, he told her he was dating someone who was spearheading a youth movement on climate change. No way she could compete with that. She wasn't that interested anyway.

This non-date with Noah, though, was the first in which she was seriously attracted to the guy. He wouldn't be the first white guy she had gone out with. He wasn't even the best-looking guy she'd gone out with. That honor went to Peter Mabhubani.

Peter looked like a young, dark George Clooney. He had intense eyes, wavy black hair and a brooding mystique that attracted female attention wherever he went. After one date, she found out he wanted Stella to sponsor him for an active Virginia real estate salesperson license. She refused to introduce him to her mother, after which she never saw him again.

Noah. There was just something about Noah. She couldn't explain what it was. He probably wanted to just be friends, but she could hope.

After trying on a few dresses, she settled for a loose peasant blouse with three-quarter sleeves, old baggy shorts, and sandals. She would be sitting on grass and she wanted to be comfortable. She applied a little makeup and released her hair from its usual ponytail. No matter how much she fluffed it, it fell to her shoulders in a straight black curtain instead of the soft waves she wanted.

"I'm leaving," she yelled to Joe as she left the apartment. She trotted down the stairs and stepped out of the stairwell at a little past five.

She was relieved to see Noah waiting outside the Laughing Buddha, as he promised he would be. He turned around when she called his name.

He wore a short-sleeve shirt and cargo pants. A backpack—very similar to the one she usually carried—was slung on one shoulder. His smile was dazzling and warm, like the sun reflecting off the Mediterranean Sea, like the promise of a spring morning.

She smiled back. Butterflies swooped and fluttered wildly in her stomach. The insects graduated to loop-the-loops and figure eights when he moved closer.

"I'm glad you didn't forget," he said. "I realized last night that I didn't have any way to contact you."

"We should exchange phone numbers," she said quickly before her courage failed her. She took out her phone and he told her his number. She called him right there and then so he would have her number as well.

"Are you hungry?" he asked when they had put away their phones. "We can eat before we walk to the mall."

She discovered she was starving, despite having had a big breakfast and lunch with her parents. "Yes, let's eat first."

"Where would you like to go?"

She looked down at her outfit. "How about somewhere casual?"

He suggested a burger place nearby. It was nicer than fast food but not nice enough to make her feel self-conscious about how she was dressed. The restaurant wasn't busy and they soon were shown to a cozy table for two. Stella would approve of his manners—he pulled out her chair for her and only sat after she was seated.

After they had placed their orders, he asked her how she liked her job. "You haven't been working for Joe that long, right?"

She was rather surprised to find he was correct. She'd been Joe's apprentice for less than two months, but it felt like they had worked together for years. "It's been great," she said honestly. "I've learned a lot about feng shui and geomancy."

"What does a geomancer do anyway?" He seemed genuinely interested.

"First, let me tell you how I got the job. The credit goes to my mother."

He laughed, his eyes crinkling at the corners, when she described how Stella badgered Joe into hiring her. Encouraged, she went on to talk about her work, although she skipped over the supernatural aspects. Joe was right about the need for discretion. And she didn't want to frighten Noah away before she got to know him better.

They were halfway through their burgers before she realized she was doing most of the talking. Noah really was good company. He prompted her along by asking good questions. He laughed at the appropriate spots, making her feel she was not only funny, but articulate. Best of all, he didn't seem to mind who she was—glasses, awkwardness and all. She was enjoying herself.

"I'm hogging the conversation," she said at last. "Please, tell me about yourself." She took a big bite of her burger to show she was serious about not talking.

He grinned. "Well, there's not a lot to say. I've managed the Laughing Buddha now for about a year and a half, and I enjoy what I do. We're turning a profit, which is good considering that most restaurants in the U.S. fail within the first year, and an overwhelming majority don't last beyond three to five years."

"Are you from the D.C. metropolitan area, or from somewhere else?"

"I was born and raised in Southern California. I left L.A. to go to Johnson & Wales University in Providence. I worked for two years in New York before I applied for the Laughing Buddha job in D.C."

"Wow. Why did you decide to stay in the East Coast?"

He paused. "I guess some people might say I'm running away from my family." He looked down at his food as if embarrassed by his own statement.

"I used to wish I could," she said wryly. "But I don't anymore. I've come to realize my mom and dad aren't that bad. I even like them as people.

I just couldn't see it when I lived with them. Okay, out with it. What's wrong with your family? Are you related to Charles Manson or something?"

He laughed. "Alright, I'll tell you. But it's your fault for asking. Have you heard of Geordie Redmond?"

The name did sound vaguely familiar. Junie gave up. "Sorry, no idea who that is. Should I know him?"

Noah looked pleased. "I'm glad you don't. You may be the very first person I've told who doesn't. He's my father and he hosts a cooking show on TV. And he owns several restaurants on the West Coast."

"Nope, still don't know him," she had to confess. "Sorry. I'm not that interested in the culinary arts and my family doesn't watch cooking programs."

"Don't apologize." If anything, he seemed even more pleased. "Anyway, I came to the East Coast so I could make it on my own. The Laughing Buddha isn't famous, or even what you might call fine dining, but it's MINE. I have only my own standards to live up to."

"So are you some kind of superstar gourmet chef like your dad?"

"Not even close. I'm not any kind of superstar, and that's part of the problem."

Junie eventually steered the conversation to Greta. She was dying to know whether there was anything between Noah and her. "So, how is Greta, by the way?" she asked with studied nonchalance.

"Greta?" He looked surprised. "She's fine. She just started at her new job."

Fudge. They must be in contact if he knew that. "What does she do again?"

"She's a social media specialist at the Four Seasons Hotel in Georgetown."

Blast. The Four Seasons was a very, very nice hotel. It sounded like Greta had a great job. "Does she like it?"

He shrugged. "I guess. I haven't spoken to her since that night we went out for drinks."

Junie smiled to herself. She liked the sound of "haven't spoken to her." She hoped he kept it that way.

He caught sight of his watch while they were arguing over what to order for dessert. "I didn't realize it was so late!" he exclaimed in dismay. "Let's skip dessert. We have to hurry if we want to catch the beginning of the first movie."

They had spent more than two hours at the burger joint. Junie was having so much fun she didn't want to leave. Not to mention she was quite certain she'd seen every movie they were showing tonight. In fact, she'd watched Jackie Chan's first *Drunken Master* at least five times in recent memory. Pa and Patrick were kung fu movie aficionados. Pa especially loved Jackie Chan and had an extensive DVD collection of his films.

Noah refused her offer to split the tab. He got up and went to the counter to pay the bill.

Junie picked up her phone to do some quick research while he was gone. She felt stupid when she realized who Noah's father was. Geordie Redmond was even more famous than Gordon Ramsay. He was involved with *many* high-end restaurants in, among other cities, Los Angeles, San Francisco and Seattle.

One venerable fine-food magazine dubbed him the "King of West Coast Cuisine." Another described him as the "legendary chef to Hollywood stars." He'd prepared meals for, among other famous people, Oprah Winfrey, Julia Roberts, Brad Pitt, Keanu Reeves, Adam Sandler and the entire cast of the old sitcom *Friends*. He'd even cooked for Jackie Chan!

The good thing was Noah didn't seem to hold her ignorance against her, at least not where his father was concerned.

* * *

The office phone rang shortly after Junie departed for her evening of fun.

Joe muted the television. He hurried out to the office and picked up the handset. "Hello?"

"Mr. Tham? It's Emma Frankel."

"Yes, Emma. And please, you can call me Joe."

"It took me all afternoon, but the utility company finally found someone to answer my questions. He says the house's safe. I'll let you in this evening."

Goodness. *Didn't she have an off switch?* Why was she working so hard on a *Sunday*? He pitied whomever she'd been pestering.

"Mr. Tham?" she prodded impatiently when he didn't immediately respond. "Didn't you say you needed access to the house as soon as possible? Your exact words, I believe, were 'the sooner the better'."

"The name's Joe, and yes, I did say that, but—"

He was about to say that he preferred to wait until tomorrow morning when she added, "Dan, Mr. Groskind, might be there as well."

He felt his spirits lift. "You managed to get hold of Dan?"

"No, I didn't speak with him," she admitted. "But I left a message that we were planning to be at the house and would like him to join us if possible."

"I've been trying to contact Dan myself," he told her. "I left many messages but he hasn't responded to any of them."

"Were you trying to reach Dan through his cell?" she asked. "I tried his cell phone a few times as well. When I didn't hear back, I called his company and got a recording telling me to leave a message or call again during regular office hours. I finally called the number that he provided Millie for emergencies. I left messages at all three places. Maybe one of them will work."

Maybe so. Emma had a proven track record of getting things done. Joe realized she was still speaking, and becoming increasingly irked at his failure to answer her questions.

"So Mr. Tham, are we meeting at the house this evening? Mr. Tham? Have I lost you? Are you still there? Hello? Hello?"

"Yes, yes," Joe said. "Sure. And the name's JOE." For some reason, his name had become another battlefront between him and Millie's capable assistant.

"Is 6 p.m. okay for you? I told Millie and Dan that's when we're meeting."

"Sure, 6 is fine. I'll see you then. And, um, thank you."

Joe hung up feeling like he'd been railroaded even though he was the one who had asked to be let back into the house. He reminded himself that the portal must be sealed. The longer they delayed, the higher the chance the yaoguai would regain enough strength to break through again. He really should be grateful to Emma for being so good at pushing things through.

He checked his watch. It was 5:25 p.m. Junie's evening out barely had started. She asked for so little time to herself that he hated to disrupt her plans.

But did he really need her there? She'd done the heavy lifting by closing the portal with the sword. To seal the gateway, the talismans' magic had to be invoked through a simple ritual. It could be done by one person. And that person didn't have to be a Dragon. He could do it himself without Junie being present.

He really hoped that Dan would be there. He was becoming more and more concerned about the contractor's continued silence.

On impulse, Joe picked up the phone again and dialed Dan's number. He growled with frustration when the call went to voice mail, even though it was what he expected. He should have asked Emma for the emergency number she mentioned. He left a new message, this time including Junie's cell number so Dan could contact her if Joe didn't pick up. He didn't want anything to interrupt the sealing ceremony, lest it result in a deficient seal.

He checked his watch a second time. He needed to hurry. He had a few items to gather and it might be difficult to catch a cab this late on a Sunday evening. He also should leave a message for Junie in case she came home early and wondered where he was.

He located a pad of sticky notes. "Junie," he scrawled, "Emma came through on house. Gone to seal portal. Hope you had a nice evening!"

He stuck the note on her bedroom door and went to his room to change.

Chapter 26

Joe was 10 minutes late. The police barrier had been removed so the taxi was able to drop him right in front of the house. He was disappointed not to see Dan when he alighted. Emma was waiting outside alone, her arms crossed and her foot tapping impatiently. She had replaced her notebook with a tote bag almost as large as his leather bag.

"Mr. Tham, I was afraid you might be a no-show." She glanced over his shoulder. "Where's your associate? Isn't she coming?"

"Junie had another engagement. Did Dan call you back?"

"No, but let's wait another 10 minutes to see if he shows up."

He decided after a brief awkward silence that conversation might make the time pass faster. He opted for the one topic they had in common: Millie. He was curious as to why Emma was so devoted to her.

"So Emma," he asked, "how long have you and Millie known each other?"

"For about five years." She glanced at him, taken aback by his sudden interest in her. "I started working for her when she and Dom returned to the U.S. You know he was a diplomat, right? He retired early from the State Department after he was diagnosed with cancer."

"Do you, uh, like what you do?"

"Sure. Millie's pretty easy to work for compared to my previous bosses. Not to mention she's a saint. She pays well too. Not that I don't give good value."

He nodded, remembering the amount on the check Millie had written him. Emma consulted her watch. She picked up her tote, signaling that Dan's time was up and their conversation was over. She reached into the bag and extracted a set of keys which she used to unlock the front door. She opened it and waved him in.

She smiled when he cautiously sniffed the air before stepping over the threshold. She inhaled as well and remarked, "They did a good job ventilating the place."

The gas was gone, but the house still was in shambles. Even worse, the utility and emergency workers had tromped carelessly over the detritus on the floor. There were filthy boot prints and scuff marks on the beautiful marble and even on some of the displaced furniture and art pieces.

"I know." Emma sighed. "The house is in a sorry state. At least we're dealing mostly with marble and wood rather than irreplaceable antique carpets. Imagine trying to get food and wine and ground glass out of those. Fortunately, Millie won't see this mess until after the housekeepers have a crack at it."

Joe continued staring at the marks on the floor. He admittedly was ignorant about tracking, but it seemed to him there was a fresher set of footprints that was different from those left by the emergency and utility employees. The prints were smaller and narrower, with tapered toes.

He was suddenly uneasy, although he couldn't explain why. His eyes flicked to the ankle boots on Emma's feet. The boots looked about the same size and shape as the prints.

"So Emma, did you take a look at the house before waiting outside for me?" He tried to keep his voice casual.

"This is the first time I've been inside since last night. It wasn't safe before. Why?"

"Oh ... um ... I was just wondering."

He let her go ahead. He thought it best not to have her at his back, where he couldn't see what she was doing.

They walked quickly to the cellar. She opened the door and stopped short when she saw the landing was lit. "Hmmm. The utility workers must have forgotten to shut off the light."

They peered downstairs—there was a dull glow where the stairs turned. Emma cupped her hands around her mouth and shouted, "Hello, is anyone down there?"

No answer. She shrugged. "At least we don't have to fumble around in the dark trying to find the lights."

Joe didn't say anything. He was too busy listening for sounds below. It was as quiet as the grave.

She was about to descend the stairs when he placed his hand on her shoulder. "Look, there's no sense in both of us going down. Why don't you wait in the house?"

"Not a chance." She looked steadily at him. "I want to see what it is you're really doing down there."

They eyed each other warily, like boxers sizing up opponents at a prize fight. He plastered a weak smile on his face. "Just a feng shui assessment," he said. "Nothing more."

Blast the woman. Something still didn't feel right to him, and he was anxious to perform the sealing ritual as soon as possible. Unfortunately, he couldn't get to it unless he could think of something to make her go away.

When they got downstairs, they found the cellar fully lit except for the tunnel and the chamber beyond it. Conscious of Emma's eyes on him, Joe took a measuring tape from his bag and pretended to measure various points.

He got a brief respite when she wandered off to examine the new gas pipe installed by the utility company, but she returned all too soon. He groaned to himself when she dusted off an old chair and made herself comfortable on it. From her new vantage point, she watched with steely eyes as he bent down and stood up and bustled to and fro with his tape.

"Aren't you going to record your measurements?" she asked after a few minutes.

"What?" He rose from his stooped position and tried to mask the desperation on his face. They were going to be here all night if he didn't come up with something. *But what?* His mind was a blank.

With her hands, she mimed writing in a book. "I can help you take down —"

She was interrupted by tinny music emanating from her tote. Joe blinked —it was one of the themes from the *Lord of the Rings* movies.

"Oh, excuse me, that's my phone." She dug into her bag. "Hello, Emma

Frankel speaking." A pause followed by a sharp intake of breath. "*Missing?*" Her voice rose in pitch. "What do you mean missing? Mrs. Scarpini could barely walk!" Another pause. "When did you discover this? Could the nurse have made a mistake? Could she still be in the hospital?"

Joe listened in consternation to Emma's half of the conversation. He was so engrossed he didn't notice the hulking presence that quietly emerged from the tunnel's murk.

Emma looked up, the phone clamped to her ear. Her brow knit; her mouth fell open. Perplexity and horror flitted across her features and she rose halfway to her feet. He realized too late that she was staring not at him but at something behind him. She screamed out a warning at the same time that he whirled around.

Millie glowered at him with beady red eyes. She was still clad in her hospital gown, but the garment strained over her massive shoulders. She lifted one arm. He saw, belatedly, the brick in her hand. The arm swept downward before he could react. When the brick made contact, he not only felt but heard the impact, like a firecracker exploding inside his skull.

Hot pain blazed above his left eye; white spots clouded his vision. He lost his balance and fell onto his knees.

The arm rose and hammered down again. This time, he fell into oblivion.

* * *

Sensations flitted through Joe's mind as he slowly regained consciousness. He felt the hard soil against his skin and a wet substance dripping down his face. His nose caught the whiff of something metallic amid the dirt's pungent stink—was that blood? Was he bleeding? His head throbbed horribly, making it hard to focus.

He tried to open his eyes. *Bad mistake.* His gorge rose and the floor underneath him tilted like a sailboat in a raging storm. He made himself lie perfectly still until his stomach settled and his dizziness abated.

He couldn't remember where he was or why he was lying on his side on the ground. A noose of some sort was snug against his throat. His hands were restrained behind him. His legs were bent at the knees, drawn up uncomfortably behind him and tied at the ankles.

With his eyes still closed, he tried to straighten his legs. The garrote around his neck tightened and he gagged. His eyes flew open and he wheezed loudly as he fought for breath. He quickly moved his legs back to their original position and the tension around his neck eased. Whoever tied him up had used a single length of rope to bind his ankles, wrists and neck. He risked asphyxiation if he moved his limbs.

He could see nothing but blackness even though he was pretty sure his eyes now were open. *Dear God, had he gone blind?* He thrashed in panic. The noose tautened again, making him gasp and choke like a fish out of water.

A light came on above him, the brightness searing his eyeballs. He quickly shut his eyes and bent his knees to slacken the pressure against his throat. A shadow fell across him.

"Ah, I see you're awake."

The voice was Millie's and yet not Millie's. Near-strangulation had quietened the angry pounding in his head and cleared his mind somewhat. Things were coming back to him. He reluctantly opened his eyes.

With the light on, he could see he was no longer in the main cellar but in the chamber. The Millie creature leaned over him. It looked even more abhorrent this close up. He noticed details he had missed the first time around. Millie's pale skin was replaced by greenish scabrous hide that was cracked in spots to reveal raw pink flesh. Its shoulders weren't just hulking, but thick and contorted. The arms that thrust out of the hospital gown's sleeves were jointed in two places, as if they had extra elbows. Stumpy legs ended in blocky feet. It had somehow managed to jam those fat feet into slim pumps.

He gazed up at the latest Millie in stupefied repugnance. "Emma," he rasped. "What have you done with her?" His injured throat burned as if on fire.

"She's right here." Millie shuffled aside and he saw Emma lying a few feet away. Her eyes were closed; the skin on one cheek was red and already starting to bruise. He was relieved to see she was bound hand and foot. The yaoguai wouldn't have bothered to tie her up if she was dead. She wasn't trussed as securely as he was. Her hands were tied in front of her and there was no strangling lasso around her neck.

"She better not be badly hurt." His statement—intended to be a threatening growl—sounded more like a shaky croak.

"You have bigger things to worry about than her." The monster's red eyes bored into his. "Where is the fledgling Dragon? Why isn't she here?"

Joe swallowed painfully; he was determined not to show how very frightened he was. "You're not the same yaoguai that we fought."

"No I'm not. Can you tell?"

"Yes. Your friend was *way* better-looking."

The creature punished him for the slight by yanking on the rope between his neck and wrists. The noose dug into his throat and he gagged. It watched avidly as he struggled to breathe, even licking its chops at one point. He was making it hungry.

The yaoguai looked disappointed when his gasping abated. "Are you surprised to see me?" it asked. "You shouldn't be. A better geomancer would have known two of us broke through. How can you call yourself a Tham? You're a disgrace to the name."

It had found a new way to torture Joe. The barb was an arrow that pierced his heart. He mentally castigated himself. The yaoguai was right. It was all so obvious on hindsight. There were TWO holes—the original sinkhole and the second tube-like hole that appeared *after* Dan and his men filled in the sinkhole. The holes should have indicated to him that there were at least two surfacings.

Stupid, stupid, stupid. He was nothing but a second-rate geomancer, if that. He wasn't worthy to carry the Golden Dragon's shoes.

Joe was still berating himself when he caught the greedy expression on the yaoguai's face. It was savoring his spiral into despair. His own contrary nature kicked in; he refused to give it what it wanted. And he had a few questions he'd like answered.

"Were you in the house during the party?" he asked.

"Yessss." The creature's smile was vulpine.

"Why didn't we see your spoor when we tracked the other one?"

"I knew when you used the sword against my brother," it said. "It burned my flesh as it burned his. When you went down the back stairs after my sibling, I crept up the foyer stairs and stayed on the second floor. I hid until I heard people running out of the house—I knew then that you had foiled his plan. Before you could come after me, I transformed into Millie. As her, I stumbled down the stairs and joined the crowd outside."

Joe was struck by one particular piece of information. He hadn't known yaoguai were telepathically linked and could share knowledge and feelings. Was it akin to the hive intelligence in ant and bee colonies? There was *so much* he didn't know about the Dragons' arch enemies.

"So it was you at the hospital?" He was going to cram in as many questions as he could. The conversation was the only thing keeping him and Emma from imminent—and probably gruesome and painful—deaths.

"Oh yesss."

"Where is the real Millie? And why did you give Emma permission to let us back into the house? You were safe as Millie—we wouldn't have found out."

"You really don't know, do you?" The monster cackled.

"Know what?"

"What's coming."

"What are you talking about?" Joe, so close to dying, had no patience for the yaoguai's riddles.

"An Alpha is on its way."

"Alpha? What's that?"

"Something much older than I am, and I was ancient before your kind existed. Alphas are the cardinal beings of my world. They are known by many names—the Elders, the Ancients, the Old Ones, the Prime. I believe you refer to them as 'mogui'."

Joe's bravado deserted him. He was lucky not to pee his pants.

"Even better, it's your fault," the yaoguai crowed. "Did no one ever warn you not to bring an object of power near a gateway unless you intend to seal it immediately?"

He shook his head listlessly. He didn't need reminding that his ignorance was infinite.

"The object acts as a beacon. Its power calls to those of us that linger in the vortexes. When you and the young Dragon placed your sword in the portal—not once but twice—its power awakened the Alpha. It's coming. Not only that—the Old One is bringing legions of my siblings with it. It won't be long now."

There was a hint of pity in its red eyes. Joe felt sick to his stomach. He was bringing on Armageddon through his profound stupidity and hubris. Why did he think himself equal to the job? This might well be the lowest point of his life yet. It had to be, if a bottom-dweller (literally!) could feel sorry for him.

The monster allowed him a brief moment in which to wallow in his misery. When it had enough, it jolted him out of his funk by kicking him sharply in the ribs with its fashionable shoe.

"I paid you a nice sum to go away, but you insisted on returning to the house." The yaoguai was intent on reminding him that it was his fault. "I could tell you wouldn't stop until you'd sealed the portal. Rather than have you sneaking around behind my back, I thought I would lay a trap and present the young Dragon to the Alpha. It and the Tham Dragons go back a long way. I will be rewarded well for delivering her.

"So I ask again," it hissed, "where is the Dragon? That's the only reason you're alive. You're bait."

"Junie can slay you with her little finger." Some of Joe's bravado was returning.

"Me, perhaps. But she can't take on the Alpha alone, especially given her inexperience. All I have to do is keep her here until the Alpha breaks through."

"Well, she's not coming. I'm sorry if that ruins your plans."

The yaoguai abruptly raised its head. Its nostrils quivered, as if it smelled something.

"Wrong again, geomancer." The creature grinned. "She's here."

Chapter 27

The Culture on the Mall outdoor screenings were held at the National Mall between the 12th Street and 9th Street expressways. The patch of green was flanked by the Smithsonian National Museum of Natural History on one side, and the cathedral-like Smithsonian Castle on the other.

The first movie had started by the time Junie and Noah got there. She was relieved to see it wasn't *Drunken Master*, but Jet Li's *Hero*. She had seen *Hero* only twice before.

It was a nice evening. The setting sun gilded the tops of the buildings and imbued the dying day with its golden light. Breezes riffled the leaves of the trees edging the mall and tumbled bits of trash and paper over the grass and along the grit paths. A large crowd had turned up, but there was more than enough space to accommodate everybody. Some people brought folding chairs while others sprawled on makeshift picnic blankets. The warm air was redolent with the smells of sunblock and snacks. At one corner of the field, small children and their parents clustered around the Smithsonian Carousel with its brightly painted wooden horses and blue and yellow striped top.

Noah stopped at a spot near the middle of the field. "How about here?" he asked.

"This is good."

He shrugged off his backpack, took out a large beach towel and spread it on the grass. Junie flopped down on the towel. He sat beside her and stretched out his long legs. "Have you seen this movie?" he asked.

"Oh yes."

"Me too." They looked at each other and laughed. On the giant 20-foot-tall by 40-foot-wide screen, Jet Li was telling the King of Qin about his fight with Long Sky.

"By the way, I also brought bottles of water in case you're thirsty," he said.

"I see you came well prepared."

The movie had beautifully choreographed fight sequences, great cinematography and lush settings. However, she couldn't keep her eyes open no matter how hard she tried. She must have been more tired than she thought. She soon was nodding off.

The next thing she knew, the dusk was gone and it was night. The little blond boy was sitting next to her on the towel. His legs were drawn up and he hugged his knees, his face pressed so tightly against the knobby joints that all she could see was his thatch of pale hair. Nobody else, including Noah on the other side of her, seemed to notice him.

She put her hand on the boy's back. "What are you doing here?"

He whispered without looking up, "It's coming." He curled into his knees, as if trying to make himself as small as possible. His little body shuddered. He was petrified.

"*What's* coming?"

"It. It's coming. Run. As fast as you can." The kid finally looked up. She recoiled at his expression of stark terror. He pressed his hands on either side of his wan face and dragged his cheeks down. To her horror, his face elongated and his eyes and mouth became black pits. She was looking at a skull.

Something bumped her and she screamed. She opened her eyes to see Noah peering at her. She'd fallen asleep against his shoulder. A few people turned around, wondering what was the matter.

"Were you dreaming?" he asked softly. "You were mumbling something about a skull."

"I must have been." She sat up straight and looked warily to her side, where the child had been. He was no longer there, if he had been there at all.

Night had fallen, as in her dream, but she couldn't have been asleep for long. Jet Li was recounting to the king that he killed Flying Snow in a duel. Noah was still looking searchingly at her. She found she wasn't in the least embarrassed about falling asleep on their first non-date. She was too filled with foreboding to be embarrassed.

She wasn't surprised when her phone rang a split second later. "I've got to take this," she told him. Phone in hand, she hurried to the edge of the field where it was quieter and answered the call.

"Is this Junie Soong?"

"Yes."

"Junie, this is Ayanna Groskind, Dan's wife."

"Yes, hello Mrs. Groskind." An icy finger traced a path down Junie's spine.

"The reason I'm calling is ... um ... I ... I was checking Dan's work emergency number for messages."

Ayanna Groskind spoke hesitantly, her voice thick with emotion. "The last message was left by Emma Frankel about a meeting tonight with Dan and your associate Joe Tham. I checked Dan's cell after that and it seems Mr. Tham left numerous messages. I'm ... I apologize for not responding earlier."

"I wasn't aware of tonight's meeting, but I know Joe's been trying to get in touch with Dan. Will Dan be at the meeting? He told us about his health issues."

A long silence. "I'm sorry Junie, but Dan won't be there. He ... um ... " Another pause, then her words spilled out in a torrent. "He suffered a series of seizures yesterday and slipped into a coma. The doctors don't think ... ah ... he ... he'll pull through. We ... uh ... the girls and I are at the hospital. He's hanging on for now, but the doctors don't think he'll make it through the night." Ayanna broke down at last and sobbed loudly into the phone.

"I'm so very sorry," Junie whispered.

"Yes, sorry to let you know like this. I should have checked Dan's messages earlier. His condition deteriorated very ... suddenly. I ... I thought we had more time."

"I'll let Joe know."

Ayanna took a few deep breaths to pull herself together. "I tried calling Joe after I discovered the messages, but he isn't answering his phone. Emma isn't answering her phone either. Fortunately, Joe left Dan your phone number in his last message."

"I'm so very, very sorry."

"Before you go … um … Dan was … uh … he had a dangerously high fever after contracting septicemia from his injured ankle. The fever is what caused the seizures. The fever also made him delirious and he said a few things. Most of it didn't make sense, but he may have wanted to tell Joe something. I only thought of it after hearing Joe's messages."

"What? What did Dan want to tell Joe?"

"He repeated it a few times. I don't know what it means. He said, 'Joe, it isn't finished. You didn't finish it. It isn't finished.' Like I said, I don't know what it means, but can you tell Joe what he said? It seemed important to Dan."

"I will. And Mrs. Groskind, can you give Dan a message from me? I know he's unconscious, but whisper it into his ear. It's very, very important."

"What?" Ayanna's grief was momentarily arrested by confusion. "What message?"

"Tell Dan that Joe and I will finish it tonight. Tell Dan he has to hang on until then."

"Is this some kind of joke?" She raised her voice, her confusion pushed aside by indignation and anger.

"No, it's not. It's not a joke. Please. You have to let him know what I said. Joe and I will finish it. Tonight."

Dan's wife didn't speak for so long that Junie was afraid they might have been cut off. She was about to hang up and call Ayanna back when she heard a soft "okay."

After Ayanna ended the call, Junie immediately rang Joe's cell. She could reach only his voice mail. She was trying without success to contact Emma when Noah came up to her, their belongings heaped in his arms.

"Is everything alright?" He stared at her in concern.

"Thanks Noah, for bringing my stuff." She took her bag from him. "I have to go."

"Where?"

"I have to get back to the office. I think something's happened to Joe."

"Oh no. I'll go with you."

Junie nodded numbly.

Noah had longer legs but he still found it hard to keep up with her. She raced ahead, stopping only when they stood outside the Laughing Buddha.

"Listen, I need a few things from the office. Do you have an Uber or a Lyft account? I need a ride to this address." She dug in her wallet and produced a slip of paper with Millie's address on it.

"Why don't I drive you? My car's parked at my apartment, which is only three blocks away. I'll wait here at the curb for you."

"Thanks again," she said gratefully. "I'll be about 10 minutes."

She let herself into the stairwell and sprinted up the stairs. She found Joe's note on her bedroom door. *Why didn't he wait for her before returning to the house?* She quickly changed into a long-sleeved T-shirt and a pair of cargo pants with handy pockets. She tied up her hair and slipped an extra scrunchie around her wrist. She replaced her sandals with tennis shoes and attached a sports strap to her glasses.

Opening the steamer trunk, she discovered that Joe had left the luopan behind. But why would he bring it? The compass was useless without her. She picked up the Energy Devourer and slipped it between her belt and waistband. She stuffed the crystal into her right front pocket and filled her back pockets with talismans. She slid her phone into a zippered pocket where it would be secure; she put flashlights in the large pockets on either thigh.

She couldn't think of anything else she might need. She was as ready as she would ever be. *But for what?* She had no idea.

She was walking out of her room when she paused. The dread caused by the little boy's appearance was still with her. She went to the closet and took out the staff. Its heft was comforting. And she felt safer with a backup weapon, even one without magical powers.

Noah was sitting in an old Toyota when she returned downstairs. He gaped at the sword and the staff and her bulging pockets but didn't say anything. He had typed Millie's address into his phone's Google Maps app while waiting for her. She tossed the staff in the back seat and got in beside him. As she fastened her seat belt, he propped his phone in the space in front of his gearshift and hit the app's start button. A pleasant female voice began issuing directions.

Junie's urgency was contagious. Noah kept his foot on the accelerator and they soon pulled up in front of Millie's imposing mansion. The house was totally dark inside. Its many windows reflected the street lamps and the light from the neighboring houses without giving away any of its own secrets.

"Looks like no one's home," he said doubtfully. "Hey, isn't this the place that had that gas leak?"

"It is. Noah, thank you for all your help."

"My pleasure. So what are we doing here? Is Joe in there? Are we going in?"

"I want you to go home," she said firmly.

"Not a chance," he replied just as firmly. "Is Joe in some kind of trouble?"

She glared at him. He stared mulishly back at her. He looked intractable in the light from the car's dashboard.

"I don't have time to explain, but it's too dangerous for you to enter the house," she said.

"Too dangerous for me but not for you?" His eyebrows rose incredulously.

"Like I said, I don't have time to explain. If you won't go home, at least promise me that you won't go in the house."

He stared at her some more, then reluctantly agreed. "Fine. I'll wait right here. Should I keep the engine running?"

Did he think she and Joe were robbing the place, and they needed a getaway car? "Um, no, you can turn the engine off," she said. "I don't know how long I'll be. It could be awhile. Just wait here, okay? Don't step out of the car. Don't go any closer to the house. Whatever happens, don't call me. It might distract me at a crucial moment."

She retrieved the staff from the back seat and got out before he could ask any more questions. She stopped midway up the front path to activate her third eye with the crystal's help.

When auras glowed all around her, she went to the front door and tried it. It was unlocked. She took a deep breath and pushed the door open.

Noah, watching from the car, was reminded of something when Junie paused on her way to the door. She gazed up at the dark house, her left hand clutching the old-fashioned walking stick. Her right hand was curled into a fist; her feet were positioned slightly apart. A street lamp shone on her like a spotlight. Tension was visible in every line of her slim body.

She looked like a warrior going into battle—powerful, yet fragile and so alone. His breath caught in his throat. He thought he had never seen anything so beautiful.

He suddenly remembered what it was that she brought to mind—a scene from the 1973 movie *The Exorcist,* when Father Lankester Merrin arrived at the mansion in Georgetown to confront the demon possessing Regan MacNeil. His aunt had given him a poster of the iconic scene, which he pinned to the wall space at the foot of his bed. For most of his teenage years, it was the first thing he saw when he woke up in the morning.

He groaned when he recalled what happened to Merrin in the movie. He wished the comparison hadn't occurred to him.

But of course, this wasn't a movie. Junie might be dealing with an emergency, but it surely didn't involve close combat. The stick and the sword must be something that Joe needed for one of his feng shui rituals.

And demons? They didn't exist.

Chapter 28

The creature vibrated, its green skin rippling as if thousands of worms twitched and squirmed just underneath. Its frame collapsed at the same time, the thick shoulders shrinking until they were narrow and slightly sloped. The long arms became shorter and skinnier. The legs grew thin and hairy. The red eyes darkened, turning into shiny black buttons.

The yaoguai's hospital gown also was changing. The part of the gown covering its upper torso became a sports coat over a button-down shirt. Its hairy legs down to its ankles transformed into pants that really didn't go with the coat.

Joe was in equal parts repulsed and fascinated by the metamorphosis. He couldn't tear his eyes away. It wasn't long before his doppelganger stared back at him.

"Like what you see?" The yaoguai smirked, seemingly satisfied by what it saw on his face. It looked contemptuously at him and the unconscious Emma and added, "Don't go anywhere."

The monster loped to the tunnel and disappeared into it with an athletic grace that Joe had never possessed. He heard it move swiftly through the passageway to the main cellar. It finally reached the staircase, its footsteps receding as it clomped upward. The cellar door slammed shut.

At least the yaoguai hadn't left them to stew in the dark. Joe blinked at the lamp above him and breathed in deeply. Light, however meager, always improved a situation. Although maybe not in this case. He glumly reviewed his options. Unfortunately, there wasn't much he could do to warn Junie. He would cut off oxygen to his brain and black out if he moved too much. Shouting was useless—she wouldn't hear him unless she was in the cellar.

Why, oh why hadn't she stayed away? What made her come? And how did the creature plan to ambush his young apprentice? Would it lure her down to the chamber, or try to trap her in another part of the house? Whichever, it would endeavor first to take the Energy Devourer away from her. She was powerless without it. He hoped it wanted her alive. If it killed her, all was lost. He and Emma were as good as dead themselves.

He refused to think of what the mogui might do once it surfaced. And it wasn't coming alone but would be accompanied by a horde of yaoguai. The outlook was dire. *Very, very* dire.

Deep in thought, it took him awhile to notice the soft scuffling sounds coming from Emma's direction. He looked over at her. She was wriggling in the dirt, maneuvering her bound hands so that she could reach into her back pocket.

"Emma! Are you okay?"

"Yes," she whispered. "Be quiet, for goodness' sake. We don't want the creature coming back."

"You were out cold for some time. Are you hurt?"

"I wasn't out cold. I was playing dead."

There was a lot more to Emma than he had thought. "Did you ... ah ... hear everything?"

"Enough," she said shortly.

She extracted something from her pocket. It was a set of keys. She fiddled with the key chain. A moment later, something gleamed in the low light. It was the blade of a small pocket knife. She angled the blade carefully with her fingers and started sawing at the rope around her wrists.

Joe could tell the knife was sharp. Even so, given its size, it would take her some time to free herself. But now, there was a glimmer of hope.

* * *

It was dark in the foyer. Junie dragged her hand along the wall where she vaguely remembered seeing a switch. She found it and flipped it. The chandelier burst into life above her like a firecracker suspended in space and time.

She was inspecting the tracks on the marble floor when she heard shouting from somewhere in the house. The sounds were clearer at the back of the foyer. Someone was calling her name.

"Junie! Junie! Over here!" It was Joe.

"Joe! Where are you?"

"I'm by the cellar door! Come quick."

She turned on one of her flashlights and ran toward the cellar. She found him standing in pitch blackness. In her beam, his aura coiled around him like an extra, living shadow. Her stomach lurched. She stopped well out of his reach and tried to conceal her shock.

"There's been an accident," he said. He placed his hand on the handle of the closed cellar door. "Emma is injured. I need your help."

He opened the door. Light spilled into the corridor from the cellar landing. He stepped in, scowling when she didn't join him. "What are you waiting for?" He pointed down the stairs. "Emma's down there. Didn't you hear me?"

"What happened?" Junie turned off her flashlight and returned it to her pocket. Her grip on the staff tightened.

"She fell down the stairs and knocked herself out. I think she may have broken something. She's also bleeding all over the cellar floor."

"Why didn't you call 911?"

"My phone's broken. I dropped it in the excitement."

"I have my phone." She tapped her zippered pocket. "I can call 911 now."

He promptly shook his head. "Not yet. Come help me first—we need to stanch her bleeding." He took a step down and waved his hand, encouraging her to follow him.

Junie approached warily, making sure she kept the staff between her and whatever it was pretending to be Joe. *What was it up to?* She couldn't let the creature suspect that she was wise to it.

As she stepped onto the landing, a frantic shout came from deep within the cellar. It didn't sound like Joe—the voice was too hoarse and wheezy—so it had to be him. A yaoguai would have done a better job. She couldn't make out his words. Nonetheless, she was filled with relief that he was alive—at least alive enough to be making those noises.

The thing masquerading as Joe moved so quickly it almost caught her by surprise. It clamped its hands around the staff and pulled, trying to haul her closer. Instead of pulling the staff back, she pushed with all her strength. The staff hit it in the stomach and pushed it off-balance.

It staggered backwards, an almost comical expression on its face. Then it was tumbling head over heels down the steps, taking the staff with it. It tried to stop its fall, but momentum and its weight worked against it. It scrabbled furiously and loudly before she lost sight of it around the bend. Deep rake marks along the walls warned her that pretend Joe had grown a serious set of nails.

She drew the sword from her waistband and crept cautiously down the stairs. Was Joe's evil double lying injured or dead at the bottom of the staircase, or was it lurking just around the corner, waiting to waylay her? Probably the latter. Unfortunately, she had to get past it before she could rescue the real Joe.

As she neared the turn in the steps, she pressed herself against the left handrail. She craned her neck, trying to see as far around the corner as she could while maintaining a safe distance. At least the light was on downstairs as well. She was thankful for whatever help she could get. A shadow shifted beyond the bend and she caught her breath. She raised the sword and bent her knees.

Before she could charge forward, the treads under her feet shook violently, pitching her hard against the handrail. As the steps jerked, she had to throw both arms around the railing to stop herself from falling face-first downward. She lost the sword and it clattered onto the landing below her.

What in the world ... had D.C. just been hit by another major earthquake?

She still remembered the big one in August 2011. Measuring 5.8 on the Richter scale, it had been strong enough to crack the Washington Monument. She was at home alone when the floor heaved, doors rattled and things toppled off the shelves. Her neighbors' car alarms squawked and dogs barked. Terrified, she crawled into her parents' bathtub and sheltered there until Stella came home.

After the event, researchers suggested that the mantle under the southeast U.S. was thinning, making the region more prone to seismic activity. Could this be the next big one?

It felt like the 2011 quake, except ... stronger, and more sustained. The initial powerful jolts had subsided by now, but the stairs—and the handrail to which she clung—were still shuddering. Bits of plaster fell from the ceiling, speckling her hair and clothes.

She heard a sharp report near her ear. The handrail was making odd noises. To her horror, a crack appeared on the wall and made its way down, zigzagging toward where the handrail was attached. The railing emitted a few more sharp protests. It sounded as though it was about to give way. *Would the stairs hold?*

The stairs stopped shaking just as the crack was about to reach the handrail. She was relaxing her death grip on the rail when pretend Joe chose to reveal itself. It bounded onto the lower landing and stood triumphantly over the sword.

"Have you lost something?" As it spoke, it began to look less and less like Joe. Its body bulged and expanded, filling up the tiny landing. Its long arms reached for her.

Before the creature's talons could close on her, the stairwell was socked by another round of forceful jolts. The yaoguai stumbled and almost fell. Its hands shot out, grappling for the walls.

She went on the offensive, seizing the opportunity that Fate offered. She released the handrail and sprang downward, slamming into the yaoguai with her shoulder. As the monster teetered at the edge of the landing, she helped it along with a hard shove. Its arms pinwheeled for a split second before it crashed down to the cellar floor, its head meeting the concrete with a solid thud.

She grasped the handrails at the landing in case the shocks returned, but they seemed to have ended again, as abruptly as they had begun. The Energy Devourer was still on the landing. She scooped it up and hurtled down the steps. The yaoguai lay on its back, stunned by its fall. The staff was just a few feet away.

She was raising the sword, about to plunge it into the monster's heart, when a third series of quakes erupted, even more potent than the previous two. The cement floor seemed to convulse; huge cracks ripped its surface. The cellar walls shivered and debris rained down on her. The tunnel at the far end let off a thunderous belch; dust billowed out of its gaping black mouth.

This time it was she who lost her balance. She tottered and fell on her backside. The point of the sword struck the floor, jarring her arm. The creature struggled to its feet and blundered up the stairs.

* * *

Joe started yelling when he heard voices in the main cellar. "Junie, stay away!" he croaked. "Don't come down here! It's a trap! It's a trap!"

Emma shushed him, warning that the yaoguai might come back to silence him. "You know Junie probably can't hear what you're saying, right?"

He ignored her. He didn't want Junie coming anywhere near the tunnel or the chamber, where she would be trapped in close quarters with his monstrous doppelganger. Emma eventually gave up, focusing her attention wholly on freeing herself.

His shouting faltered when he felt the earth throbbing. The throbbing rapidly intensified into tremors, then violent shaking. He howled in alarm as the ground heaved beneath him and his body was slammed repeatedly against the hard-packed earth. The chamber's support beams groaned and chunks of wood fell from the ancient ceiling.

Emma curled into a fetal position until the quaking subsided. "Dear Lord," she mumbled, "is that an earthquake? Could the situation get any worse?" She sawed even more vigorously with her pocket knife, her face streaked with grime and grim with determination. She was almost done with the rope around her wrists.

Was Emma correct that this merely was an earthquake? During the worst of the upheaval, it felt as though something was pounding forcefully and repeatedly at the ground directly under him. *As if something was pounding* ... A muscle twitched under his eye. His insides felt like an icebox. He was quite certain it wasn't an earthquake. He would give his right arm for it to be an earthquake.

Even worse, the earth seemed to be rising under him. He could feel a distinct lump under his right side. Based on his position under the lamp, he had to be lying almost exactly where the portal had been, the portal he and Junie had closed only last night. Something—no, some *things*—were now hammering at the closed gateway in a bid to reopen it. The thing leading the charge had to be massive—COLOSSAL—to make the ground heave like that. At this rate, the mogui would soon break through. The yaoguai's words came back to him: *It won't be long now.*

The creature had deliberately positioned him so that when the Alpha surfaced, he would be the first thing it encountered. He was a side offering, an appetizer to whet the mogui's appetite, a tidbit to assuage its rage over the indignities it had suffered at the hands of the Tham Dragons. Junie—the latest Dragon—was the main course.

He couldn't let that happen. He might die, but Junie had to survive. It was his duty to ensure that the Dragons lived on. But what could he do?

While Joe was taking stock of their predicament, Emma worked furiously at her bonds. The earthquakes, and the laboring ceiling above them, were a huge impetus. She was a lot faster once her hands were free. She had sliced through the rope around her ankles by the second series of quakes. She was crawling toward Joe when the third lot hit.

The tunnel collapsed with an earsplitting boom, enveloping them in dust. The room's support beams creaked even louder. The lamp hanging over Joe gyrated wildly, heightening her disorientation. She dropped to the ground and covered her head with her arms, sure the chamber's ceiling would give way next. Miraculously, the ceiling withstood the violent shaking. And the bulb wasn't damaged, so they still had light.

Emma rose tentatively to her feet when the ground stopped moving. She wiped her streaming eyes and coughed and spat to expel the muck in her mouth. She lurched over to the tunnel mouth and found it blocked by debris. There was no way out of the chamber. She smacked her fist against the wall in frustration.

"Emma!" Joe wheezed. She turned.

"Cut me loose. Quickly. I have work to do."

She limped back and crouched beside him. "How do you feel?" she asked.

"Fine," he growled. "Stop wasting time and cut me loose."

He winced when she touched his forehead. She showed him her fingers, red with his blood. "You have a nasty cut on your forehead and it's still bleeding," she said.

"We have more important things to worry about. Like I said, I have work to do. Cut. Me. Loose."

She sat down and started hacking at the rope between his neck and wrists with her pocket knife.

"Do you know what happened to my phone?" he asked.

"Sorry buddy. The thing that beat you up took your phone while you were unconscious. He stomped on it, and stomped on mine as well.

"*Bastard,*" she added with feeling. "I *loved* that phone."

Chapter 29

They heard clattering within the tunnel. Emma slashed harder at Joe's bonds. She was close to freeing him, and they had no idea who, or what, was trying to get through. At least the quakes appeared to be over for the time being.

"Joe! Joe!"

He started at the sound of Junie's voice.

"We're in here!" Emma shouted as she cut through the last strands of rope. Joe moaned with relief when the pressure against his throat went away. She deftly unwound the rope around his wrists and ankles, and gently worked the noose off his neck.

"Emma? Is that you? Where's Joe?" Junie sounded close to tears. "Why isn't he saying anything?" They heard more clattering, banging and thudding.

"He's okay," Emma hastily shouted. "A little beat-up, but okay."

She helped Joe to his feet. He yelped and sagged when pins and needles viciously stabbed his limbs. It felt like he was under attack from a thousand sharp instruments. He could barely walk after being tied up for so long. She had to practically drag him to the mouth of the tunnel. He peered in dismay at the large pile of rock, sand and wood that clogged the passage. The barrier looked impregnable.

"Joe? Is that you?" Junie's voice came through a small space above the blockage.

"What is—" Joe cleared his throat and tried again. "What is the situation out there?"

"A bunch of weird earthquakes caused part of the tunnel to collapse. The quakes seem to come and go. The damage is mostly at your end. I'm trying to climb the rockfall to see if I can get to the hole at the top. It's hard—things keep shifting and rolling around. If we work together, we might be able to make the hole bigger so you and Emma can get out before the quakes return."

"Junie, you need to leave right now." Joe tried to sound as authoritative as possible. "Not just the tunnel. I want you gone from the house."

A silence. "I'm not leaving," she said mutinously.

"You must. It'll take too long to explain, but something's coming. Remember what I told you about mogui? You need to leave NOW. Time is of the essence."

An even longer silence. "Is that what's coming?" she finally asked.

"Yes. It's trying to break through. That's what's causing the quakes. Emma and I will try to stop it by sealing the portal, but you need to leave in case we fail."

"You and *Emma*?" Junie was astounded.

Joe glanced at Emma; she stared wearily back and gave him a thumbs-up. Whatever he had to do, she was game.

"Yes. Me and Emma."

"Well, while you perform the ritual, I'll stay here and guard the entrance in case the yaoguai comes back. Say, did you know there's a second yaoguai? I'm pretty sure this isn't the one I chased into the sinkhole yesterday."

"Yes, it's a different one, but … but forget about yaoguai for the moment," he spluttered. He was getting desperate. "You need to understand—I can't let the mogui kill you. You may be the only one who can defeat it if it comes through the portal. But only when you're ready, which you're not."

He spoke faster. "If I don't make it out of here, I want you to call my mother, Elsie Tham. Her phone number should be somewhere in the office or apartment. She may be reluctant to talk at first, but tell her about the mogui. She'll know what to do. She'll help you. You may need to hole up in Florida with her. Hide so the mogui can't find you."

"Joe, *you're* the one who doesn't understand." Junie's voice was like steel. "I. Am. Not. Leaving. You."

He sighed loudly in exasperation and glanced again at Emma. She shrugged. "Look, there's something else you can do," he said gruffly.

"Okay. I'm listening."

"I think Millie might still be in the house. Find her and get her to safety."

Emma gave him a sharp look when she heard Millie's name, but didn't interrupt.

"Millie!" Junie gasped.

"Yes," he said. "It wasn't Millie at the hospital, but a yaoguai posing as her. Two of them came through the portal."

"That's what I've been trying to tell you. This second one's stronger, smarter and *meaner* than the first one. It does a pretty good imitation of you as well."

"Where is it now?"

"I think it's somewhere in the house. It ran up the cellar stairs before I could kill it. So you think the real Millie is here as well? Where could she be?"

"My guess is she's still in her bedroom. We never actually searched the room. I don't think the firefighters did a thorough search either."

"Alright Joe. I'm going to look for her."

"Before you go, did you see my bag in the cellar?"

"No, but I wasn't really looking."

Damn. "I need a talisman and a few other things for the ritual. They were in the bag."

"Do you need a talisman? Give me a sec."

Before long, something poked out at the top of the rockfall. Joe was astonished to see it was his father's old staff. Junie had wrapped two talismans around its tip, securing them with one of the things she used to tie her hair. Emma jumped and grabbed the staff with the tips of her fingers. Pebbles and dirt poured down on her as she pulled the rod through.

She was handing the staff to him when Junie shouted, "Watch out! I'm sending something else. Just in case you need it."

A black object shot out of the hole. It dropped onto the dirt floor and rolled to a stop near Emma's feet. It was a flashlight. She stooped down and picked it up.

"What else do you need for the ritual?" Junie asked.

The floor began to vibrate, signaling that the quakes were about to start up again. "Junie, go now!" he yelled. "Remember what I said about my mother. And please, be careful."

There was no response. He didn't know if she caught his last words. Emma grasped his elbow and pulled him away from the tunnel mouth. The small stones at the very top of the blockage were trembling and knocking so hard into each other that they sounded like chattering teeth.

The quakes hit with full force when they were halfway across the chamber. The violent shocks sent them sprawling to the ground.

"So, did I hear you say you and I are going to perform a ritual?" Emma asked as the floor bucked and rocked under them.

"I don't know if we can. I don't have all the materials I need."

"Dude, if this is as important as I think it is, then we've got to at least try." Her gaze was fierce. "Can we improvise? What do you need?"

Joe gulped and nodded at the same time. It was difficult to marshal his thoughts with his head aching so badly—and the shaking didn't help—but she was 100 percent right. This wasn't the time to give up. "I need materials that represent the five feng shui elements: wood, fire, earth, metal and water," he said. "I also need a compass to tell me where the four cardinal directions are."

She combed the chamber with her eyes. "Well, we have earth and wood right here in this room. That leaves fire, metal and water, correct? Let me think about those while you set up the ritual. Where will it take place?"

"Right there." He pointed at the ground under the swinging lamp. The bulge was even more obvious now, and still growing. How long did they have before the Alpha broke through?

"Goodness." She stared at the protrusion. "I can't believe I missed that. Was it always there?"

"No."

"Wow." It was her turn to gulp. "Does this mean it's urgent?"

"*Very.*"

"How are your legs?"

"Better, I think." He tried rising to his feet. It was tricky with the floor swaying so much. He found he could stand with the staff's aid.

She stood as well. "Let's get to it then."

"Let's pretend the hump is the center of a compass," he said. "I need the four main compass points marked clearly around it. Accuracy is key, and without an actual compass, I'm afraid I won't be exact."

"That's easy. You don't need a compass. You have me. Let's see, the house's front door and foyer face west." She braced her left hand against the groaning wall and spread her legs wide for extra balance. "The cellar is at the back, near the side entrance." She shut her eyes to better visualize the orientation of the mansion and its underground components. "The room is accessed via the tunnel at the back of the cellar. That must mean … "

She raised her right hand and pointed it in various directions, mumbling to herself all the while. When she was done with her mental exercises, she wobbled around the jouncing room collecting bits of wood.

She returned to the hump. "This is north." She dropped a piece of wood on the ground.

The fragment, tossed around by the tremulous ground, jiggled and hopped away from the spot. Joe got down on his knees, dug a shallow trench with his fingers and pressed the wood into it.

"Okay, that seems to work." Emma pointed with her foot to indicate where he should next dig. "This is south. Alright?" She dropped the south marker and he pressed it into the dirt. "And this is east. And that's west."

The quakes had quietened by the time they finished marking all four cardinal directions. Joe removed one of the talismans from the staff and put it on the hump. He placed a rock on one corner of the yellow rectangle to ensure it wouldn't slide off when the shaking resumed.

"Can we begin?" she asked.

He nodded. "Basically, the ritual invokes ancient Chinese protection magic," he said. "We're calling upon the Celestial Beasts of the Chinese constellations, also known as the Five Feng Shui Guardians, to help make the talisman seal unbreakable. Each Beast utilizes the element with which it's associated to amplify the seal's power.

"The ritual is conducted in Mandarin and special words are used to entreat the Beasts." He frowned. "I don't think it has to be in Mandarin;

that's what my father spoke, but any Chinese dialect would suffice. I don't remember the exact words—bear with me, I only saw my father perform the ceremony once—but I have a rough idea of the phrasing. This morning, before I went to the hospital to see Millie, I cobbled together an approximation of the Mandarin incantation with the help of Google Translate and other translation apps, so I would be ready to perform the ritual.

"Unfortunately"—he sighed heavily—"I left my notes in my bag. So … um … I'm going to just wing it and, uh, perform the ritual in English."

His stress levels shot up as he listened to his own rambling explanation of the ceremony and what he planned to do. Beyond the incantation, there was so much of which he was uncertain. He and Emma were about to find out whether the Guardians approved of his improvisations.

If their makeshift ritual failed, it was GAME OVER. The talisman wouldn't work and the portal couldn't be sealed. And the mogui and its minions would be let loose on the world.

At that thought, fear uncoiled in his stomach like a viper preparing to strike. He was more afraid than he had ever been at any point of his wasted life. But he couldn't afford to let his feelings paralyze him.

Emma's face was tense as she listened carefully to his every word. She could tell—as could he—from the shimmying light overhead and the rumbling under their feet that the jolts were about to recur.

"When we petition the Beasts, we must face the direction each represents or it won't hear us," he said hurriedly. "We also must perform the ritual in the correct order, which is east first, then south, west and north, so as not to anger the Guardians."

"Wait," she interrupted. "There are four cardinal directions but five Guardians. What does the last Guardian represent?"

"The center," he clarified.

"And that's the hump?"

"Correct."

He picked up a small piece of wood from the ground and placed it in his pocket. He went to the east marker and stood over it with his back to the bulge. He smacked his palms together in a single, resounding clap. Keeping his hands in the prayer position slightly below his nose with his elbows almost fully extended, he bent at the waist in a deep bow.

"Green Dragon," he chanted in a singsong voice. "Most Honored Protector of the East, I call to you. I humbly beg your indulgence. Please make this seal invincible."

He raised his head. In one smooth movement, he took the wood out of his pocket, turned and tossed the chip at the talisman on the hump. The minute the two touched, a puff of green smoke appeared from out of nowhere and the wood disintegrated. His jaw dropped even as his knees buckled with his profound relief.

"I didn't think this would actually work," he admitted. "I guess Chinese magic is very accommodating."

"Maybe the Chinese gods understand how serious the situation is," Emma muttered. "And Joe, please don't take this the wrong way, but stop with the negativity. It's not constructive."

He was taken aback by how much her criticism stung. He would have thought after a lifetime with his mother that his epidermis now was virtually impenetrable. Oh well. If they survived, he and Emma would go their separate ways. He never had to see her again.

She must have seen his hurt expression. She opened her mouth, about to say something else, when the floor yawed—the quakes were back. The chamber's aged ceiling rasped and screeched, likely at the end of its endurance. They heard a low rumble followed by a loud, strident crack.

A large chunk of rotted joist crashed down in one corner of the room. They held their breaths. Another piece of joist gave way, then another. When the ceiling in that portion of the chamber began to tilt, they dove to the ground, expecting the entire framework above them to fail.

That didn't happen. After a few minutes of almost unbearable suspense, Emma staggered to her feet. "Let's hurry along," she said, her tone mild but her body rigid with strain. "I don't think we have much time." She reached over to help him up.

"The next direction is south. South is fire. Oh no, I need fire." He tried to contain his panic. "Where are we going to get fire?"

They looked around wildly. Emma's eyes suddenly widened. She dug in her back pocket and produced a small badly squashed package. There was one stick of gum left in it. "I have an idea," she said. "Where's that flashlight?"

They hurried to opposite ends of the room to hunt for the tool. She had set it on the floor while searching for wood markers. *Where had it gone?*

Joe finally spotted the flashlight in the corner where the ceiling sagged. The quakes had ebbed again. How long would their reprieve last this time?

The flashlight was lying directly under the fallen joists. Luckily, it had rolled under some ancient shelving or it would have been crushed or buried. There was no telling how long the shelves could take the weight of the lumber. They probably wouldn't survive the next bout of shaking.

He lay flat on his stomach and used his elbows and feet to push himself under a large beam resting precariously on the shelving. The flashlight was just within reach. He extended his arm and carefully rolled the cylindrical device toward him with his fingertips. He had the flashlight in his hand and was about to crawl out when the shocks started up once more.

He hadn't expected them to return so soon. The interval between the earthquakes was getting shorter. This latest episode was a bad one. He froze, staring as the shelving above him splintered and cracked. The decrepit shelves creaked loudly, as if in pain, and abruptly disintegrated, showering him with wood bits and dust.

The beam slid downward. He was about to be flattened like a bug under someone's shoe.

Chapter 30

Junie sprinted through the tunnel, trying to avoid the rocks that tumbled from the ceiling. The rest of the passageway collapsed just as she flung herself out of the brick archway. She hit the ground hard and rolled, coming to a stop a few feet away. When she looked over her shoulder, rocks spilled from the archway as though it had just vomited.

She rose shakily to her feet. How would Joe and Emma get out? Should she call the police? But not just yet. She had to give him time to perform the sealing ceremony. The task was even more important, the stakes higher, now that they were trying to prevent a mogui from reopening the gateway. She could only pray to whatever gods were listening that the chamber hadn't caved in as well and crushed the two of them.

A lump rose in her throat and she forced herself to breathe slowly: in and out, in and out, in and out. The simple act of inhaling and exhaling calmed her. Whatever happened, she couldn't allow herself to lose heart. She had to find Millie and keep the yaoguai occupied so Joe—assuming he and Emma still were alive—could finish sealing the portal. She would fail if she didn't focus on those objectives. As she had warned Joe, this yaoguai was harder to handle than the first one.

She took a quick look around the main cellar to make sure the creature hadn't sneaked downstairs while she was in the tunnel. There was no sign of it. It must still be holed up somewhere in the house.

The staircase was still standing, to her relief. She better get upstairs quickly during this lull in the quakes. She hadn't enjoyed being tossed around in the stairwell. And surely the structure could take only so much vigorous jolting before it gave up the ghost.

She tried the first step. When it and the next few treads didn't buckle under her feet, she continued around the bend, her sword held ready. The creature wasn't lurking anywhere on the stairs. Above her, the cellar door hung ajar. Through the small opening, she could see the house lights hadn't been turned on. She extracted her remaining flashlight from her cargo pants and flicked it on.

She experienced a strong feeling of *deja vu* as she warily mounted the steps—or, more accurately, reverse *deja vu* since she was *ascending* (rather than *descending*) the cellar stairs into darkness to hunt yaoguai. *Had it been only last night that she tackled the first monster?* Saturday seemed like a lifetime ago.

She paused on the upper landing to take a few more calming, deep breaths. In and out. In and out. In and out. Her heart rate slowed, falling in sync with her breathing. When she felt ready, she raised her sword, kicked the door wide open and rushed over the threshold. Nothing loomed at her from out of the dark.

Like its predecessor, this yaoguai was playing hide-and-seek.

* * *

Junie was disconcerted to find that upstairs, the powerful episodic earthquakes were reduced to a slight shivering of the floorboards and a quavering in the walls. For some reason, the house was insulated against the worst of the shocks. Why? Did that mean it was safe from collapse?

She headed for Millie's bedroom, since that was where Joe thought Millie might be. She was midway up the back stairs when she heard someone calling for help.

"Help, somebody! Help me! Where is everyone?"

It definitely was Millie's voice. The plaintive wails came from the direction of the foyer. Junie was about to run up the stairs when she hesitated. The second floor was the quickest way to reach the foyer—she could cut across the corridor to the foyer stairs—but the corridor had too many doors behind which the creature could lie in wait. And while it might take her longer to reach Millie from the first floor, it also offered more escape routes should the cries for help prove to be a trap. She turned around and tiptoed back down the stairs.

She made her way through the dark house, turning off her flashlight when she was at the back of the foyer. The chandelier was still lit, the way she had left it. Millie was standing at the front door, clad in a silk dressing gown, her feet bare. She wept piteously as she clawed and beat at the door, as if she had forgotten how to open it.

"Millie?"

The woman turned around uncertainly. "Who's there?" Her voice quivered with fear.

Junie stepped out from the shadows. "It's me, Junie, Joe Tham's associate."

"Where's everyone?" The woman wrung her hands. "Why is the door locked?"

Was this another of the yaoguai's tricks? Junie slipped her hand into her pocket and clasped the crystal as she cautiously approached Millie. Before her third eye could open, she heard tinkling from above. She looked up; the chandelier's piercing light made her blink. She blinked again and her mouth fell open. A giant green lizard was curled around the lamp's mounting bracket.

She recognized the yaoguai when the lizard's red eyes gleamed. The chandelier's pendulous gems shook even more vigorously. Junie's stomach plunged to her toes—the monster was about to drop the heavy fixture on Millie. She dashed forward and launched herself at the woman. A split second later, the light abruptly died and 300 pounds of Austrian crystal came crashing down.

The expensive glass baubles hit the unforgiving marble floor and exploded into a million jagged shards. The two of them would have been badly hurt if she hadn't managed to push Millie and herself behind the heavy sculpture by the door. The large art piece made for bad feng shui but a pretty good shield. Its copper surfaces took the brunt of the razor-sharp slivers that ricocheted off the floor and walls.

In the pregnant silence that followed, Junie gazed upward, searching for the yaoguai. There was enough ambient light shining into the foyer from the street lamps outside for her to make out a sinuous shape on the ceiling. The shape fell to the floor with a meaty plop and pushed its way through the glass, its movements twisting and snake-like. Quickly, before she lost track of it in the gloom, she whipped her flashlight out and trained its beam on the undulating figure. Her heart stuttered in her chest when she saw what it was heading for.

The Energy Devourer lay under what remained of the once-magnificent chandelier. She had dropped the sword in her haste to save Millie.

The lizard creature seemed impervious to the broken glass. The sword was a different matter. The yaoguai yowled when it plucked the weapon out from under the ruined lamp. It hung on to the sword in spite of its obvious pain. It shot her a baleful glare before slithering swiftly out of sight.

Junie's fingers tightened around the flashlight; she felt like yowling herself. The yaoguai had employed a ruse to separate her from the Energy Devourer. And even though she had anticipated some sort of a trap, that hadn't prevented her from walking blithely into it.

She edged out gingerly from behind the sculpture. Glass fragments crunched under her feet; the marble floor glistened as though it were made from diamonds. She looked longingly in the direction in which the yaoguai had gone, anxious to retrieve the sword. But she had to get Millie to safety first. She tried the front door. It was locked and couldn't be opened without a key.

She glanced at Millie, still huddling behind the sculpture. She seemed to have fallen into a catatonic state. Her dazed expression didn't change when Junie spoke to her and waved a hand in front of her face. *What had the yaoguai done to her?*

Junie tried lifting her to her feet, but the older woman outweighed her by at least 50 pounds. She had no choice but to leave Millie where she was, at least for the time being. That was the only spot in the foyer that was relatively sliver-free. Millie's feet would be cut to ribbons if she ventured out from behind the artwork.

A movement caught her eye. The front door's handle was jiggling. Looking out through the foyer's glass walls, she saw Noah trying the door. At the curb, the Toyota's interior light was on and the driver-side door wide open. He must have come running when he saw the chandelier fall. What else did he witness? She tapped on the glass and he looked up.

He left the front door and came over to where she was standing. He shouted something but the plate glass was too thick for her to hear what he said. Finally, he put his hand to his ear, miming to ask if she needed him to call 911. She shook her head and pointed to the car. When he hesitated, she adopted a stern expression and pointed to the car again. After a long and silent battle of wills, he turned around and stalked back to the Toyota.

She knew by the set of his shoulders that he wasn't happy. However, she couldn't worry about him for now. Where was the yaoguai and what was it planning next? The monster hadn't tried to kill her even though it must have known she was defenseless without the sword. Did that mean it wanted her alive? Was it saving her for the mogui? If so, it would try to keep her in the house until the other monster arrived, unless Joe managed to seal the portal.

She had no intention of trying to escape while she could. She also wasn't going to sit around waiting for things to happen. She shone her flashlight around the foyer. She needed another weapon posthaste.

Chapter 31

Joe felt warm hands around his ankles. He was yanked out from under the beam just before it toppled to the floor.

"I'm glad you didn't let go of the flashlight," Emma said dryly as she released him. "Give it to me."

He stared wordlessly at the jumble of brittle old wood reduced to smithereens by the heavy beam. *That could have been him.*

Emma said something else. When he didn't respond, she impatiently extracted the flashlight from his limp hand and brought it back to the ritual site.

He tried to follow after her but his legs were like putty. The latest quakes had ceased by the time he had recovered enough from his close brush with death to see what she was up to. She had placed her empty gum wrapper on a flattish rock and was using her pocket knife to slice the foil into three thin strips that were narrower in the middle, like a bow tie. Her nervous chewing showed where the gum had gone. The hard-won flashlight lay on the ground beside her—she kept one foot on it to ensure it didn't wander again while she cut up the wrapper.

She handed the strips to him when she was done. She picked up the flashlight and took out one of its double A batteries.

"This is what we're going to do," she explained. "After you recite the words for the next Guardian, I'll take one of the strips and press each end to the ends of the battery. It has to be the metallic side of the strip, not the paper side, that connects to the battery or it won't work. The energy flowing through the foil should generate enough heat to ignite the strip. Once it's on fire, I'll throw the strip at the talisman, like I saw you do with the wood element."

She took a deep breath. "Let's hope this works. I read about it in a survivalist newsletter but haven't actually tried it. Are you ready? We should do this now while it's quiet. It'll be harder if things, including my hands, are shaking."

Joe nodded. He gave her one of the strips and went to stand at the marker indicating south. After clapping sharply, he bowed deeply and chanted, "Vermilion Bird. Most Honored Protector of the South, I call to you. I beg your indulgence. Please make this seal invincible."

Emma pressed the ends of the strip to the battery's metal caps. She grinned triumphantly when the strip's thin mid-section smoked briefly and burst into flames. With a flick of her fingers, she flung the burning strip at the talisman. To their dismay, the flame died in mid-toss before it hit the yellow paper.

She took another slip of foil from him and tried again. She yelped and dropped the strip after it flared. "Sorry, sorry. That got a little too hot." She sucked her index finger.

He passed her the last strip. "It's the only one left," he warned, stating the obvious.

"Before I waste this one as well, let's try to find something I can set on fire that won't burn up so fast," she suggested. "Do you have a used tissue or something like that?"

Joe didn't have a tissue, but he dug out his wallet and produced a handful of receipts. "Will these do?"

"Yes." She twisted the bits of paper into a taper. "Here. Hold this while I set the strip on fire."

She was handing him the taper when the floor jounced, throwing them together. The quakes had returned. "Given that it's our last chance, let's hold off until the next quiet period to lower the risk of the flame going out," she said grimly.

They waited in nervous silence. When the shocks passed, Joe straddled the south marker, clapped, bowed and repeated the invocation to the Vermilion Bird, in case the Beast had forgotten that it was the one being addressed. At the end of the incantation, Emma touched the ends of their last strip to the battery. The strip ignited and Joe held his wad of receipts to the flame. The taper caught fire and he gingerly lowered it onto the talisman.

The burning receipts disappeared in a puff of red smoke. They let out whoops of joy and hugged each other. "It worked," she cried, pumping her fist.

Their celebration came to an abrupt end when the talisman—and the rock anchoring it in place—slid off the hump. They gaped at the protuberance. It was growing wider before their very eyes, its sides rising and pushing the directional markers out of place. It now was shaped more like a mesa than a hump.

Joe retrieved the talisman and held it down with trembling fingers on top of the swelling pile of earth. "We can't stop," he said urgently. "Something is close to coming through. The next direction is west. I need metal."

She pulled a ring off her finger. "How about this? It's silver. I think. Mostly."

He nodded. Emma scooped up four pieces of wood and marked the cardinal directions again, this time further from the center of the growing mound. She held the talisman in place while Joe stood over the new west marker and invoked the White Tiger. When she touched her ring to the talisman, white smoke rose and the silver band crumbled to dust.

"What's next?" she asked breathlessly.

"North. We need water."

"How much water?" She eyed the blood on his temple.

The mesa emitted a deep groan before Joe could reply. Emma felt the talisman move under her fingers. She lifted it, revealing a small crack in the middle of the mound. They watched in horror as the crack lengthened. Other cracks appeared and radiated down the mound's sides. The mesa looked like it was about to blow its top.

"Put the talisman back down," Joe ordered.

He hopped over to the north marker and chanted to the Black Tortoise. At the end of the incantation, he returned to the protuberance and bent over it. Emma barely had time to remove her hand before he spat. The water droplets hissed on contact with the talisman and disappeared in a wisp of black smoke.

The mesa groaned again. The cracks under the talisman visibly widened. The paper charm started to list. She snatched at it but before she could pluck it up, the talisman slipped into a large gash that almost bisected the mound's top.

She was about to reach into the gash when Joe roared, "Don't do that!" He looked around for the staff and spotted it lying between the south and east markers. He brought it back to the mesa, which had grown about two feet high and almost four feet across. He cautiously poked the stick into the gash and wiggled it around.

The mound's top erupted. Joe's ears were assaulted by a loud blast before hot air singed his skin. An instant later, he and Emma were knocked off their feet. They cowered as sand, dirt and rocks pelted them. When he finally peeked out from under his arms, the mesa was gone, in its place a pit. The light above swung in wild spirals but amazingly, it was intact despite its proximity to the eruption.

He rose unsteadily to his feet and hobbled over to the cavity. It was large, larger than the original sinkhole had been, and it reeked. The odor was reminiscent of sulfur and blocked sewers. He was pushed to the brink of despair when he saw something red and glowing, like luminescent lava, deep within the shaft. A tiny yellow speck floated in the middle of the redness.

Emma came up beside him and gasped. "What … what in the hell is that?"

"I think … " He clenched his jaw to still his chattering teeth. The room was warm from the blast but his whole body felt chilled. "I think we're looking at an eye," he whispered. "Or rather, part of an eye."

"*Holy smokes.* The thing must be gigantic if that's its eye."

"It's finally broken through," he said sourly, "and now it's determined to make an entrance."

Emma gasped again. The red substance was rising rapidly to the surface.

* * *

Junie went to the kitchen and took out the largest cleaver in the knife block. After a brief reflection, she replaced the knife and picked up a rolling pin.

As a child, she had been warned repeatedly not to run with sharp objects. It was a tough life lesson to shake. She suspected that with the cleaver, she was far more likely to hurt herself, or others, by accident than the yaoguai by design. And she liked how solid the rolling pin felt in her hand. It reminded her, albeit vaguely, of the Energy Devourer.

Thus armed, she crept through the mansion's murky interior, searching high and low for the yaoguai. She finally found it on the second floor.

The monster was in Millie's bedroom. It wasn't even trying to hide. It stood brazenly on the balcony with its back to the room. Absorbed in the house's beautiful grounds and the lights of the city beyond, it didn't turn around when she entered. Was the creature daydreaming about all the human suffering it would feed upon once the mogui ascended through the portal?

Her pulse quickened when she spied the sword on the bed, half-wrapped in a dishcloth. The yaoguai must have found the Energy Devourer too painful to handle after all.

She sneaked toward the bed, her heart pounding so hard in her chest she was afraid the creature would hear it. She was less than 10 feet away when the yaoguai strode through the balcony's French doors. It went to a lamp and turned it on. Its eyes and teeth gleamed in the mellow light.

It had taken on Millie's guise when it was on the balcony; that mask began to transform into something greenish with a sloping head that resembled its lizard incarnation.

"Why are you here?" It looked somewhat perplexed. "You should have stayed away. I won't kill you—I'm leaving that to the Alpha—but that doesn't mean I can't hurt you badly."

It eyed her rolling pin. "And that, fledgling Dragon, is no substitute for the sword. Didn't the geomancer teach you better?" It grinned nastily. "Of course, he may not know any better."

The bed stood between her and the yaoguai. She was nearer to it than the creature was. She darted forward, hoping that with the advantage of surprise, she would get to the sword first. But she badly underestimated the creature. It moved so swiftly that all she saw was a blur of legs and arms before it was next to the bed and gingerly grasping the sword with the dishcloth.

"Looking for this?" Its face twitched unpleasantly as the weapon seared its flesh through the thin cotton. Without warning, it raised its arm and pitched the sword through the open French doors. She watched in disbelief as the Energy Devourer sailed over the balcony railing and out of sight.

"Now that we've got that out of the way, it's just you and me now." The monster's grin widened, revealing pointed teeth set apart like a picket fence. "You'll be sorry that you came looking for me. I'm sure the Alpha won't mind if I rough you up just a little, since you're the one who provoked the fight."

Before she could react, it sprang over the bed like a giant jackrabbit, lifted her by the armpits and threw her across the room. She slammed against the far wall and fell to the carpet. She was too stunned to resist when it scurried over, grabbed her again and flung her in the opposite direction. This time she came down hard on Millie's coffee table. She landed awkwardly on her right arm and felt something snap between her wrist and elbow. She moaned as a wave of pain shot up her shoulder.

Seizing her upper arms, the yaoguai hoisted her off the table until her feet dangled in the air. She pursed her lips, trying to hold in her screams from the manhandling of her broken arm.

"You're not so strong without your sword, are you, Dragon?" it snarled, its breath hot and fetid. The monster's reptilian visage took on a pensive expression.

"If I smash you down hard enough, I can break both your legs at the same time," it said in a conversational tone. "Or I can snap your spine so that you're paralyzed from the neck down. Either way, you won't be able to escape when the Alpha arrives. Which shall it be? Do you want to pick or should I?"

The yaoguai pretended to drop her, but snatched her up by the arms again before she hit the floor. It shook her, chortling when she yelped from her arm being jogged. She was as helpless as a rag doll in a cruel child's hands.

"Can't make up your mind?" it asked at last. "I'll do it then. I think I'll break your"—it paused for dramatic effect—"spine." It bared its picket-fence teeth. "You'll be completely incapacitated. Whether or not the Alpha kills you, you'll never recover from this, even with Dragon powers."

It dropped her, chuckling with delight when she clutched her right arm and wailed in agony. It bent over her and pressed one of its narrow hands on her collarbone. The other hand clasped the nape of her neck and lifted her head slightly off the carpet.

She looked into its red eyes, wondering whether the creature would be quick, or take its time.

Chapter 32

"Can you complete the ritual?" Emma asked frantically as the redness soared inexorably upward.

"I'm waiting until I can see the talisman clearly," Joe said, steadying himself with the staff as the ground jolted and rocked.

The quakes this time were the worst yet. A pair of support pillars close to where Joe had found the flashlight squealed harshly and suddenly gave way like snapped toothpicks. The ceiling previously held up by the pillars —including the portion that already was tilting—collapsed next with a deafening crash. The room now was reduced to half its former size.

He hummed to himself to tune out the noise of the beams and joists shrieking in protest above and of the violent shock waves coming from below. He focused on the talisman which, riding like a speck of dirt in the mogui's eye, was getting nearer.

When the yellow paper was close enough for him to discern its symbol, he clapped and bowed over the pit. "Yellow Dragon," he intoned solemnly. He took especial care not to rush his words for fear of offending the last Guardian, which happened to be one of the most important beings in the Chinese constellations.

"Most Honored Protector of the Center of the Cosmos and Sovereign of the Celestial Dragons, I call to you. I crave your indulgence. Please make this seal invincible."

He scooped up a handful of dirt. However, despite his best efforts to time it just right, he waited a tad too long. Before he could drop the dirt onto the talisman, the red substance rose to the mouth of the hole and jutted out, proving to be more solid than it appeared. He stumbled backward as the earth around the pit heaved and cracked from the straining of the monster underneath. The cavity crumbled at the edges and became even larger, allowing more of the eye to extrude.

Joe swore and discarded his handful of soil. He couldn't seal the portal while the monster was trying to come through. He raised the staff with both hands and lunged at the eye with a bray of defiance. He was answered with an angry roar so low in pitch they felt it in their feet through the ground's reverberations rather than heard it. The Alpha backed off; its eye disappeared down the hole.

"Emma!" he shouted. "See if you can spot the talisman while the eye's still underground and lob some dirt at it. Earth is the last element we need!"

He couldn't tell if she heard him. The mogui's eye was squeezing through again. As he jabbed at the red substance, he realized that Junie's second talisman was still attached to the staff's tip. The charm's protection magic must be what was keeping the behemoth at bay.

The eye retreated into the hole. The Alpha uttered another of its booming infrasonic cries. He thrust the staff deep into the aperture and waved it around, hoping to discourage the creature from rising to the surface. He caught movement at the periphery of his vision. Emma came up beside him, her hands full of dirt.

"Where is it?" she asked. "Can you see the talisman?"

"No! I've been kind of busy."

They hunched over the cavity, trying to locate the small yellow rectangle amid the red, shining mass. The eye was rolling around, making it even more difficult. Concentrating on the hole, they were caught off guard when something pierced through the ground behind them.

Joe was swept off his feet. Emma was knocked to one side. They stared in abhorrence at the tentacle that loomed over them. It was the color of diseased flesh shot through with veins of red, as thick as a tree, with suckers the size of dinner plates. The giant appendage withdrew into the ground as quickly as it had emerged. Another tentacle shot up on the other side of the pit and smacked into the fragile ceiling. Wood pieces and fragments rained down. The tentacle disappeared as swiftly as the first one.

"Joe, what should we do?" Emma's face was filled with horror.

"If it keeps hitting the ceiling, it's going to bring the whole thing down on us," he said. "That's probably its plan."

"*Shit.* What about the ritual?"

What about the ritual? They were so close, yet so far. "We can't seal the portal if any part of the mogui is in our world," he said desperately. "The seal won't be tight. And the earth element must connect with the talisman for the ritual to take."

He hadn't finished speaking when a third tentacle punched out of the ground and struck the ceiling directly above them. The beams groaned and sagged, shedding debris like tears.

Emma stood up and wrested the staff from his hands. When the tentacle retracted back into the earth, she scampered to the pit and hammered at its edges with the rod, screaming all the while like a demented banshee. The dirt fell away at her onslaught, further enlarging the cavity.

"Emma, what in the world are you doing?" he asked, bewildered.

"I'm. Increasing. Our. Chances. Of. Survival!" she screeched, timing her words to her ferocious pounding. "Maybe. Something. Will. Fall. On. The. Talisman."

Joe crawled to her side. He kicked and pushed at the soil around the pit. More dirt fell in.

She suddenly clutched his shirt and pointed. He froze when he saw amber smoke curling out of the pit. As the haze drifted upward, a deep hush descended as if everything in the chamber—human and inhuman, animate and inanimate alike—was holding its breath.

The smoke hung in the air for a brief moment before dissipating. When the last of it was gone, the pit began to change, so subtly at first that he couldn't tell what was happening save that there was increasingly frenetic movement within its depths.

The activity intensified and became more visible. He could now see that soil was ascending from below and adhering to the sides of the shaft. The earth swarmed up as though borne on the backs of millions of tiny, hardworking ants. The pit was rapidly closing over. And not just the pit—every single puncture hole left behind by the Alpha's tentacles was closing as well.

When the last piece of dirt slid into place, he sank to his knees and sent heartfelt thanks to the Yellow Dragon and its Heavenly Cohorts. The ground was now smoothed over except for a few odd ridges where the pit had been. Curious, he traced the bits of raised soil with his index finger. It dawned on him that they were a larger version of the talisman's symbol embossed, as it were, on the earthen floor. It was confirmation that the portal was sealed.

Emma collapsed beside him. "Is it over?"

"I think so."

But he spoke too soon. The mogui wasn't finished with them yet. They heard, or rather felt, the monster's furious bellowing. The deep bellows were accompanied by a chorus of keens and ululations that, while not pitched for human hearing, raised the fine hair on the napes of their necks and made the tips of their fingers tingle.

The chamber shivered; it felt like something was shaking it from far, far below. A heavy post thudded to the ground a few feet away, making them both jump. Their eyes swiveled upward in alarm.

"Oh no," Emma said in a small voice.

They ducked as a joist tore away from the ceiling and fell, barely missing them. Joe, cowering on the ground, heard a sharp creak overhead. There was a soft pop, then a rasping groan, followed by a resonant crack. They both looked up again.

"We're not going to make it," he said.

* * *

The yaoguai was just about to twist Junie's neck and sever her spine when it paused. Its bay of rage almost deafened her. It released her and ran to the bedroom door.

She curled into the fetal position, using her body to shield her broken arm. Her left hand brushed against something long and round on the carpet. It was the rolling pin. She pulled the implement toward her and tucked it against her stomach.

The bed blocked most of the yaoguai from view so she couldn't tell what it was doing. The creature seemed to be standing stock-still at the doorway, as though listening or waiting for something.

After a long while, it let loose another howl of rage and stomped back to her. She remained in the fetal position, not moving even when it bent over her.

"It seems there's been a change of plans," it hissed in her ear. "The fake geomancer sealed the portal after all. The Alpha isn't coming. That means I am free to kill you."

Junie's heart leaped with joy at hearing that Joe had succeeded in his mission. *He and Emma were still alive!* She hid her elation, pretending to whimper as if terrified by the yaoguai's words. It grabbed her shoulder, trying to haul her up. She turned suddenly and jammed the rolling pin with all the force her left hand could muster against the underside of its chin. The yaoguai's picket-fence teeth snapped shut audibly and it staggered backwards. She swiped the rolling pin viciously at its legs, causing it to trip and fall on the bed.

She was on her feet and sprinting toward the balcony before the creature could recover. She risked a peek when she was at the railing. It was struggling to get up.

Their eyes met; the monster managed to convey through its malevolent red glare that when it caught her, she would die in the most horrible way possible.

For her part, she was doing her best to survive. She climbed onto the railing and jumped.

* * *

Junie knew from Saturday's pursuit of the first yaoguai that the balcony hung almost directly over the swimming pool. The balcony was about 12 feet off the ground, and the clearance between the balcony's edge and the pool was about six feet. As she leaped, she sent out a hasty prayer asking for three things.

First, she prayed she had pushed off from the balcony with enough force to land in the pool rather than the concrete deck around it. Second, she prayed the water was deep enough for someone jumping from such a height. Fortunately, based on the position of the diving platform, she was plunging into the pool's deep end and not the shallow portion. Third, she prayed that when the sword sailed off the balcony, it landed in the pool and not somewhere else.

She was asking much of God, or the gods, or whichever benevolent being that by chance was listening. As an agnostic, she wasn't sure to whom she was praying, but she knew she was as good as dead if any of her prayers wasn't answered. Even if she didn't die from the fall, the yaoguai would come and finish her off.

She plummeted downward, her left hand holding her right elbow firmly to prevent her broken bones from being joggled too much. The pool's electric lights were off, like the lights in the rest of the residence. The water, however, glimmered faintly in the soft glow from the tall solar lamps edging the deck. She felt as if she was about to pass through an enormous looking glass, like Lewis Carroll's young heroine Alice.

Her feet hit the water with a big splash. Her body prickled from the shock of the cool water and bubbles rose in a white froth all around her. She took a deep breath just before she went under.

The water slowed her fall, but she did her best as well by kicking her legs vigorously. She still shot to the bottom, which was about 10 feet deep at that point, coming to an abrupt halt when her waterlogged shoes hit the tiled floor. Her gorge rose from the pain of her jarred arm but she fought down the nausea. She bent her knees and waved her left arm in an upward motion to keep from floating back to the top.

She was at ease in the water, and that was due in no small part to her brother. Patrick, competitive from the day he was born, had taken great pride in trouncing her academically and athletically when they were children. But she found one activity in which he couldn't beat her—holding her breath and swimming underwater—and she practiced and practiced until she excelled at it. She never thought the skill—if it could be labeled a skill—would come in so handy. Her mother had her eternal gratitude for insisting on swimming lessons.

She looked up from the bottom of the pool, squinting to see if she could spot the sword floating anywhere on the surface. Her glasses had been pulled off her face when she entered the water but that was fine—spectacles were useless underwater anyway. At least she hadn't lost them; the sports strap kept them around her neck.

The lack of lights in the water was both a boon and a bane. While the murkiness hid her from the yaoguai, it also made it harder for her to see. The solar lamps cast light trails but they were few and far between. As far as she could tell, the sword wasn't in the pool.

Crap and double crap. Her time was running out. She didn't have a Plan B. The yaoguai must surely be about to barrel into the pool after her. Or it could at this very second be coming through the sliding doors into the backyard.

The longest she previously managed to stay underwater was just shy of four minutes. She had no idea how long she had stayed under this time. Whatever it was, she was almost at the end of her limit. She had to surface soon to take a breath, which definitely would give away her position. Should she sneak out of the pool and try to escape through the gate at the other end of the walled grounds? She could try, but she knew she couldn't outrun the yaoguai.

She moved, not wanting to be directly under the creature should it jump from the same spot she had. She kicked something when her feet slid along the tiles. She crouched lower and felt the object with her left hand. *It was the Energy Devourer.* Apparently, wood from the sacred groves of the Shen Ting Mountains—what the sword was made from, according to the first yaoguai—wasn't buoyant. Who knew?

Just then, the water exploded and a large whale-like shape loomed above her. The monster had just dived in. She raised the sword in her left hand —her right arm was virtually useless—and kicked hard against the pool floor to propel herself upward. She had one shot to get this right.

The monster plunged swiftly downward at the same time that she thrust upward. The yaoguai hadn't expected her to be on the offensive. It yipped in surprise and pain, thrashed and swallowed water when the sword pierced forcefully into its abdomen.

The sword was wrenched out of her hand by the creature's downward momentum. When it smacked the bottom, she quickly swam to it, pulled the sword out and kicked her legs strenuously to bring herself to the surface. The yaoguai floated up while she was taking long, shuddering breaths of the night air.

It floundered feebly, half-drowned, stunned by its hard impact with the tiles, and bleeding from its stab wound. She didn't know yaoguai *could* bleed. Dark blood streamed from its belly, looking like chocolate syrup in the light from the solar lamps.

When the creature drifted close enough, she kicked strongly again and launched herself half out of the water. As she fell back in, she stabbed the sword downward into the monster's chest.

It shrieked. It jerked and flopped and writhed as the sword greedily sucked away its life force. Its desperate struggles turned the pool into spume and white water, making her feel like she was caught up in powerful rapids. She hung on grimly, no matter how much her broken arm hurt, using her weight to keep the sword inside the creature. Her very life depended on her killing the yaoguai first.

It tried to push her away, but it was weakening, and shrinking rapidly. She had to kick and scissor her legs to keep them both afloat. The creature stopped moving by the time it was the size of a cat. She pulled the sword out but the corpse continued to shrivel and curl in upon itself.

It eventually became a small, roundish mass that bobbed in the water. She was staring at it, wondering whether there was something else she should do, when it burst like a ripe seedpod, ejecting thin black tendrils. The tendrils quickly dispersed in the water and disappeared.

The instant the last of the yaoguai was gone, the adrenaline that had kept her going leaked from her. She felt like a deflated beach ball; she barely had the strength to tread water. She clamped the sword under her right armpit and awkwardly dog paddled to the shallow end of the pool, where there were wide steps descending into the water. She hauled herself up the steps and collapsed with half of her body still in the water. She passed out from pain and exhaustion.

She looked around wildly when she came to, temporarily disoriented. She had no idea how long she had been unconscious. The Energy Devourer was on the pool's top step, pinned under her body. Holding on tight to the sword, she staggered out of the water and turned to stare at the sliding doors. Were they locked? Could she use them to get back into the house?

She blinked hard, trying to focus her eyes in the poor light. Something was wrong with the doors. Baffled, she dried her wet glasses as best as she could and put them on.

The doors were crooked, as if they had fallen off their tracks. The tempered glass pane on one of the doors was completely shattered, reduced to pellets that peppered the porch's gray cement pavers.

She lurched over to the doors and peered through them into the sitting room. She gasped when she saw the canted furniture, the sloping floor and the giant dip in the room's middle. Her shock slowly was replaced by ice-cold dread; fear settled on her chest like a heavy weight that made it difficult to breathe. Wasn't the chamber—the underground chamber in which Joe and Emma were trapped—situated somewhere under the room?

She tucked the sword in her waistband and pulled her phone out. She tried to turn it on, which proved challenging because her one good hand couldn't stop shaking. When the device refused to turn on, she cut across the grounds and let herself out through the gate in the stone wall. She dashed down the alleyway between the garage and the side of the house and sped across the front garden, trampling over Millie's neat flower beds in her haste to get to Noah.

He jumped out of the car when he saw her. "Why are you sopping wet?" he asked in amazement.

"Call 911," she shouted urgently. "Tell them the cellar collapsed, with Joe and Emma inside. There's another person at the front of the house as well."

She got into the car while Noah spoke with the emergency dispatcher. She was shivering by then, from reaction as much as her damp skin and sodden clothes.

After he hung up, he wrapped her in the beach towel—the same one they had sat on at the mall—and turned on his car's heater to give her some warmth. She wanted to ask what time it was, but her teeth were chattering too much for conversation. Her watch had stopped working, along with her phone, when she was immersed in the water.

Her shuddering gradually eased while they waited for the emergency responders. He placed his hand gently on her back. "What happened?"

"Did you feel the earthquakes?"

"*Earthquakes?*" He goggled at her. "What earthquakes? Are we talking about figurative or literal earthquakes? It's been quiet out here."

She shook her head and stared apathetically out the passenger-side window, too spent to answer any questions, or even care about what he was thinking. He was right though—it was peaceful, a summer night in the city just like any other.

She heard a toot of car horns in the distance, a snatch of laughter, rap music from a passing SUV. Flickering light in windows showed that a few night owls were still glued to their televisions. For the most part though, Millie's neighbors slumbered, cocooned in darkness, insulated from the true darkness that had temporarily invaded her glass mansion.

So much had happened that Junie couldn't believe it was still nighttime. The moon and the stars shone impassively above, bright beacons in the vast ocean that was the night sky.

Chapter 33

The neighborhood's serenity was rived by brilliant flashing lights and strident sirens.

The D.C. Fire and Emergency Medical Services Department arrived in two fire engines, two ambulances and a sport utility vehicle, followed closely by several marked and unmarked police cars. The firefighters spilled out of their trucks and hurried to the house to assess the situation while the police set up a cordon and directed traffic.

Junie and Noah spoke to a man who got out of the SUV. He seemed to be in charge.

"There are three people in the house," she said breathlessly. "One by the front door and two more in the cellar."

"Are you the ones who called 911?" the man asked. They nodded.

"The cellar caved in at the back, where there's a passageway leading to a storage chamber," she said. "My boss and the homeowner's personal assistant are trapped inside the chamber. If you go round the back to the porch and pool area, you can see where it's collapsed through the house's sliding glass doors."

"Alright, we'll take it from here," the man said authoritatively. "Please step back to where it's safe." He looked at her wet hair, the towel around her shoulders and the manner in which she cradled her right arm against her body. "Are you hurt? The paramedics are over there."

An EMT was bracing her arm with a padded board when the emergency responders brought Millie out through the front door on a gurney. Junie was too far away to see whether she had snapped out of her apparent catatonia. She was conveyed to an ambulance that zoomed off with its siren wailing.

The EMT finished splinting and bandaging Junie's arm. He fashioned a sling for her out of bandages and told her she needed to go to a hospital to get the arm x-rayed.

"It looks like a bad break," he said. "Could be multiple bad breaks. The X-rays will tell you more. You also have several nasty contusions. Are you hurting anywhere else? I can transport you to the hospital now and have you thoroughly checked out by an emergency room doctor."

"I'm not going anywhere until I know more about what's happening with my colleague," she said stubbornly.

She was still arguing with the paramedic when a young police officer came to take her statement, with Noah in tow.

"Ms. Soong? Are you done here?" The officer glanced at the EMT, who nodded irritably and began to stow his equipment.

"I'm Officer Gerald Weems from the Metropolitan Police Department. I've talked to this gentleman"—the policeman tilted his head at Noah—"and I'd like to hear your version of what happened. Are you ready to speak with me?"

Junie *was* ready. She had spent the few minutes before the first responders arrived to think up a plausible story. She kept in mind Joe's advice to be discreet. She knew half-truths were the best lies.

"Just the facts, right?" she quipped.

His face wore a pleasant smile, but his toffee-colored eyes were guarded.

She told the officer that a concerned client called her saying she couldn't get in touch with Joe. She herself became worried when she couldn't reach him. She knew Joe had gone to Millie Scarpini's house with Millie's assistant, Emma Frankel, so she asked Noah to give her a lift to the residence.

Once she got there, she found the front door unlocked. She went in and discovered Millie in a confused state. Millie told her that Joe and Emma were outside. When she went out to check, Millie locked her out. She went around to the back compound hoping to get into the house through the sliding doors. The backyard was poorly lit. She tripped and fell into the swimming pool and broke her arm.

After she clambered out of the pool, she went to the sliding doors and saw the state of the sitting room. Her cell phone was damaged by the water, so she ran out to Noah and asked him to summon the authorities.

Weems recorded what she said in a notebook. He consulted his notes and said, "Mr. Redmond told us you and he arrived here shortly after 9 p.m. Is that right?"

She nodded uncertainly. "It could be. I'm not sure. I wasn't checking my watch at the time."

"It's now 3:30 in the morning. What did you do in the house that took nearly six hours?"

Careful. The officer was more alert than he looked. She shrugged. "I didn't want to leave Millie alone while she was so frightened and confused so I stayed with her awhile. I was also trying to find out from her where Joe was." She crossed her fingers, hoping Millie wouldn't remember what had happened and contradict her later.

"Why didn't you call immediately for an ambulance? You knew Mrs. Scarpini should have been in the hospital. The hospital filed a missing person report last evening."

"Actually I *didn't* know," she said. "When I saw her, I thought she had been discharged."

"You said she seemed confused." Officer Weems stared at her. "Didn't you think you needed to call somebody?"

She shrugged again. "I tried to call Joe, but he wasn't answering his cell. I didn't have Emma's number, and I didn't know who else to call."

"Mr. Redmond mentioned that the chandelier fell."

"That's right, it did." She kept her gaze on Weems, not looking at Noah. "I attributed that to shoddy construction. It didn't hit us, so I thought Millie, or Emma, would call the contractor the next day to sort it out."

"So why, exactly, were Mr. Tham and Ms. Frankel at the house?"

"Mrs. Scarpini wanted us to bless the house. Joe had her permission to be on the premises."

"*Bless* the house? What do you and Mr. Tham do?"

"Uh, we're feng shui practitioners."

The policeman looked blank. "It's an Asian thing," Junie explained. "Our customers hire us to … um … unblock the stagnant energy in their homes."

Still looking blank, Weems moved on to his next question. "What do you think Mr. Tham and Ms. Frankel were doing in the cellar?"

"Joe told me that's where he wanted to perform the blessing. I didn't ask why. When you rescue him, you can ask him."

Weems said he had no more questions, but warned that he might need to speak with her again. She reminded him that her cell phone was broken. He departed after she provided him with her office number and address and her parents' phone number.

Noah looked at her arm in the sling. "What did the paramedic say?"

"He says I need to get the arm x-rayed. He thinks it may be a bad fracture."

"Let's do it now. I can drive you to the nearest emergency room. Oh wait, I can't." He smacked his forehead with the heel of his palm. "My car is blocked in by the fire engines. They probably won't take kindly to me asking them to move."

"I don't want to leave before finding out about … survivors." Her voice cracked.

He nodded sympathetically and they hurried over to a group of firefighters standing by one of the fire trucks.

"Any news yet?" she asked anxiously. "Has anyone tried to enter the cellar?"

A fireman shook his head. "We're still analyzing the extent of damage to the house," he said apologetically. "We won't enter the cellar unless and until we're certain the house itself is stable and not about to collapse. The gas leak on Saturday adds another layer of complexity. We'll have to check for gas before going in. We don't want to make things worse by being too hasty."

Another firefighter in the group was staring at her. It was the woman who had escorted her and Joe out of the cellar.

"Why am I not surprised to see you here?" the firefighter said when she saw that Junie recognized her. "You and your business associate just couldn't stay away, could ya?"

Junie teared up, and the firefighter immediately looked contrite. "I apologize," she hastily said. "I shouldn't be making light of the situation." She placed a reassuring hand on Junie's good arm. "We're doing everything we can. You just have to hope for the best."

The firefighter's eyes flicked to Noah. "You take care of her, you hear?"

Noah glanced at Junie. He still recalled, so clearly, the sight of her standing before the house and the feelings it had evoked in him.

"I'm pretty sure Junie can take care of herself," he said.

* * *

Junie took the firefighter's advice to heart and tried to hope for the best, but the emergency responders still hadn't entered the cellar when dawn broke. The area outside the police tape was thick with newspaper and TV reporters by then. Noah refused to leave without her, and she finally suggested that they ride back to the office via one of the rideshare services.

"Why the office? Why not go straight to the hospital?"

"I want to get out of these wet clothes first. And I need to put some things away."

"Okay, but we're going to the hospital after that."

Before their Lyft ride came, they returned to the Toyota so Junie could retrieve the sword and Noah his backpack. They rode in silence back to Chinatown. The Lyft driver dropped her in front of the Laughing Buddha. She went up to the apartment while Noah waited with the driver.

She stored the Energy Devourer and the crystal in the trunk. She took the remaining talismans from her back pocket and gently smoothed them out, trying not to smudge their red symbols. The charms were still a little damp so she draped them on the bathtub's edge to dry.

She found Elsie's phone number pinned to the refrigerator and copied it on a piece of paper. After that, she struggled to change her clothing, hampered by the padded board splint around her arm. She gave up after a while. Her clothes were dry by then anyhow, albeit badly wrinkled.

The Lyft driver shot her an irritated look when she finally made it downstairs. The drive to the hospital was another silent one. She borrowed Noah's phone to call her father while they were waiting for a technician to x-ray her arm. When she hung up, she told him to go home.

"I'll be fine, and my parents are on their way," she said. "You've been up all night. You need some sleep."

He wearily massaged the skin above his eyes. "I should head back to my apartment and get cleaned up." He peered at his watch. "I have to open the restaurant in about an hour's time."

"Thank you so much for everything," she said awkwardly. "And I forgot to thank you for a lovely evening. The first part, that is, not the last bit."

"I had a great evening too, and I was happy to help." He hesitated. "I didn't tell Officer Weems everything. What *did* you do while you were in the house?"

She wondered how much she could divulge without scaring him away. He had been wonderful thus far, but she wasn't ready to reveal everything. And she really had no idea how he would react. When it came down to it, she didn't know him all that well, although she hoped to. She decided to play it safe for now.

"Like I told Officer Weems, I stayed with Millie and tried to comfort her," she said.

"What you told the police doesn't square with what I saw," he said stiffly. "I didn't see you get locked out of the house. Once you went through the front door, you didn't come back out again. I'm sure I would have noticed. And I could have sworn I saw something else in the foyer with Millie, just before you came and the chandelier fell."

"What did you see?"

"I … I don't know what I saw," he admitted. "I was afraid I might have fallen asleep and been dreaming. That's why I didn't say anything to Weems. Was there something … someone else … in the house? Besides you, Joe, Mrs. Scarpini and that Emma person, I mean."

He looked hurt when she didn't respond. "Okay." He stood up abruptly. "I'm leaving. Get that arm taken care of. Phone me if you have any news about Joe." He turned and walked quickly away.

She wanted to call him back but didn't know what to say. She was still looking in the direction in which he had gone when her parents came up behind her.

"Junie!" Stella cried. "Why in the world did you return to that house?"

She burst into tears at the sight of their worried faces. "Ma, Pa," she sobbed, "Joe might be dead!"

Junie told her parents roughly the same story that she told the D.C. police officer. Unlike Weems, they didn't feel the need to pry every last detail out of her.

* * *

The X-rays revealed that her right arm was fractured in three places. An orthopedic technologist placed her arm in a fiberglass cast, after which she was sent to a doctor's office to discuss the injuries. He brought up the X-rays on his computer and pointed out the breaks in her ulna and radius with a pen.

"You're lucky you didn't need an operation to insert pins to hold the bones together. You say you sustained the fractures last night when you fell into a swimming pool?"

He stared at the X-rays and frowned. His pen tapped the table gently as he fidgeted. "It's strange, but I'm seeing a few hairline cracks that look as if they're far along in the healing process." Bemused, he scratched the top of his head with the pen.

"How long do I have to wear the cast?" she hurriedly asked.

"About six to eight weeks. We'll schedule a checkup in around a month's time to make sure everything is on track. Do you need anything for the pain?"

"No, I'm fine." In fact, the pain was steadily subsiding. She had a feeling her arm would be back to normal in a few days' time.

She went home with Stella and her dad returned to his patients. After Stella finished fussing over her, she fished out the piece of paper in her pocket and used her parents' landline to call Joe's mother. The phone rang for the longest time before it went to voice mail.

"Mrs. Tham? This is Junie Soong, Joe's colleague. I'm afraid there's been an accident." She paused. "Joe was in a building that collapsed. The rescue workers are still trying to extract him. Can you … can you call me? You can reach me at this number."

She shook her head as she hung up. That sounded awful. She should have rehearsed what she wanted to say. She should have softened the blow somehow. She chided herself for not throwing in a few platitudes, such as,

"He's fine, no need to worry." This was all new to her—she had never been the bearer of bad news before.

She was perturbed when Elsie didn't call her back immediately. She paced up and down her parents' living room, waiting for the call that didn't come.

This was the woman that Joe thought she should turn to in the event of a mogui emergency? Perhaps Elsie was away, or one of those people who didn't bother checking their phone messages. She slumped on the couch in front of the TV and spent the rest of the day disconsolately flipping through channels for news updates on the collapse.

"It is unlikely that the two individuals known to be in the cellar at the time of the collapse are alive," one newscaster said. "Emergency responders have not identified the two, but sources tell us one of them is Emma Frankel, Millicent Jenks Scarpini's personal assistant. It is not known why she and the other person were at the residence so soon after it was evacuated Saturday due to a gas leak. Mrs. Scarpini, who was also at the house, has been hospitalized. Her doctors aren't allowing any visitors."

Stella sat down beside her. "I'm so sorry, sweetie," she said. "Joe was a nice man."

"I don't care what anyone says," Junie said fiercely. "I won't believe he's dead until they drag his body out."

Stella put her arm around Junie's shoulder and nodded sadly.

Late that night, her mother came to her bedroom to tell her she had a call. Junie went downstairs and picked up the phone. "Hello?"

"Any news yet of Joe?" The woman's voice was low and refined, and she had a slight British accent.

"Who is this?" Junie asked suspiciously.

"This is Elsie Tham."

"Mrs. Tham." She became flustered, having given up hope that Joe's mother would call. "Um, no, there's no news yet. Will you—"

Junie heard the disconnect tone and stopped speaking. She stared dumbfounded at the phone in her hand. Elsie was no longer on the line.

Chapter 34

Junie was pulled out of a deep, dreamless sleep by persistent knocking on her bedroom door. Her father poked his head in.

"Sorry for waking you so early, but there's breaking news on the cave-in," he said excitedly. "Come down to the living room. I've got the TV on."

The D.C. Fire & EMS official was in the middle of announcing that the department believed there was at least one survivor. He recounted that rescue workers had lowered into the collapsed site a sound location device linked to microphones. The microphone system had picked up tapping noises, and they were able to pinpoint the location from which the sounds came.

"As in any rescue effort, time here is of the essence. We have no way of knowing how badly injured the individuals are." The official pointed to a diagram of the cellar. "We'll be trying today to go in through this tunnel here, rather than come from above through the house, for fear of bringing more rubble down on any of the survivors."

After the segment ended, Raymond changed the channel to a cable news program in which a pundit theorized that the gas leak and the cave-in were connected. The pundit—who described himself as a fire safety consultant—knew about the sinkhole in the cellar. According to him, gas leaking from the Saturday incident had become trapped in the sinkhole. Although the hole was filled, there must have been air pockets in which the gas collected. The trapped gas somehow ignited and exploded, leading to the collapse of the adjacent structures.

Junie supposed the theory was as good as any other.

* * *

In the end, it was Wednesday before rescue personnel were able to access the collapsed area. According to the news flash, they found two survivors.

A little later, a brief news item showed emergency workers carrying a stretcher out of Millie's front door. The footage was blurry, but Junie was certain Joe was the person on the stretcher.

"Ma!" she screamed. "They've been found."

Stella rushed out of the kitchen and jumped up and down with her daughter. Junie's face streamed with tears of joy.

Junie called Elsie after her mini celebration with her mother. No one picked up. When the call went to voice mail, she left a message about Joe's rescue. She didn't expect a callback. She didn't receive one.

She also called Noah, but he already had seen the news. She hung up after a stilted conversation. He hadn't yet forgiven her for her lack of trust in him. Or was he distant because he didn't trust *her*? He knew she lied to the police.

Whichever, it seemed the relationship was over before it even began.

* * *

Joe drifted in and out of consciousness as the ambulance weaved through the busy D.C. streets. He woke up to find a team of doctors probing his head wound.

When they saw he was awake, the lead physician shone a small flashlight into his eyes and asked him questions—"What is your name? What year is it? How old are you?"—to test his mental acuity.

He drifted off again when they were pushing him into a magnetic resonance imaging machine to do a scan of his brain.

The next time he opened his eyes, he found himself in a semi-private hospital room. His head was heavily bandaged, and intravenous fluids dripped into his system via a needle inserted in his arm. Monitors beeped softly but insistently around him.

Emma sat on a chair by his bed. She was dressed, as he was, in a hospital gown. Her face was a patchwork of cuts, scrapes and bruises. He must look worse; he certainly felt worse. Aside from his sore head, his entire body felt like someone had run it over a few times with a snowplow.

"Hi Joe." She took his hand and pressed it gently. "I guess we made it after all."

Her words stirred up a surge of nightmarish memories. They swirled to the surface of his foggy brain, as if she had dragged a stick through a pond's muddy bottom. His eyes snapped shut, but the memories kept coming.

* * *

The ceiling emitted a deep groan of surrender. As it—or what was left of it—fell, Joe reflexively folded his arms around Emma and sheltered her with his body. He closed his eyes, expecting to be pulverized at any moment by the weight of the house above. He hoped his life wouldn't flash before his eyes—he didn't want to relive any of it, however briefly, except maybe the years that he spent with his father.

He could hear large objects crashing and falling around him, but nothing actually struck him. They weren't ground to pulp. He opened his eyes to pitch blackness. Their friend, the steadfast lamp, finally had been extinguished. He couldn't see anything, not even Emma, although her shoulder felt comfortingly solid under his arms, and her stertorous breathing was loud in his ear.

He dropped his arms but discovered he couldn't move much beyond that—he and Emma were wedged together by what felt like large slabs of wood, plaster, cement and insulation. The air was thick with dust.

She coughed and spat. "Why aren't we dead?" she whispered.

"I don't know," he replied with wonder.

They should be dead by all rights, squashed under part of the house. *Why were they still alive?* It was as if they had an invisible shield around them. He straightened his cramped limbs with difficulty and felt under his legs. His fingers confirmed what he suspected: that he and Emma were sprawled on the dirt ridges reproducing the talisman's symbol. Had they been saved by the charm's sphere of protection? Were they alive solely by the grace of ancient Chinese magic? That was the only explanation he could come up with.

But they were by no means out of the woods. The two of them now were crammed in a stifling space of no more than three feet high and about two feet wide, with no water, food, or light. And how long would their oxygen last?

"Don't get too excited," he warned. "We may die yet."

"Great," she mumbled. "My last days on earth, and I have to be stuck with a die-hard pessimist."

He found he was too dog-tired, too drained, to take umbrage. "They'll find us. Junie knows where we are." *But what if Junie were dead?* He swallowed hard, unwilling to go there.

"We have to make some kind of noise," he continued, "to help them locate us under all this debris."

"How about we both yell at the top of our lungs?" she suggested.

"No, we should try to conserve our oxygen. Can you move your hands? You can? Try to find a handy rock or something and bash it against something else. Be careful. We don't want things shifting around too much. The wreckage could still come down on us."

Groping blindly in the dark, he felt something thin and long against his legs. It was the staff, partially buried. He gently worked one end of the stick free and thumped it up and down on the ground. The noise it made was muffled, and not very loud. He tried moving the rod sideways and it struck what sounded like rock. He moved it sideways again, harder this time, and was rewarded with a loud tap.

Emma managed to nudge loose a hunk of wood. She got a satisfying thunk when she smacked the wood against another piece of lumber.

Together they thumped and rapped, rapped and thumped, stopping only when their arms grew too weary. They allowed themselves short respites during which they tried to keep each other's spirits up.

Joe surprised himself by opening up about his childhood with the Golden Dragon. It must be because, if these indeed were his final hours, he wanted to dwell only on his happiest times. In turn—and perhaps because she felt the same way—she told him about growing up in Vermont, of days filled with mountains and streams and endless woods and meandering country lanes. She lived with her grandparents on their rural property —complete with red barn and goats, pigs and chickens—until she was 12. They lived off the land through subsistence farming, hunting and fishing.

But the thick dust clogged their throats and their conversation petered out. Not able to see their watches, they lost track of time. Eventually, exhaustion caught up with them. Instead of signaling their location together, they took turns. Even so, the silent periods became longer and longer. Their rapping became weaker as thirst, hunger and despair took their toll. Joe's injured head was throbbing again and he found it harder and harder to keep his eyes open.

He thought he was dreaming at first when he heard the sounds of rubble being cleared and people shouting. Then his eyes, accustomed to total darkness, were blinded by a piercing beam of light. Strong hands reached in and pulled Emma and him out, freeing them at last from their tiny, tenebrous prison.

* * *

Emma quietly left the room when she saw that Joe had fallen back to sleep. His battered face twitched with the force of his dreams.

Chapter 35

Emma returned the next day. Joe's eyes fluttered open when she sat down.

"They still haven't found you a roommate, huh?" she said, glancing at the empty bed next to his. "Anyway, I brought you a gift."

She pointed to the staff leaning against her chair. The spare talisman, looking a little worse for wear, was still tied to the rod's tip with Junie's scrunchie. "The rescue workers told me they had to pry it from your hand. I informed them that it was a valuable antique and insisted they hand it over to me for safekeeping."

He sat up with a groan. She was glad to see him looking more alert.

"Why are you in so much better shape than I am?" he grumbled. "You're up and about and walking around."

"Good genes, I suppose. That and the lack of a brain injury." She quickly added, "In all seriousness though, we're lucky to be alive. The doctors can't stop telling me how lucky I am, and how amazed they are that we're not more badly hurt."

He laughed wryly and she smiled. "I came by to return the staff, but also to let you know that I'll be out of here probably by today. They couldn't find anything wrong with me other than dehydration and a few minor abrasions. I have to go—I need to find out what's happening with Millie."

Joe inexplicably felt abandoned at the thought of her leaving. He stared at his hands, hoping his face showed no sign of his emotions. "We … made a good team," he said at last.

"We did."

"You were *awesome*."

"You were pretty awesome yourself." She smoothed down her hospital gown and cleared her throat. "So, um, before I go, I wanted to th—" she paused and raised her chin, distracted by a slight commotion outside the room. "I think your family's here."

Joe shook his head. He opened his mouth to tell her he didn't have any family that would be visiting him. Before he could say anything, the door cracked open and Junie poked her head in.

"Are you decent?" she asked. "Can we come in?" A balloon floated above her head. It exhorted in capital letters and bright colors: "GET WELL SOON!"

He nodded weakly. Emma stood up. "I'll see you later," she said, patting his hand.

When Emma tried to squeeze past the Soong clan, including Patrick, Stella blocked her way. "Don't go," Stella cried. "We have muffins."

The Soongs hadn't only brought muffins. They also bore flowers, cards and gifts from Joe and Junie's customers who also were Stella's friends. They crowded around Joe's bed, talking all at once.

"I didn't believe, not once, that you were dead," Junie said fervently.

"We were all so worried," Stella said gently.

"How do you feel?" Raymond asked solicitously.

"What does it feel like to be trapped in a collapsed building?" Patrick asked curiously. "Is it true about what they say about your life flashing before your eyes? And about your head trauma—would you mind coming up to Baltimore to do some tests? After you're discharged, of course. I'm interested in the level of deterioration to your cognitive abilities."

Patrick ducked when his father pretended to cuff his head.

Joe wasn't used to so much goodwill and warmth. Or having so many people concerned about his well-being. He found himself choking up, and blamed it on delayed reaction to the stress of almost dying. He was thankful his mouth was full of muffin so he didn't have to talk.

Emma managed to escape while Stella's back was turned. Raymond made everyone except Junie leave when he saw Joe's eyelids drooping. "Let the man rest," he said. "That's the best thing for a head injury."

Finally, Joe and Junie were alone. She took the chair previously occupied by Emma. He eyed her arm in the cast. "What happened to you?"

"The yaoguai broke my arm just before I killed it. I'll give you the full details later." Raymond had shut the door behind him but she kept her voice low out of an abundance of caution. "The arm should recover soon, but I plan on wearing the cast for a month so no one asks questions. By the way, are we done with the portal?"

"Yes. I sealed it with the talisman, with Emma's help."

"What happened to your head? Was that caused by the cave-in?"

"Yaoguai," he said tersely. "Hit me with a brick. Any news about Millie?"

"My dad said she's been transferred back to his hospital. She seems to have slipped into some kind of deep coma and is unresponsive. Speaking of unresponsive, I contacted your mother to let her know about the collapse, and the rescue."

"What did she say?"

"Not much."

He nodded morosely. "That sounds like Elsie. Any idea how long I'll be stuck here?"

"I was getting to that. My dad spoke with your doctors, who released your information only because we're relatives. Pa may have slightly exaggerated how closely related we are. Anyway, the gash in your head required stitches. Fourteen, to be exact.

"The good news is there's no swelling or bleeding in your brain. They say you can be discharged as early as tomorrow afternoon, as long as there's someone around to make sure you aren't having seizures or throwing up. Today's Saturday, by the way, in case you didn't know. I'll return tomorrow to fetch you back to the apartment."

"You don't have to do that."

"Of course I do," she said in surprise. "I can't let you go home by yourself. Since it's the weekend, you can pay me overtime if that makes you feel better."

* * *

To his disgust, they made him sit in a wheelchair while he signed his discharge documents. An attendant wheeled him out. Junie walked alongside carrying the staff and his belongings. Stella picked them both up in her car.

Stella pulled up in front of the Laughing Buddha and Noah hastened out. He opened the car door before Joe could. "Glad you're still with us, Joe."

Noah avoided making eye contact with Junie when he reached in to help Joe out of the car.

At the stairwell, Joe insisted he didn't need further assistance so Noah went back to work. However, Junie couldn't be dissuaded from holding onto his arm as he tottered up the stairs.

To his dismay, his progress up the two flights was painstakingly slow, even with her help. He was winded, and slightly dizzy, when he finally made it to the top. Junie steered him carefully through the office and into the apartment.

He reached his boiling point when she tried to fluff the sofa cushions with her good arm before he sat down. "I'm not an invalid," he barked sourly.

"You are," she said patiently. "For the time being anyway."

* * *

Junie phoned Dan's wife, Ayanna, on Monday. She half-dreaded what Ayanna would say.

"Mrs. Groskind, it's Junie Soong."

"Junie, I'm so glad you called." Ayanna's voice was warm, and Junie released a fervent sigh of relief.

"How is Dan doing?"

"He made it through the night we spoke and has been steadily improving ever since. I'm here now at the hospital with him. Would you like to speak with him?"

Junie put her cell phone on speaker mode and joined Joe on the sofa. "Hello Dan, how are you?" he asked.

"Fine." Dan's raspy voice sounded almost back to normal. "The doctors have given me a preliminary clean bill of health. They're patting themselves on the back and pronouncing it a goddamn miracle. I know, though, where the credit should go. I'm grateful you two could finish the business. I think my life kinda depended on it."

"You're welcome. Our lives kind of depended on it as well."

"Yeah, I heard about your adventure," he said dryly. "Why did you have to trash the house after I expended so much effort into building it? All jokes aside, I'm glad you and Junie are safe. Did the blueprints help?"

"They helped tremendously," Joe said. "We couldn't have done it without you."

"My pleasure. I hope you kicked some ass. Is it finally over?"

"Almost. There are still a few loose ends we have to tie up."

After they ended the call, Joe told Junie one of the loose ends was Millie. "Let's see her today. The yaoguai is gone—her health should be improving, like Dan's. Why is she comatose? Can you call Emma and arrange a visit at the hospital?"

"No, Joe," she said firmly. "You're still recovering yourself. Pa warned me in strict terms not to let you do anything too taxing or exciting. You're supposed to take it easy for at least seven to 10 days, remember?"

In the end, he reluctantly agreed to put off the visit for a week.

Chapter 36

Emma met them at the door to Millie's room. It was the same one she—or more accurately, her yaoguai double—had occupied before.

"Any change in her condition?" Joe whispered.

"Yes, but not for the better." Emma crossed her arms tightly across her chest. "Her vital organs are beginning to shut down. The doctors are flummoxed. They don't know what's wrong, other than the fact that she's slowly dying. They've performed every test they can think of. All the tests, including PET—positron emission tomography—scans of her body and brain, have come back normal. It's like medically she's fine, but somehow she's lost the will to live."

She stared miserably at Millie, whose eyes remained stubbornly closed.

"How are *you* doing?" he asked after a long silence.

"Good, good." Emma brushed a lock of hair back behind one ear. She looked much better than the last time he saw her. She was allowing her brown hair to fall forward so that it framed her face and concealed some of her healing cuts and bruises. He thought the effect very attractive.

"How about yourself?" she asked. Her tone was casual, but her gaze intense as she examined his face.

"Getting better every day."

"And you?" She glanced at Junie's arm in the sling.

"I'm fine, thanks," Junie said. The sling was only for show. She had already removed the cast with Joe's help, giving up on her plan to wear it longer. It was just too much of a hindrance.

While the other two continued talking, Junie circled the bed. Millie, her skin waxen, lay very still against the white sheets, like a carved effigy on a marble tomb.

She felt somewhat responsible for Millie's condition. Should she have done more for her at the house? This was far worse than the catatonic state in which she had left her. At the time, at least her eyes were open. Now there was no sign of life other than the almost imperceptible rise and fall of her chest.

Junie stopped short on the other side of the bed, her attention arrested by a silver picture frame on the bedside table. The photo in the frame showed a much younger Millie, a man and a small boy. The man rested one hand on Millie's shoulder; her arms were clasped around the boy. Her smile was radiant; her eyes sparkled with joy and pride. The boy was blond and cherubic, his hands thrust out toward the camera as if reaching for the world.

Emma noticed Junie studying the photo. "That's Millie with her husband and son," she said.

"Son?" Joe queried. "She's never mentioned a son."

"Yeah." Emma dropped her voice. "It's pretty sad. The boy passed away at a young age. I believe it was brain cancer. Cancer got her husband too, but her son's the reason why she contributes so heavily to pediatric oncology research and causes."

Emma picked up the frame. "She treasures this photo. She told me it shows her at her happiest, before she and her husband learned about their son's condition. I asked the firefighters to retrieve it from the house, pleading that it may help in her recovery. I didn't realize at the time that she might not ever wake up." She shrugged helplessly.

"Do you know the son's name?" Junie asked, her eyes still fixed on the photo.

"Oliver. His name was Oliver. Actually, he was named Dominic Oliver Scarpini Jr., after Millie's husband, but they called him Oliver."

So the little blond boy had a name. *Oliver.* It suited him.

Emma peered quizzically at her. "Why are you so interested in the picture?"

Joe was looking at her as well. "What is it, Junie?"

"Joe, that's the blond boy I keep seeing."

"What do you mean?" Emma asked in bewilderment. "You can't have seen him. He's dead. He's been dead for almost three decades. He died before you were born."

"When was the last time you saw him?" Joe asked.

"I told you, remember? When Noah and I were at the Mall, just before I got Ayanna's call. Oliver appeared and warned me that the mogui was coming."

"Have you seen him since?" he asked.

"No."

"Can you recall when you *first* saw him?"

"I think it was the first night I slept in your spare room. It was the same day that Dan told us about the cellar and asked us to check on Millie."

"And all this time I thought the boy was your alter ego, like that weird kid and his finger in the movie *The Shining*." Joe took the frame from Emma. "Was this in Millie's room all this time and we missed it?" He stared intently at the photo.

"If Millie is lost somewhere in her own mind because of the yaoguai, I have an idea of how we can communicate with her," he said at last. "Perhaps Oliver can be of assistance."

Emma gaped. "*What?* Do I have to keep reminding you two that the boy's dead?"

"Junie can try to contact him. She and Oliver seem to share a special connection. He views her as his ally." He turned to her. "But be careful. Remember what I said about sentient ghosts having their own agendas."

"You handle ghosts too, not just demons and feng shui?" Emma asked.

"Yes," Joe said dryly. "We're a full-services practice."

"Joe, what kind of agenda can Oliver have other than protecting his mother?" Junie was indignant on her little friend's behalf. "He can't be more than five years old!"

"Ghost children are the worst," he said soberly. "They're all impulse, without any regard for consequences. They're difficult to reason with, they're challenging to restrain and they're impossible to predict. In short, a ghost child behaves exactly like a living child."

"Are we going to banish him with the bell, like we did with all those ghosts in the cellar?" Junie looked aghast.

"We'll worry about that when the time comes. For now, let's just try to summon him."

"Wait a minute, did you just say there were ghosts in the cellar?" Emma was more bemused than ever. "Why is this the first time I'm hearing about it?"

Joe quickly explained what he and Junie had done that day when Emma first met them and let them into the cellar.

"I wondered what all the loud clanging was about," she said when he finished. "So you want to summon Oliver here?" She indicated the door. "Someone could walk in at any moment."

"You're right," Joe acknowledged. "We need somewhere more private. I don't want a doctor or nurse barging in. Let's do it at the office."

Emma insisted on coming along, so they rode back in her car. Once there, Joe shut and locked the door and let down the blinds.

"Ghosts prefer a poorly lit environment," he said. "To be clear, they can appear in day- or nighttime, but it's harder for them to manifest in bright sunlight, don't ask me why. Perhaps it's something to do with the sun's ultraviolet rays.

"Ghosts also can be either sentient or non-sentient. It's a spectrum, like anything else. The totally non-sentient or residual ones haven't caught up to the fact that they're dead. They haunt specific places. When they appear, they repeatedly perform an action that was significant to them in life. They're not aware of the things around them.

"Sentient ghosts, on the other hand, are more likely to haunt people, although they can haunt places as well. As I reminded Junie, they usually have an agenda or some unfinished business that may not be obvious to us. Oliver clearly is sentient since he interacts with Junie and reacts to the things happening to his mother."

"Why do you think he's appearing now?" Emma asked. "Was it something to do with the yaoguai?"

"I think he's always been with Millie," Joe said. "She herself may not have known because not everyone can see or sense ghosts."

He rubbed his chin absently. "That would make sense," he muttered to himself. "A child dying too young, a mother who can't let go of her grief. A mother's yearning can be powerful enough to tether her deceased children and prevent them from moving on."

He frowned at Emma. "I have a question for you. Did you notice any changes in Millie's behavior right around the time that the sinkhole appeared?"

"Hmm." She chewed her bottom lip. "I remember thinking she was a little scatterbrained at times, which isn't like her. She's usually laser-focused, and very organized. And she was upset about the contractor's heart attack, of course. But she bounced right back after that, as sharp as ever, and brimming with ideas for the party."

She hesitated. "No, wait, that isn't totally accurate. She was *mostly* herself after she announced she was going to have the housewarming, but there still were a few occasions when she seemed out of it and couldn't recall what we'd previously discussed or agreed to do. But those times were so few and far between that I didn't think anything of it. I just assumed she was distracted by all the things she had to do to get the house ready for the party."

He nodded. "I would say by then that the sharp Millie was the yaoguai, and the forgetful Millie the real one."

"On reflection, it *was* like two completely different people."

Joe brought the conversation back to Oliver. "When the first yaoguai broke through, Oliver's ghost may have benefited from the power seeping up through the portal, like the spirits in the cellar," he said. "If so, the first thing he would do with his new strength is reach out to his mother. If my theory is correct, Millie has been seeing her son since the sinkhole opened. Did she ever mention anything?"

Emma shook her head, but promptly added, "Even if she did see him, I don't think she would have admitted it. I mean, confess that she's seeing her *dead son*? The old Millie would have immediately checked herself into the loony bin. However, let's say you're right that Oliver piggybacked on the vortex's energy, like the other ghosts. Now that the portal is sealed, won't he revert back to being invisible and powerless?"

"No. The seal prevents more energy from escaping the vortex, but it doesn't affect the energy that's already leaked. And remember, when Junie and I dissipated the energy of the cellar ghosts, Millie wasn't at home, which means Oliver wasn't either. So his energy hasn't been dispelled and he's still potent. And he must be pretty potent if he can appear to Junie anytime he wants."

"What do you think Oliver can do to help Millie?" Emma asked.

"If Oliver is as potent as I think he is, he can bring her back from wherever she's gone," Joe said. "At the very least, he can try to find out what's happening with her."

"So how do we summon him?" Junie asked impatiently. "And what do I say to him?"

"Summoning is the easy part. Just make yourself comfortable and call to him. You can do it aloud or in your head, whichever you prefer. He'll hear you either way if he's still around. Once he answers, ask him why his mother won't wake up."

Junie pointed to her desk. "Can I do it from here?"

When Joe nodded, she sat down and shut her eyes. "Oliver! Oliver!" she said to herself. "Can you hear me?" She mentally willed the ghost child to respond.

Dead silence. Emma cleared her throat, the sound loud in the quiet room. "Sorry," she whispered when the other two turned to her. "Throat itch."

Junie gave up after a while. "He's not answering," she said flatly.

Joe patted her arm. "Maybe I'm wrong and he's gone on. But it was worth a try."

After Emma left, Junie asked Joe how he knew so much about ghosts. "I know you can't see them. Did your knowledge come from your father? Weren't you only 10 when he passed away? How did he manage to teach you so much?"

He looked slightly guilty before divulging that most of his information came from watching ghost hunting programs on cable TV.

"They're actually very instructive," he said stiffly.

* * *

Oliver came to Junie that night. "What do you want?" he asked. He sat cross-legged at the foot of her bed, as he had done the first time she saw him.

She was in that state where she was sleeping, but awake enough to direct her dream. "We're concerned about your mother," she said. "She won't wake up. Do you know why?"

He beamed. "She won't wake up because she's with me, Junie. We're having fun together."

"Oliver, you know she can't stay with you. She needs to wake up. You have to tell her to wake up."

He drew back as though she had struck him. His little face crumpled, then his features scrunched up in a mutinous scowl. "Why? I like having her with me. She can't ignore me like she used to. I was mad before when she acted like I wasn't there even though I shouted and shouted as loud as I could. But she can see and hear me now. I want us to stay like that forever. I want her to stay with me forever."

"Oliver—"

He rose and stamped his foot, his face black with anger. "I don't want her to wake up. I won't let her wake up! I WON'T LET HER WAKE UP!"

Junie was wrenched abruptly out of her dream state. Her ears were still ringing when she sat up in bed. It was a steamy night outside, but her room was freezing. She discovered her upper arms were riddled with goosebumps.

Beyond the cold, she felt something she had not experienced before in her interactions with the little boy: heart-thumping fear.

Chapter 37

She told Joe about her encounter with Oliver in the morning.

"That's not good." He frowned and made her repeat what the ghost boy said. "It sounds as if Oliver's the one keeping Millie in her vegetative condition. He seems to have more agency than most ghosts, certainly more than the apparitions in the cellar. The little hellion must have been hoarding energy from the vortex all this while, until we finally sealed the portal."

"He was furious, so furious he couldn't stop shaking," Junie said worriedly. "And why does he need her in a coma? Why can't she be awake? I've seen him when I wasn't sleeping."

"Perhaps it takes more energy for him to manifest to those who are awake," he said. "Or maybe he has more control over her when she's asleep."

"I can't say I blame the little fella." Joe ran his hand over his stubble while he brooded. "Ghosts, sentient or non-sentient, generally are to be pitied. They're stuck in place while the people they loved continue with their lives. Many of them are doomed to relive their worst moments over and over again until something happens to break the cycle. Even the sentient ones may not realize they're dead, so they feel abandoned or rejected by their friends and loved ones."

He sighed. "It's an unenviable plight. It explains why so many of them have disagreeable dispositions. Even the nicest people can become certifiably insane after years and years of isolation and hopelessness.

"In Oliver's case, anger is common with spectral children, especially those who died very young. He doesn't fully comprehend what's happened, or why people, especially his mom, keep pretending he isn't there. Most ghosts need a little help to move on—you know, go into the light—but I believe Oliver has enough power to do it on his own. If we can persuade him to do that, he might also willingly release Millie."

"Can you be more specific about 'moving on'?" She was uneasy, still feeling protective of the child despite his tantrum last night. "Where exactly do they go?"

"I don't know," he admitted. "Different religions and philosophies posit different destinations. But unless he takes that step, he'll remain a child forever, chained to Millie until she dies, in which case he will be stuck alone in that shadow realm between the living and the dead, otherwise known as 'limbo'. Surely moving on—which after all is part and parcel of the natural cycle—is preferable to that."

"It may be a tough sell," she said doubtfully. "He seems pretty happy now. And if Millie dies, won't she just join him in whichever plane of existence he's in? Won't he and his mother be together forever, like he wants?"

"There is no guarantee. It takes quite a lot of determination and stubbornness to linger on, and even if Millie wants to, she may not have that kind of resolve. In any case"—Joe tapped his index finger on the table to emphasize his point—"she has a life to live, and the dead shouldn't be allowed to interfere with the living. Not to mention she's our client and she hired us to protect her from supernatural beings. That includes her spectral progeny. We haven't finished the job as long as she's in danger from him.

"Now if Oliver can't be persuaded to leave of his own volition, we may have to do it the hard way, which is to forcefully banish him with the bell. The risk of doing that is Millie might not be able to wake from her coma without Oliver's help."

"What's the difference between what we did in the cellar and forceful banishment?"

"Technically, in terms of what *we* have to do, not much," he said. "The difference has to do more with the entity's state of mind at the time of the exorcism or banishment. If the entity is ready to go, then it views the ritual as a release. If it wants to stay in the material plane, it will view the ritual as a forceful eviction. As it passes on, any feelings of rage, bitterness or frustration can have negative connotations for its afterlife, or the next phase, or whatever you want to call it."

Junie recalled how relieved Matias looked when they freed his apparition in the cellar. Oliver, on the other hand, would hate being torn away from his mother again, especially now that she was acknowledging him and responding to him. Junie couldn't bear to punish the little boy when he had been such a great help.

"Let's try persuasion first," she told Joe. "I think banishment should be the last resort."

A new thought struck her. "Joe, what if Millie actually *wants* to die and join him?"

"Well, it'll be nice if she can communicate that somehow," he said dourly. "Is it our fault if the client can't issue clear instruction?"

* * *

Joe phoned Emma to make another appointment to visit Millie. "Is there any way in which we can be assured of some privacy, say for about half an hour?" he asked.

"What are you thinking of doing?"

"We're going to try to contact Oliver at Millie's bedside."

He recounted what the wraith said to Junie in her dream. "Oliver's mad at Junie, so he probably won't come when she calls. However, we can increase our chances of summoning him by doing it at the hospital, since he's probably sticking close to his mother's corporeal body. Junie will try to reason with him. If the kid won't listen to reason, we'll proceed to banishment, which involves ringing the bell. It's going to be loud, and it may alarm some, or maybe most, people."

"A hospital's already a pretty noisy environment, what with all the chirping machinery, loud ventilation systems and crackly intercoms," Emma said. "Add to that doctors, nurses, orderlies and visitors talking and bustling about. If you have to ring the bell, just do it. I don't see that we have much choice. If you wait any longer, Millie's health will continue to deteriorate to the point of irreparable damage.

"Anyhow, what's the worst that can happen if someone notices the ringing or is bothered by it? They'll just ask you to leave. Or throw you out.

"As an extra precaution, I'll stand outside the door and keep watch," she added. "If anyone approaches, I'll try to stop him or her from entering, or at least give you a heads-up if the person insists on coming in."

"Thanks. How will you stop them from entering?"

"Let me worry about that," she said. "You get Millie out of her coma."

* * *

They brought the luopan as well as the bell in the new leather bag Joe bought to replace the one that was still in the cellar.

When he and Junie trooped in, Emma took a chair from the room and placed it just outside the door. She closed the door behind them and sat on the chair, prepared to head off other visitors and nosy hospital staff.

"Hello Millie." Joe felt compelled to greet her even though he didn't expect a response. And he didn't receive any. Her face was impassive and relaxed, as if she had no more worldly cares.

He handed the luopan to Junie. When she touched it, the device's needle moved until it pointed downward, at the south-southeast direction of an ordinary compass.

"I think that's what's called a 'sinking' needle," he said. "It signals the presence of a restless spirit. I think we can safely assume that he's here."

She passed the luopan back and sat cross-legged on the carpet, believing the little boy would be more comfortable if she were at his eye level. "Oliver! Oliver!" she thought without saying his name out loud. "Come. We need to talk."

Nothing happened, but she could tell from the pregnant atmosphere that something was listening.

"*Oliver!*" She injected more urgency into her summoning. "*Oliver!* You better come now or we're going to do something you won't like."

She felt a momentary chill, as if a cloud was moving past the sun. She blinked and Oliver materialized in front of her, seated on the carpet like she was.

"What do you want?" he asked belligerently.

"You left before we finished our conversation. We were talking about your mother."

"I told you I don't want her to wake up. If she wakes up, she'll go back to ignoring me. I don't like to be ignored."

He glowered at her. "I'm little," he whined. "She's not supposed to leave me on my own. She's my *Mommy*. She's supposed to take care of me and love me. I don't want her to stop loving me. I don't want her to stop being with me."

Junie pointed to Millie on the bed. "It's not good for your mom to sleep like that. She has a life to live."

"Why can't she live her life with me?" His eyes welled up with tears, and she felt terrible for making him cry.

Joe couldn't see or hear Oliver, but he could see Junie and hear her half of the conversation. He saw her hesitate. "Don't let him manipulate you," he warned.

Was Oliver manipulating her? The tyke seemed genuinely distressed. She softened her tone. "Oliver, you have to let your mother go. You have to move on. It's part of the natural order. What you're doing isn't how things should be."

The boy's cheeks were flushed. He was about to fly off the handle again.

"Oliver," she said sternly, channeling her fiercest teachers in elementary school. "You must listen to me. I'm trying to help Millie."

He clambered to his feet, his pudgy hands balled into fists, his demeanor threatening. "It was me!" he shouted. "I was the one who helped Millie, not you. *I* helped Millie! She doesn't need you. All she needs is me!"

She and Joe jumped when the bathroom door suddenly slammed shut. One of the chairs beside Millie's bed toppled over. A bedpan hurled itself across the room, narrowly missing Junie, who ducked just in time. The metallic pan hit the door with a loud clatter and fell to the floor, a large dent in its side. Fortunately, it was empty. It left a deep gouge in the door.

Emma's alarmed face peeped in through the door's narrow glass panels. One of the machines surrounding Millie emitted loud, insistent beeps.

"Junie." Joe placed his hand on her shoulder. "Millie's heart is racing. Someone will be coming in soon."

Oliver was gone. Junie stood up just as the door burst open. A nurse dashed in and fiddled with the beeping equipment. "I'll have to ask you two to leave," he said distractedly.

Joe grabbed Junie's shoulders and propelled her out of the room. Emma accompanied them to a secluded corner. "What happened?" she asked. "When that pan smacked into the door, I was so startled I almost fell off my chair."

"Oliver," he said tersely. "Oliver happened. The boy was having a major snit fit."

"He wouldn't listen to me," Junie said. "I tried to tell him we were helping his mother, but he claimed he was the one helping her, not us."

Joe knit his brow and sighed heavily. "I think we have no choice but to do it the hard way."

"No," Junie cried. "Let me try again. I'm sure I can get through to him."

He looked somberly at her. "Did you see what he did? He aimed that bedpan at you. You could have been badly hurt. Don't be fooled by the kid's cute exterior. I think the power is going to his head. It's corrupting him. It's amplifying his innate willfulness. He's no longer that innocent, defenseless child he once was. He likes being the strong one. He likes having his way. We must stop him before he does more damage to Millie or anyone else."

"But if we banish him, won't Millie be trapped in the coma?" she protested.

"We'll have to take our chances," he growled. "If we don't deal with Oliver now, he'll only get bolder and more out of control."

"What would the Golden Dragon have done?" she asked desperately.

"The Golden Dragon wouldn't have thought twice about banishing the boy. He didn't have much patience for wayward spirits. You're a *Dragon*, Junie. You cannot afford to be soft. You have responsibilities."

She locked eyes with him and stared him down. "Well, Joe, as a *Dragon*, I say we give the kid another chance." She quoted one of her father's maxims. "Compassion doesn't cost anything, and its rewards are beyond measure."

He looked away first. Junie was the new Dragon, and she had the final say in how she exercised her abilities.

"Alright," he said with ill grace. "Spare me the fortune cookie platitudes. It's your call."

Chapter 38

They returned the following day. "Good luck," Emma said. She gave them hearty pats on the back for good measure before going outside and parking herself at the door again.

Junie sat on the floor. Joe knelt in front of her.

"Be careful, okay?" He glanced over his shoulder at Millie, as if afraid she was eavesdropping, and lowered his voice. "Having routed you once, the boy will be even more confident now."

She nodded. As she prepared to summon Oliver, she couldn't help but notice that Joe stepped as far away from her as he could to the other side of the room.

She didn't have to wait long this time. The spectral child whirled into being as if riding in on a storm. Her hair blew away from her face with the force of his manifestation. Before she could utter a word, he boomed, his voice like a clap of thunder, "Go away! Go away!"

He came close to her and glared, his face barely an inch from hers. His eyes burned like lit coals. His cherubic countenance was replaced by something much older, vastly uglier. For a moment there, he didn't look like a child, or even human. She flinched when he snarled like a feral animal.

Joe was right. The boy was reveling in his own power.

"Go away! GO AWAY!" Oliver's shouts grew steadily louder. He repeated the words faster and faster until they became unintelligible. "GO AWAY!   GOAWAY!   GOAWAY!   GOAWAY!

GOAWAYGOAWAYGOAWAYGO—"

The items on Millie's bedside tables quivered. The furniture itself started to tremble. The bathroom door slammed, like it had done yesterday. Millie's heart rate sped up. Joe stealthily took the bell from his bag. He held it aloft and tried to catch Junie's eye.

"Wait." She held up her hand. "Oliver," she said sharply. "Oliver. Stop shouting. Listen. To. Me."

The boy closed his eyes and rammed his fingers into his ears. "GOAWAYGOAWAYGOAWAYGOAWAY!" He was now screeching at the top of his lungs. His words became a shrill, relentless keening that drilled into her brain.

She clapped her hands over her own ears. Her eardrums and her brain hurt. Over Oliver's strident shrieking, she somehow heard Joe calling her name. He got one clang out of the bell before it flew out of his hands.

Joe kept calling her name. Oliver's screams rose in pitch and volume, if that were possible, and drowned him out. Still seated, she threw her arms over her head and scrunched her face down between her knees. She didn't know how much longer she could withstand the piercing aural attack. Her head felt like it was about to explode.

She was caught completely by surprise when an invisible force gripped her and flung her roughly onto her back. As she lay supine, her whole body pinned to the floor, Oliver's screeching stopped. The child climbed on her and jumped up and down on her ribs as though he was in a bouncy castle.

"Junie, look," he suddenly said. "Look! I'm a wheelbarrow."

She gasped when the tyke's weight abruptly increased. He sat down cross-legged on her chest and carefully observed her panicked expression.

Joe dashed over when he saw her flop backward. While he was oblivious of the phantom child, Oliver was highly entertained by Joe's attempts to lift her.

"Junie, Junie, now I'm a car!" The boy became even heavier.

Junie's gasps changed to labored wheezing. It felt as if an actual automobile was balanced on her chest and compressing her lungs. The specter watched dispassionately as she struggled to breathe. She seemed to him no more than a bug he had found in the tall grass.

"Junie, now I'm a ... tank!" Oliver proudly announced.

Joe was distressed when Junie's face turned a mottled purple and her limbs twitched. She was suffocating, although he couldn't understand why. He gave up trying to raise her and ran for the door. There were doctors outside who might be able to help, or at least figure out what was going on.

He discovered that the door was stuck; he couldn't open it no matter how hard he twisted and jerked the knob. Looking up, he saw faces, including Emma's, peeking at him through the door's glass panels. Voices yelled at him to let them into the room. He could do nothing except kick and pound the door in frustration.

Junie was on the verge of blacking out when she thought she heard something. She almost missed the soft voice amid the cacophony of Joe's cursing and furious assault on the door, the shouting outside and Millie's beeping devices.

"Oliver," the voice said again, a little louder this time. "Oliver. Oliver."

The ghost obviously heard the voice as well. He turned his head toward the bed. Even though he was still sitting on Junie, the weight on her chest magically disappeared and she gasped greedily for air.

Joe glanced over his shoulder at the sound of her raspy breathing. "What's happening?" he asked frantically. He followed her gaze to the bed. All he saw was Millie lying on the white sheets, no different from before.

Junie saw what Joe saw, but she also could see a second, younger Millie perched on the bed's edge. She strongly resembled the Millie in the photo, except she was slightly translucent at the edges.

"Oliver." Young Millie spoke gently but firmly. "Oliver, it's time for you to go."

"Mommy." The boy hopped clumsily off Junie's chest and ran to the woman. "I don't want to go," he said. "I want to play some more. Junie can play with us. We can all play together for always.

"Oliver." Young Millie spoke gently but firmly. "Oliver, it's time for you to go."

"It's time for you to go," Young Millie repeated. "It's time. I have to let you go. I release you."

"I don't want to go," the child grumbled. "I don't want to leave you."

"You must," she said. "You can't stay anymore. You're free." Tears started down her cheeks. "You're free."

She rose swiftly from the bed and swept Oliver up in a fierce hug. He resisted at first, shoving her and slapping at her hands, but she didn't let go. "You're free," she reiterated. "You're free. I'm setting you free." She kissed the top of his tousled head as he writhed in her arms.

He finally stopped fighting and buried his face in her chest. "You're free," she kept whispering. One hand stroked her son's back. She kept the other clamped tightly around his waist to make sure he couldn't get away.

"Do you love me, Mommy?" he mumbled.

"I love you to the moon and back," she said.

"I love you to the sun and back," he replied. He sighed and snuggled against her. "I'm tired, Mommy." He stuck his thumb in his mouth.

"Shhhhh," she said. "You've had a long day."

"I've had a long day," he echoed obediently. His arms crept around her neck, his legs around her waist. He lay his head on her shoulder.

"Close your eyes," she said. "Go to sleep now. My most precious boy, my baby, it's time for you to rest."

Junie sat up and wearily rubbed her hand across her face. Young Millie carried Oliver to the door, murmuring endearments all the while. Mother and child were becoming so faint they could hardly be seen against the hospital's tasteful beige and white décor.

Junie watched them disappear through the door. She started when she felt pressure on her shoulder. She looked up to see Joe nodding at the bed.

Millie, the older version, was awake. Her face was cradled in her hands; she sobbed as if her heart was not only broken but cleaved in two.

Junie heard the door crash open behind her. Emma, a doctor and an orderly spilled into the room and rushed to Millie's side.

Joe picked up his bag. "I think," he said as he helped her to her feet, "it's time for us to go."

Chapter 39

Emma phoned two weeks later. "Can you come to the hospital? Millie would like to see you and Junie."

Millie sat up when they stepped into the room. She looked wan, but at peace. Her experiences had aged her, but they also gave rise to a new serenity. There was little trace of the restless urgency that had spurred her former hectic life.

"I'm glad to see you doing better," Joe said.

"Thank you. I'm doing so well they're releasing me this afternoon."

"Will you be recuperating in D.C.?"

"Actually, Emma is driving me to my beach house in Maine." She smiled at Emma. "I'll be doing nothing except lying back and enjoying the sun, the sand and the sea. Well, maybe I'll throw in a little sailing and fishing, and maybe some light reading and casual beachcombing. And lots of good food—my housekeeper there also is an excellent cook." She grinned, looking for a split second like the young woman in the photo.

"Sounds like heaven," Joe said. "What are your plans after Maine?"

"I'm going to focus on my charity, which is geared toward childhood cancer research. I think Emma may have mentioned it to you. It's called Oliver's Moon and Sun Foundation."

Millie's eyes sought out Junie. "The foundation is named after something I said to my son every night when I tucked him in bed."

Junie dipped her head slightly to indicate that she understood the reference.

Emma cleared her throat. "By the way, I wanted to let both of you know that the police have concluded their investigation of the cave-in.

"They called this morning. They've determined that the incident was an accident—or at least not caused deliberately or with ill intent. It was something to do with the collection of natural gas in the sinkhole. The independent consultant who came up with the explanation apparently is quite the expert."

"That's good," Joe said. "What will you do with the house?"

"I'm focusing on the immediate future, which is fixing whatever's necessary to make the house habitable again," Millie said. "Once that's done, I may—depending on my mood—sell it or move in again. I don't know yet. I haven't decided."

Junie, spying Millie's pensive expression, wondered if she could ever feel safe in the house again.

"I'd like to suggest a safeguard." Joe glanced at Emma, tacitly asking whether she had filled Millie in about the yaoguai. She nodded, and he told Millie and Emma what he had in mind.

"That should protect the seal and ensure the portal never is opened again," he said.

"Emma will call Dan before we leave D.C.," Millie said. "Will that be the end of it?"

"I sincerely hope so," he said.

His words were followed by a long silence. Joe caught Junie's eye and shuffled his feet.

"Before you go," Millie said quickly, "I have something I'd like to get off my chest. It's something I've held on to for far too long."

Her eyes flicked once more to Junie. "You have to understand that *my* Oliver was the sweetest child. He was also smart as a whip, funny, and quirky, and kind. He loved pancakes, and ice cream, and fudge, and chocolate syrup. He loved tumbling down hillsides and racing against the wind and catching snowflakes on his tongue. He loved to dig for earthworms in the rain and jumping in puddles. His laugh was infectious; his smile lit up my world. The boy you saw in the hospital wasn't *my* Oliver. It's important to me that you know that. You never saw Oliver at his best."

Her gaze slid down to her clasped hands. "He was four years, seven months, 20 days and eight hours old when he passed away. Despite having money and the best doctors, we discovered the cancer too late—it was inoperable by the time they found it. He never had a chance.

"And my baby was brave up to the very end even though he suffered excruciating pain. It was I who was the coward. I couldn't bear a life without my little boy. As the cancer ravaged his brain, I kept telling him to hang on. I kept hoping and praying for a miracle so he wouldn't leave me."

Her words spilled out in their haste to be released. "I hardly left his bedside during his last days. But one night, a night when my husband wasn't at the hospital with me, I just felt overwhelmed. I was suffocating in that room watching my son wither away. When I couldn't take it any longer, I left the hospital and walked around the block to clear my head. On the way back, I stopped at a cooler for a drink of water. I couldn't have been away for more than 20 minutes, but when I returned, Oliver was gone. He didn't ... he couldn't wait."

She dashed away her tears with the heel of her hand. Emma moved toward her but she fiercely waved her away. "I was prostrate with grief," she continued, "but I also was consumed by rage. I was angry with God for taking my child; I was angry at the world. Most of all though, I was angry at myself. I couldn't forgive myself for letting Oliver die alone. And I"—her breath hitched—"I couldn't forgive him for not waiting.

"I think I was more than a little unhinged that night. I wouldn't leave him and they had to pull me off. I was hospitalized for some time. A piece of me died with my son and I've never felt whole since. If not for my husband, I don't think I would have been able to go on.

"Time passed. The minutes became hours; the hours turned into days, the days lapsed into months, then years. I learned to cope. My husband and I never stopped mourning, but we had a good life nonetheless. After Dom died, I soldiered on and tried to do some good with my money.

"Then out of the blue, I had that frightening experience in the cellar. I called you and Dan, and I was relieved, and a little ashamed at my own histrionics, when you found nothing more eerie than a sinkhole. But the weirdness didn't end after you left. It only got worse.

"I began to see and hear Oliver in the house. It was just glimpses at first, then he started staying longer. One night while I was sleeping, he came right up to the bed." She touched her forehead. "He kissed me there ... I could actually feel his lips ... and he told me he never left, he'd stayed by my side like I begged him to.

"As you can imagine, part of me was overjoyed at having my little boy back, and part of me was scared that I was losing my mind again. But I couldn't help myself. I kept asking him to come back. And the more real Oliver seemed, the less real the world became. It was as if I was stuck in a dream that wouldn't end. I started losing track of time. I had blackout periods in which I couldn't remember where I had been, or whom I had seen and spoken with. People contacted me about plans I didn't remember making."

"It wasn't you," Joe said. "You were under a monster's thrall."

"I know," Millie said. "The death of that nice construction worker —Matias—was like a bucket of ice-cold water thrown in my face. It temporarily drove away the fog that enveloped me. It was only then that I realized there was something else in the house with me and Oliver. At that point, I told Dan to stop work and leave the site. I couldn't let another death be on my conscience. But I couldn't keep the fog away, and things got hazy again. The housewarming itself is a complete blur.

"But I didn't really care, because Oliver was with me. I was so happy that I never wanted to wake up again. And it wasn't really much of a choice, because every time I woke up I was terrified."

She paused to stem a fresh flood of tears. "I would have been content to be with him forever, then I saw how he behaved when Junie tried to talk to him, how he tried to hurt her." She turned to Junie. "Please believe me when I say that raging boy wasn't the son I knew. I realized then that it was my fault. I *caused* him to become that monster. My pain and anger were holding him back; my selfishness was harming him. I knew I had to release him, for his sake as well as mine."

"Is he gone?" Joe asked cautiously.

"Yes, I think so." Millie picked up the photo in the silver frame and held it to her bosom. "I told him to look for Daddy. I hope he and Dom are together now. I hope they're waiting for me and that I'll see them again when it's my time."

Another long silence. Joe was dying to know what happened when

Oliver "crossed over." *Did it involve some kind of a threshold? Did Millie steer her ghost child toward a tunnel of light?* However, she didn't elaborate and, despite his disappointment, he couldn't bring himself to press for details. His avid curiosity was a little unseemly under the circumstances. He sighed to himself and shuffled his feet again.

"Just one more thing before I'm done," Millie said. She nodded to Emma, who presented Joe with a check. As before, he was rendered speechless by the amount written on it.

"Thank you for not giving up on my child," Millie told the geomancer and his apprentice. "Thank you for helping us both to move on."

"In truth, you were the one who exorcised Oliver," he interjected. "I'm not sure I can accept—" He stopped when Emma elbowed him sharply in the ribs. He humbly pocketed the check.

They warmly shook hands and exchanged goodbyes and good wishes. Millie promised to contact them when she returned to D.C., or if she made up her mind about the house.

Emma walked Joe and Junie to the elevators, where she pulled Joe aside. "Can I borrow him for a second?" she asked Junie.

"Sure," Junie said. "I'm going over to the vending machines to get a soda. Come get me when you're done. Take as long as you like."

Emma and Joe stared awkwardly at each other. "I never got the ch—" she said.

"I should have—" he said at the same time.

They laughed. "Me first," she said. "I wanted to thank you for allowing me to help save the world, or at least D.C."

"I couldn't have done it without you. And thank you for pulling me out when part of the ceiling fell. You saved my life."

"It was pretty intense, wasn't it?" Emma smiled. "In hindsight, it was kind of a blast, although nothing I could share with anyone. Who'd believe it?" She paused for a beat and added, "I liked hearing the stories about your father."

"And I liked hearing about your childhood. Is the farm still in the family?"

"Uh, no. After my grandfather died, my grandmother couldn't make the mortgage payments so we lost the farm. My grandmother and I were homeless for a while after that."

"Oh. Gosh. I'm sorry. Did things work out?"

"No. She died and I was placed in foster care."

Her revelation took him by surprise. To his dismay, he couldn't think of an adequate response.

To fill in the uncomfortable silence, she quickly said, "But that's all behind me. What I really wanted was to ask … um … would you like to go out sometime? I mean, I'm off to Maine with Millie, but when I get back, maybe the two of us can grab a coffee or something, or maybe dinner. I'd like to hear more about you and your father's exploits."

He gaped. Was she asking him out on a *date*?

"Or not," she said hurriedly. "It's perfectly fine if you're not interested. You can turn me down. I can take it. I'm a big girl."

"I thought you said I was negative," he blurted out.

"Ah." She eyed him gravely. "Those damn earthquakes interrupted me before I could finish what I was trying to say. Joe, admit it, you're a bottle-half-empty kind of guy. Before you start anything, you've already convinced yourself that you're going to fail. And yet"—she shook her head in wonder—"you do it anyway, to the best of your ability, without hope of wealth or glory, and even if it might cost you your life. You do it because you believe in something beyond your own self-interest. That's truly admirable. In my book, that's the definition of a 'hero'."

"Junie's the real superhero," he stammered.

"Junie is amazing, but how does that negate your own commendable qualities? In fact, you're incredibly brave given that you *don't* possess superpowers. Almost anyone can smash you to a pulp, yet you're willing to take on terrifying supernatural monsters."

"Maybe I'm foolhardy."

"We both know you're well aware of the risks, but you do it anyway because you believe in saving the world. That's noble, and heroic."

No one had ever called him a hero before. *He could love this woman.* He stared mutely at her and she blushed.

"Like I said, you can always turn me down," she said. "I won't hold it against you, I promise."

"No, no," he said hastily. "I'd love to go out with you." He raised his voice, anxious that she would withdraw the invitation.

"Okay, okay. No need to let the whole hospital know." Her face was still red. "I should go now—there are a lot of things to do before Millie can be discharged. We're driving to Maine tomorrow. We should be there only for a couple of months. It's hard to keep Millie from D.C. She has too many roots here."

"I've always been curious—why are you so devoted to her?"

"It's a long story. Let's just say that when I was at my lowest point, she stepped in and offered me a job when no one else would."

Joe wondered what could be harder than losing the family farm, or homelessness, or being an orphan. "What was your lowest point, if you don't mind me asking?"

"When I was discharged from the army."

His mouth fell open. "You're ex-military? Why were you discharged? And what did you do there?"

"Gross insubordination. Military police." She glanced at her watch. "I'll tell you more later, if you really want to know. In the meantime, I'll be in touch about what Dan and Millie decide to do about the cellar."

She brushed her lips against his cheek and strode away.

Joe watched her until she was out of sight. He felt like he was dancing on a cloud with angels.

* * *

On the way home, Junie told him she wanted a raise.

"When I agreed to the pay, I had no idea the job would require me literally to risk life and limb," she said. "I also want health insurance. And we should raise our prices. I've compared our rates to other feng shui practitioners and they're abysmally low. Some outfits charge by the square foot rather than the job, which I think is a good idea. At the very least, we should try to raise our profit margin."

His excellent mood was in danger of evaporating. "What's wrong with my prices?" he demanded. "They've been the same for years, and no one's complained."

Junie didn't bother to respond. He sighed. "I suppose we can set our rates higher. And I should pay you more, and offer you health insurance.

Millie's two checks should cover those, at least for the next few months.

"How about this? I'm promoting you to senior associate, effective immediately. I'll even put your name on the door. You've definitely earned it."

She brightened at the praise. "Wait till you see what I'm planning on social media," she said happily. "It'll knock your socks off. Do you think we can get permission from Millie to take a few photos of the Kalorama house? That'll look impressive on our website. I'm sure it photographs well as long as we don't include the collapsed areas."

"It won't look good if customers find out part of the house collapsed shortly after we were hired to improve its feng shui," he said. "And they'll surely find out—the gas evacuation and the cave-in were widely reported in the news."

"Oh, right." Her face fell. "Oh well. Maybe Shirley Yang will let us photograph her condo. Ma says the new color scheme is stunning. Or how about Ginnie Poon's hair salon? We maybe should have a web page dedicated to small-business owners. We could highlight a different owner every week."

While Junie chattered on, Joe stared glumly out the cab's window. Raindrops slid lazily down the glass, blurring the harsh lines of the sodden city through which they drove. His good mood, like the sun, had disappeared.

He had no problem with letting her advertise the business, but a small part of him wished that things could stay the same. He thought wistfully about the good old days, when he had hardly any customers, and people left him alone.

Epilogue: *Six Weeks Later*

Dan was waiting for him at the front door. Aside from a slight limp, the contractor seemed to have fully recovered from his ordeal.

"You look good," Joe said.

"I feel good," Dan said as he unlocked the front door. "Where's Junie?"

"She decided to stay in the office to work on our website. It's coming along nicely, she says. How are you doing on the house repairs?"

"It was in pretty bad shape after the cave-in, but we've been slowly and methodically putting things back together. The hole in the sitting room is gone. We installed new foundation and support beams in the cellar and reinforced what we didn't rip out. We replaced the cellar stairs and also overhauled the lighting system. We'll be moving next to the painting and cosmetic fixes for the rest of the house."

Joe looked up when they stepped over the threshold, curious to know what had replaced the foyer's opulent chandelier. The hunk of glass and steel that squatted in the middle of the ceiling was modern and serviceable, but certainly not as resplendent as its predecessor.

In addition, Millie's lovely furniture and artwork were gone, reducing the mansion to nothing more than a cold, empty husk. It could be that she had removed her belongings to make it easier for Dan to carry out the repairs. However, it seemed more likely to Joe that she didn't plan on returning.

They chatted as they proceeded through the house and into the cellar. Finally, they were where the tunnel used to be. The archway was completely bricked over. The new wall blended in almost seamlessly with the other walls. The work was so skillful that most people would be fooled into thinking there was no more to the cellar.

"What do you think?" Dan asked proudly.

"I'm impressed. This is great brickwork, exactly what I wanted."

Joe had asked Dan to pour a cement slab over the entire floor of the chamber to prevent anyone from tampering with the raised dirt that formed the talisman's symbol. He also requested that the tunnel be bricked up so that it, and the chamber, could no longer be accessed. This was the only way they could ensure that the seal would forever remain undisturbed.

Dan smoothed the wall with his hand, brushing away bits of mortar that were sticking out. "Will this and the slab actually keep the monsters at bay?"

"Let's just call them extra precautions. The seal will do the heavy lifting. Did you make sure it wasn't damaged when you poured the slab?"

"Yes. We were very careful. I put my best employees on the job and supervised it myself."

"Good. Very good."

They left the cellar and went back upstairs. They shook hands at the front door.

"Thanks again for everything," Dan said. "And don't forget, we're expecting you and Junie for dinner next week. Did you get Ayanna's email?"

"Yes I did. We'll be there."

Walking to the main road, Joe texted Emma and Junie to let them know the chamber was bricked off. After that, he tried phoning Elsie again.

It was only recently that he felt up to calling his mother. He was still resentful that she hadn't made any attempt to contact him after his rescue, but he needed answers regarding his father's death. She couldn't avoid him forever, could she?

As always, the phone rang and rang. Then it went to voice mail.

About the Author

Yin Leong was a journalist and editor in Washington, D.C. She grew up in Singapore listening to her mother's ghost stories. She now lives in Virginia with her husband and dog. This is her first novel.

From the Author

Thank you for joining Junie and Joe on their feng shui adventures. I hope you had as much fun reading the book as I had writing it.

Feedback is important for authors. Please consider leaving a review or a rating on Amazon, Goodreads or the website of your choice, especially if you enjoyed the book!

I'm working on the next installment in *The Geomancer's Apprentice* series.

If you would like to know when the next book is released, please subscribe to my blog or follow me on social media:

Blog **www.kampungkreepy.com**
Website **www.yinleong.com**
Twitter **@kampungkreepy**
Facebook **www.facebook.com/kampungkreepy**
You can also contact me at **author@yinleong.com**

Made in the USA
Columbia, SC
14 May 2023